THE REJECT

Edyth Bulbring

First published in 2018 by Tafelberg, an imprint of NB Publishers
This edition published by Edyth Bulbring, 2021

ISBN: 978-1-990941-28-3

For Julia, wonderful Savage

PART ONE

1

THE MESSAGE

The bird swoops over me, her outstretched claws skimming my head. She pelts the deck of the seacraft with scat, then shoots into the sky. I watch her fade to a speck until my eyes become a blizzard of spots.

Princess Fanny visits me every afternoon. Some days, like today, the hadeda taunts me. Other times, she brings me news. The last time she told me, crowing with glee, that the state of Mangeria and its Locusts had cornered the rebel Savages. They were packed like rats in the underground sewers of Posh City, starving as supplies ran out. Their only source of water the putrid liquid dripping from the pipes.

"They will all go to Savage City." The teller tapped her beak on the deck to mark time. Tick-tock. Tick-tock. Tick-tock. Mucus leaked from her scarred eyes as she glared in my direction.

I spat at the bird. She was saying it to torment me.

The rebels are led by my father, Handler Xavier, and Kitty, my best friend from the orphanage. I look across the ocean to the shores of Mangeria. Slum City is burning, the fires grow every day. The rebels will fight to the bloody end – they will never be taken alive. They know what capture and a sentence to Savage City prison means: torture and then slow death from heat and starvation. Freedom or death!

I hear a shuffle of footsteps on the deck. "What news from the bird, my beauty? Has the time come for us to leave?"

I am not alone on the seacraft. Reader, the blind past trader who taught me my letters as a child, is my only companion. He bribed his way onto the craft with a suitcase full of books that would teach me how to sail. But only Reader knows how to read the dots. When I have learnt his blind language, I will turf him overboard and push his head beneath the water. Hold it down.

"There's no news, old man. Stop asking."

Reader arches his neck and sniffs. "I smell moisture in the air. Tell me what the sky looks like."

I peer up. The sun is a smear of pus against the dark sky. It is cloaked in black clouds.

"There's not much to see. The sky is full of smoke. And the sun is very faint," I tell him.

"The smoke is deceiving us. Rain clouds are lurking. We cannot wait much longer, faithful Juliet. The season has turned and the seas are perilous when the storms come."

"Hold your tongue. I've told you: I won't leave until I have news. Go back to your berth. You disturb my peace with your prattle."

The old man chuckles. "Oh, my beautiful Juliet. You have no peace for me to disturb. I hear you at night when you cry out in your sleep. It shreds my dreams." He stretches out his hand.

I turn away. Nothing can comfort me.

My beloved Nicolas and I were supposed to run away across the sea to discover what lay beyond. We tricked The Machine and killed the marks on our spines. But instead of sailing away together, I took our seacraft and left him behind.

I was faced with an impossible choice: My half-sister, Larissa, was dying and Mistress, the woman I recently discovered to be my mother, wanted me to save her. But to do this, I would have had to betray Nicolas by telling Mistress where he was. Nicolas's father, the Guardian of Justice and Peace, believed the rebels had taken his son hostage – until Nicolas was returned to him, the Guardian refused to let Larissa have the procedure that would save her life.

Unable to make a choice between Nicolas and Larissa, I have waited for fate to decide. Until I know whether Nicolas is back with his father, or that the Guardian has relented and allowed Larissa's procedure to take place, I cannot leave these shores.

Reader sighs. "While we linger, let me read to you from one of my books. You are slow to learn my blind language and there is much you need to know. You have mastered the sails and the tiller, but you have not learnt how the sun and stars can guide us. I have an excellent book in my collection about how Polynesian sailors from the old world navigated the seas without instruments by observing the sky and the swell of the waves."

He gives a sly smile, his toothless gums as pink as a baby's. He knows that for as long as he is useful to me, he has a place on board. He is old and past his time, but he is still cunning.

During the past three months, while I have waited for news from the bird, we have sailed out of sight of the coastline during the day, dropping anchor close to shore only at night. We are careful to keep out of sight of the Locusts. I have become skilled at raising and lowering the sails; I have learnt how to helm, and how to lash the wheel to hold the boat steady while I sleep, but I am still battling to read the skies.

As Reader fumbles his way across the deck and disappears into his berth below, I hear the cry of the teller again. She has come back to provoke me. Princess Fanny spins wildly around the mast and suddenly dips towards the seacraft, crash-landing onto the deck.

She is not a beautiful bird. Not anything like the pictures I've seen of other birds in books Reader has lent me over the years. But now Princess Fanny looks more hideous than usual. Her feathers are covered in oil and her talons are stained with blood. She pulls herself across the deck, dragging a ragged wing behind her.

I give her some water – she is no use to me dead. The bird drinks, and dunks her head into the bowl. She searches her feathers. She finds a fat louse and crunches it in her razor-sharp beak.

"Do I have to wring your scrawny neck to make you speak? Tell me about Larissa and Nicolas. And don't lie to me."

She scowls at me with scarred eyes. The Muti Nags who make magic in Slum City blind the chicks when they hatch so they have sight of the future. The tellers are unable to lie. But I do not trust this ugly bird. Her loyalty is tied to Larissa.

Larissa found Princess Fanny as a chick and promised she would never blind her, but gouged out her beloved bird's eyes when she thought the rebels had kidnapped me, the drudge carer she had grown to love. She wanted the blind teller to help her find me.

The bird has not forgotten my part in this betrayal.

Princess Fanny's voice is hoarse. "Your sister will have her procedure tonight. The Guardian of Justice and Peace has given his blessing. They have found a Savage girl who is a perfect match. My Little Miss will be well again." She empties her bowels on the deck and utters a strangled howl.

A slab of concrete lifts off my chest. Larissa will live!

And after the procedure, the Savage donor will die. Tomorrow, some mother and father will wake up in Slum City to the news that their daughter has been sacrificed to make a Mangerian miss well again. The girl is probably a drudge like me. Someone of no value.

"And Nicolas? Is he alive? Is he still free? Tell me."

The teller stares blindly across the water. "Nicolas is alive." She probes her bloody talons with her beak, picking, then spitting out bits of flesh. She senses how much news of Nicolas means to me.

The bird hobbles towards the edge of the deck. "The Locusts have laid down their weapons, the Savages too. The

7

fighting has come to an end." She vomits on the deck and releases an ear-splitting honk.

The war is over, and perhaps the Savages have won. Nicolas is alive, and possibly free. And my sister will be well. I have been tormented by a nightmare that my refusal to choose between them condemned both to die. But fate dealt the cards kindly and favoured them both.

"You must set sail across the sea. The tellers have foretold that you are the one. There is a journey you must take. Until you leave, you cannot return. The clock is ticking. Go now and fulfil your destiny." Princess Fanny launches herself into the air and is swallowed by the billowing smoke.

Destiny! Prophecy! The one! The tellers have been squawking this nonsense about me before I was born. But they are wrong. Kitty is the one. She fought the war to free the traders of Slum City. All I wanted was to leave with Nicolas and have a new life, not fulfil some foolish prophecy. I do not fight other people's wars. I fight only for myself and for Nicolas.

Reader totters onto the desk clutching a book. "I heard that noisy bird. What is the news?"

I cannot help myself. I laugh. "The teller says my sister will be well again and Nicolas is alive. The war is over."

"If you are sure, my lovely. You are certain the bird never lied?"

The old man is ignorant. Tellers do not lie.

The seacraft lurches as a wave beats against the beam. Reader clutches the book in his arms and grabs the railing.

"We must anchor close to shore for the night. Tomorrow we will sniff the stench of our homeland for the last time and say goodbye."

"No, at first light tomorrow we're going home. There's something I have to do. Then we can go on our journey." I will find Nicolas and ask him to come away with me as we planned. There is no one else in Mangeria for me to stay for. Not Mistress, my mother, who as a young girl took up with a Savage boy from Slum City and bore his child. I do not trust that she'd believed I had died at birth, that she had not abandoned me. She would have been at the forefront in the war against the rebels, fighting my father, Xavier. The man she once loved.

I will not stay for him either. He does not even know I am his daughter, and would probably care rat scat if he did. As for Kitty, she would not thank me for refusing to join the rebels.

But ... there is my sister. Larissa does not know we share blood, and Mistress will make sure I never see her again. I shake my head. In time, Larissa will forget me.

"This is not wise, Juliet. I do not trust the bird. It might not be safe. Sometimes lies are told not in what is said, but what is not said. We must hoist the sail tomorrow and leave as the sun rises."

The old man cannot stop me. I have to go back. If Nicolas won't forgive me for deserting him, I will go on the voyage without him.

Reader wets his finger and holds it in the air. "We do not

have much time to dilly-dally. I fear a storm is coming to these shores."

I wake suddenly in the middle of the night. I cannot breathe. A dead weight sits on my chest and my arms are pinned down.

A hand smothers my mouth and nose. I am suffocating.

A monster peers down at me, its face cut in half by the faint light of the one-eyed moon. Black eyes stare into mine.

"Don't make a sound, else I'll slit your throat." The voice is male. His eyes are round. His hair is a savage mop of barbed wire. Not a monster: a boy from Slum City. He presses something cold against my neck.

I kick out, but my legs are tied. I try to bite his hand, but it presses down harder, grinding my head into the deck. I force a harsh sound out of my throat, stripping it raw.

"Stop messing around and shut your gob-hole," he says.

A foul smell fills my nose. The boy stinks of rot, and oil. I make my body slack and he pulls away a rusty knife. I run my tongue over my lips and taste the filth from his hand.

"Who else is on this seacraft? How many of you? And don't lie to me else you'll get what's coming to you."

Lying is one of my natural talents, one I have nurtured these past fifteen years. It has saved my skin in many tricky situations.

"Five others. Scavvies. They're sleeping below," I tell him. "When they catch you, they're going to rip you apart."

Scavvies – the Necromunda who scavenge for relics in the city that was drowned when the seas rose after the conflagration.

They are the toughest scum from Slum City; burnt black by the sun, their skin salted from the sea.

He grabs me by the hair and drags me across the deck. I am trussed up to the mast like a piece of meat ready for the fire. Fit for some Posh's dinner. He tucks away the knife in his satchel, his grin mocking me. His teeth are jagged and sharp like bits of bone.

"And the old man I found wandering around below, babbling to himself? Did you forget to tell me about him?"

If the boy has hurt Reader, I will claw that smile off his face and make him eat it. "He's just a past trader, a useless piece of rubbish. I hope you pushed him overboard."

The boy chuckles. "He said the nine Locusts on board would break me in two and use my spine to beat me before dragging me off to Savage City." He saunters around the mast, checking the knots on the rope and pulling it tighter around me. He grins when I wince.

"So, I'm right in thinking it's just the two of you on this sloop. No Scavvies, no Locusts. It's a big seacraft for one skinny girl and a blind old man."

He could not know that the sloop belongs to Nicolas's father, that he sails it in summer to the pleasure resorts along the coast. If the boy swam out in the dark, he will not have seen the family emblem, a gloved fist, branding the front of the bow.

But the seacraft is mine now. I will not allow this Captain Hook and his stinking knife to steal it from me.

"What do you want? I've got food and water. Take what you need and get off my sloop."

"Yours? I don't think so. I've always wanted to be a captain." He limps over to a container of water, dragging his foot. He is injured. Weak.

I could fight him. If I could untie my hands.

The boy sprawls out on the deck and massages his foot. No, he is not wounded. His foot is a bunched club. He takes off his shirt and uses it to clean the oil off his body. His skin is brown, covered in a fine pelt of black hair. Scars criss-cross his bony back. They are old scars, like red twine bulging through his skin. The base of his spine is clear: there are no six numbers marking him.

My mark is still on my spine, the same as all citizens of Mangeria – Posh and Scum alike. It determines what trades we'll have and who our fate-mates will be. But The Machine cannot track me now. My mark is dead.

As the boy scrubs his face I see his features. His face is dark and gaunt, hungry like a rat. Squatting above his eyes are growths like two small horns. My stomach knots with disgust. A club-footed devil with horns on his head, and no mark on his spine. A Reject: the worst scum. The Machine would have found him useless at birth. He would have been dumped in the landfills outside Slum City. And then, because he survived, he would have been bonded as a slave to another Reject. The scars on his back tell me he is an obstinate piece of trash.

"Duh! I'm a Reject. You can stop staring at me with those big eyes of yours." He fills a bowl with water and drinks. Burps. "Now, where's the food, Cow-Eyes?"

Cow-Eyes. It's a name I have been called many times. My eyes are too big on my face, my body too long and skinny, my hair too Savage, my skin too pale. I am the ugly friend of Kitty, the beautiful pleasure worker. But Nicolas found me beautiful. And when I was with him, I felt beautiful.

"Juliet! Juliet, my lovely. Are you alright?"

The Reject turns as he hears the cry from below deck and groans. "I think I'll take your advice and push the old rubbish overboard. Gab-gab-gab, gab-gab-gab, the whole time I was tying him up. I had to punch him in the head to get some peace."

I hiss at him. He will regret using his fists on Reader.

"Hang on." The Reject stares at me slyly. "Juliet? That's a name I've heard in the market. There's a price on your head, Juliet Seven." He rubs his fingers together. "A large number of credits."

I strain against the rope. Rejects are loyal to no one – the traders of Slum City treat them with as much cruelty as the Posh do. The boy would sail the sloop back to Mangeria and trade me to the Locusts.

I look towards the horizon. Reader was right, a storm is brewing. The sun is rising in the grey sky, and clouds are massing above Slum City. But it is not smoke – the fires have died down. The bird did not lie.

"The war is over," I say. "No one will pay credits for me. I'm worth nothing to you. Let me go."

The Reject laughs. "The price on your head stands. There're a few Guardians who want a piece of you. You must have pissed off a lot of people."

Mistress, my mother. She will not have forgiven me for sabotaging the procedure and endangering Larissa's life. And Nicolas's father. He will want to teach me a lesson for kidnapping his son, or so he believes.

"What's your name?" I ask. If this Reject is going to sell me for credits, his name will be the last curse on my lips.

He shrugs. "I've been called lots of things by my masters. A name means scat to me."

I smile through my teeth as I bunch my fists. "I think I'll call you Gollum. It's a favourite of mine." Gollum, the hideous creature from a book Reader once lent me; despised and cursed for stealing a precious ring. "You look like a Gollum. A handsome, sweet-tempered boy with goodness in his heart." My words drip with honey. "If you release me, Gollum, I'll show you where we keep the food. I can cook you porridge. And maybe you'd fancy some banana?"

And when your back is turned, a knife between your shoulder blades.

The Reject nods. "Gollum's a strong name, better than most. And maybe I will let you cook and serve me before I hand you over to the Locusts. But if you burn my food, Cow-Eyes, I'll beat you." He grins. "I think I'll beat you anyway."

The noise of banging comes from below deck. "Juliet, please answer me. Tell me that you are alive. The storm is coming. We are not safe. We need to raise the anchor and set sail before it is too late."

"Raise anchor? I can do that. Then I'll take you home. There's a cell in Savage City with your name on it." Gollum crosses the deck and begins to winch up the heavy chain. He has no meat on his bones, but as he secures the anchor on deck, I see that his arms and back are strong. "Time to head on back to shore."

Suddenly a rogue wave smashes against the hull of the seacraft. Gollum falls and scrambles to his knees, but the sloop broaches and water sweeps him along the deck. The mast groans against the rising wind.

Laughing like a madman, Gollum crawls down the length of the deck. He clings to the railing as a giant wave breaks over the stern, drenching him in sea water. His satchel is whipped down the deck towards me. I stretch out my foot and trap it. I know I've found the knife when it stabs my hand. I pull it out and attack the rope around my waist and my ankles. The wind screams in the rigging and I cling to the mast.

As Gollum reaches me, another wave hits the seacraft, throwing it over on its beam ends. My hands slip; the wind pulls me towards the railing. Before I can be swept away, Gollum grabs me, pushing me against the mast, and wraps his arms around me.

2

THE PIRATE

I stumble out of the cabin onto the deck. Pain slices through my shoulder; the side of my head is caked with blood. I shade my eyes against the sun. There is no sign of land, only an endless stretch of black sea. Hot wind swirls across the deck.

Someone moans behind me. Gollum is curled in a ball around the mast. I kick him in the gut, grab his face and push it down. "Don't breathe. Don't move. One sound and I'll make your face uglier than it is already."

Tears bite my eyes as the bones grate above my breast. I ignore the pain and tie his hands and feet, and loop the rope around his neck. I wrench up his head and fasten the rope tight to the mast. It's his turn to be trussed up like a slab of meat.

"Looks like you got hurt, Cow-Eyes. And from the way you're huffing and puffing, it sounds like maybe you broke something." Gollum swallows, and moistens his lips. "I need water. Get me some. I'm asking nicely now. Pretty please."

I raise my arm and the movement makes me gasp. I press the tips of my fingers across my shoulder blade. It is tender.

Scanning the deck, I see that our water provisions are gone, probably swept overboard. Containers are upturned, rope and sheeting turfed out of their boxes.

Banging and muffled cries come from below.

I slam back the bolt on the door to Reader's berth. He's lying tied up on the floor with a jumble of books and clothing, staring blindly at the ceiling. I kneel and trace my fingers over the blue-and-purple bruises on his cheek. I think of Gollum's stinking fists beating this old face. I think of all the things I am going to do to the Reject when I get above deck. When I am done with him, he won't smirk at me with that broken-toothed mouth again.

Reader jerks. "Juliet, is that you?"

"I see you put up a good fight, old man. Lie still and let me untie you."

"You sound breathless, Juliet. Are you hurt? Did that boy harm you?" Reader shakes his hands free of the rope and flexes his fingers, rubs his feet. He sits hunched over, his head in his hands.

"Stop fussing. The storm came just as you said it would. I thought it would crush our seacraft or we'd capsize. It's stopped now, but I think it will be back."

Reader lifts his head. "The boy took me by surprise. I tried to warn you but he was too strong. I could not bear to think what he was doing to you. I lay here like a foolish parcel unable to do anything. Did he hurt you? Did he?" Tears leak from Reader's eyes and he sobs.

"I've dealt with the boy. He won't mess with us again.

Come, have some water. You've drained most of it from your body with all that wailing."

We climb up on deck. The sea stretches forever. Black glass, cracking. The giant at the top of Jack's beanstalk is smashing the surface with a hammer, creating sharp splinters and jagged peaks. Waves pummel the hull and the contents of my stomach rise in my throat. I lean against the railing and gag. Water and bile pours out of my mouth.

Reader turns at the sound of my retching. "Juliet, you are ill? Is it the sun sickness?"

I know those symptoms: a hot head, dry mouth, a bleeding rash on the skin. I touch my forehead. Not sun sickness: it's the choppy sea playing pat-a-cake, pat-a-cake with my stomach.

Cries come from the mast: "I hear you, old man. I hear you." Gollum's voice is hoarse. "You're going to have to untie me. The girl's hurt. She's useless. The storm has blown us far from home and you can't sail this sloop without me."

"That boy. He is still on board?" Reader moans. "And he says you are hurt. This is bad news, Juliet. I am old and there is little strength in these feeble bones of mine."

It's true that Reader and I are as much use as a pair of gloves to a fingerless Reject. I grip the rope around Gollum's throat. "I could toss you overboard. It's something I'd enjoy more than anything. But I've hurt my shoulder and we can't sail without your help."

Gollum arches an eyebrow at me. "Why should I? What's in it for me?"

Reader groans. "Foolish boy. You must help us, otherwise we will bob around this terrible sea until our water and food runs out. That is if the next storm does not take us to a watery grave. Do you understand me? And when we reach the shores of Mangeria, you will go on your way and leave us in peace."

Gollum closes his eyes and is silent for a few moments. "Okay. It's not like we've got a choice. So let's all play nicely until we get home. No tricks – I'll be watching. Now get these bloody ropes off me."

"Let the rascal go, Juliet. Then he must bind your shoulder before we set sail."

The Reject will be watching me, but my eyes are sharper. I untie the knots around Gollum's hands and feet, and loosen his neck from the noose.

He shakes himself free. "Water, where's it?"

I point at the hatch and a few minutes later he returns, wiping his mouth.

"You said there was food, Cow-Eyes, and there's sacks of the stuff. I'll be eating all of it before we get back home."

Nicolas stocked the galley with dried mango and banana and strawberry and pumpkin smuggled from The Laboratory. It was for our journey together.

"And from now on, matey, you must call me Captain Gollum." Gollum salutes me. The cap on his head is embossed with gold braid and bears the emblem of the Guardian of Justice and Peace. He has changed out of his rags and is wearing Nicolas's shirt and a pair of his trousers. How dare he!

"Take those clothes off," I hiss.

"They're mine now. Fit for a captain." Gollum struts on the deck. The shirt hangs loosely and the trousers are held up by a piece of rope. "Come, let's have a look at that shoulder of yours."

I pull my shoulder back and stand upright while he rips canvas from an old sail.

"Strip. I need to see what I'm working with here." Gollum has a hard glint in his eye.

I take a deep breath and fix my gaze on the two devil horns on his forehead. I yank off my dress and stand naked in the warm air. Nicolas is the only boy who has ever seen me without my clothes, or touched my skin. And now this Reject.

He stares at my bare chest and colour rises in his face. He touches my shoulder and feels along the bone above my chest. The skin on his fingers is rough, but he probes gently.

"It's your collar bone. I've seen the same kind of injury on the Pulaks."

The Pulaks of Mangeria are harnessed in pairs and pull taxis squashed full with passengers. Most of the Pulaks are not able to serve in their trade for longer than seven years. Then they are taken to the Reject dumps, broken and crippled.

Gollum knuckle-taps along my bone. "You're lucky. Those poor buggers never get a chance to heal. This isn't such a big deal. In a couple of months the bones will knit good as new." He stands behind me for a moment, and then laughs. "So, you're just a smelly old drudge! The Machine decided you'd wipe Posh kids' arses and scrub their floors."

I fold my hands over the numbers at the base of my spine. I am no longer a drudge – the mark on my spine is dead. But this boy will always be a Reject, a nothing. He was never meant to be anything.

He twists the canvas around my back, immobilising my shoulder. He makes a sling and straps one arm against my body. He pulls on my dress, leaving my other arm free.

"Come now, *Captain* Gollum," I say. "You must set sail away from the sun. And tonight Reader will tell you how to plot a course home by the stars. I'll go below and cook some food. You can trust that it will be most tasty."

And when I can manage this sloop on my own, I'll poison you and watch you rip your guts to ribbons, vomiting to death. You won't have the chance to sell me to the Locusts when we get home.

"Yes, of course I trust you, Drudge." Gollum laughs.

The days drift into each other, a pattern of unrelenting sun and vicious storms. The sloop is tossed between the wind and towering waves in a spiteful game that often blows us off course. Some days there is not a whisper of a breeze, and the seacraft bobs stagnant in a sea smothered in a mass of plastic.

Plastic bottles and packets and containers for as far as the eye can see on the dead sea. Bubbling blankets of plastic mush. Rotting green and black and yellow, a lifeboat for the flies that feast on its trapped filth.

Back in Mangeria, everything is made of plastic. The air

smells of plastic. My food tastes of plastic. When I sweat, my skin is coated with abnormally shiny beads. And here on the sea we are besieged by the old world's plastic legacy.

On these calm days, we take the oars and try and free the sloop from the prison of plastic. But it is useless. So we wait for a wind to rise and fill our sails.

I have made it my duty to cook breakfast for Gollum at sunrise when he ends his evening shift. Boiled oats, a spoonful of spit and a sprinkling of spite. The food is ready for him on deck once he has set the sloop on its morning course, and is done washing himself.

Under the blistering sky, he scrubs his hairy body with our precious water, singing bawdy songs that infect my ears. He keeps his captain's cap on when he bathes, never removes it. During the long, hot days, he sleeps restlessly, sprawled out over the hatch to the galley where our supplies are kept – a rat guarding its food.

If I surprise him while he is washing, he never covers himself. He does not care if I see him – his scarred back, legs all knees, thin body. It has grown in terrified spurts and formed weirdly in places. When he catches me looking at him, he sings even louder. He is more Savage than any person I have known. I envy his defiance. Mine is sapping away with the endless days on the sea.

He eats with a ferocious appetite, shoving food into his face with dirty fingers as though he suspects someone might steal away his bowl before he is finished. "Is there any more porridge? A slab or two of mango? You can't expect your captain to only eat banana for breakfast." His stomach is never full.

I do not eat with him. I tell myself that the sight of him guzzling our food disgusts me. But food repels me now, especially the smell. When I was an orphan in Section O, I could not stop stuffing my face. How Kitty would laugh if she could see me now, gagging at the sweet smell of my favourite strawberry.

Maybe Kitty is free now, feasting herself fat on mango.

Maybe my beautiful friend is missing me too.

My sickness is worse in the morning. There are days when I have to turn away from cooking breakfast and race on deck to hurl into the sea. I am an empty sack; my energy has leaked from my bones.

"You never eat, Drudge. Are you sick?" Gollum shovels porridge into his mouth. "When I slaved at the pleasure clubs for one of my masters, I saw girls and boys like you who also never ate. Some pleasure workers had the sickness, a grubby gift from their Posh patrons." He runs his hands together. "The rub-a-dub-dub, they called it. They were fit only for the dumps. Diseased and useless."

Gollum's eyes slide over my body.

"Girls weren't always sick, mind you. Just gone down the river. They ate very little during the first months, tried to hide the swelling. But their bellies grew until they got rid of their burden. Another of my masters dabbled in that line of work. A lucrative trade. Then, if the Locusts didn't catch the slaggets under the bridge, they came back to work at the clubs. The lucky ones."

I touch my stomach. "I like to wait until Reader wakes. He prefers not to eat alone."

Most of the days are calm; the storms come at night. Reader and I huddle down below in our berths, bolts drawn against any treachery. Gollum stays on deck. He says he likes the storms. I cross my fingers and hope he gets swept into the sea.

He watches me watching him. And takes to wearing a waist harness attached to the mast when the sea is rough. And hides the galley knives. I keep a broken bottle under my mattress. And wait for my collar bone to heal. Plain-purl. Plain-purl. Plain-purl. Faster, faster. Knit those bones.

Reader spends the early part of the evenings instructing Gollum where to sail and, when the course is set, the old man leaves him to get some sleep. I hear them, sometimes, as I toss about in my berth trying to ease the burn in my chest.

"Tell me how the stars are arranged against the sky so that I can direct you. I have an excellent star chart in this travel history by a brave fellow called Joshua Slocum, who navigated these oceans in a sloop just like ours hundreds of years ago. What do you see tonight, my captain?"

Reader has told me he merely humours Gollum, calling him "my captain". But as time passes, I sense he says it out of respect. He tells me Gollum is a fine sailor. As a young boy, Gollum was bonded to a Reject master who worked for the Scavvies. Then he moved on to various other trades, some dark and terrible. Our captain has perfected many crafts. I do not want to hear about his horrible talents.

At first Gollum scoffed at Reader: "What can those stupid dots in old books teach me about navigating the sea? They're rubbish. You're hurting my ears with your gab-gab-gab."

But as the days and the sea stretches before us, and every morning brings no sight of land, Gollum can do nothing but trust the knowledge from Reader's blind books.

"There's a cross of stars that marks the sky tonight. And a belt that draws a circle around a dagger. Should I helm a little to the west, Master Reader?"

Master Reader! Gollum knows how to charm the old fool.

On calm nights, Reader teaches Gollum the alphabet. My old teacher is more patient with the pirate than he was with me. Gollum uses a piece of coal to make the letters on the deck, and Reader has taught him the alphabet song. Gollum's voice sinks and rises in the air: "Ela-menna-pee. Queue-are-ess, tee-you-vee …" Over and over. I could scream.

Gollum is quick to learn the twenty-six letters and Reader teaches him how to write his name, and short sentences. To encourage his progress, the old man has given Gollum a journal he found in the Guardian's trunk. At the end of each day, Gollum writes an entry into what he calls his "captain's log". It records all the important occurrences on board, the weather, the navigational details and, of course, the captain's keen observations of the sea. He keeps the book in a pouch strapped against his stomach. Only the captain may make entries into the log, Gollum tells me. So smug.

Reader says Gollum is the smartest student he has ever taught. "Yes, even smarter than you, Juliet. I wonder how it is possible that this fine mind belongs to a Reject."

Soon Gollum will be able to read, beginning with nursery rhymes. Reader has already taught him some songs, and Gollum buckles his shoe (one, two), knocks on the door (three, four) and follows Mary and her little lamb all the way to school until I want to slaughter him and his woolly sheep. They are my rhymes. *Mine.*

And now his. Next Reader will tell him fairy tales, and before I know it, this Reject thief will have stolen all of my stories.

During the day, when Gollum sleeps, I take the helm and keep the seacraft's course. Today, as the sun begins its descent in the bloodied sky, Reader joins me on deck.

He places a bowl of mango and a cup of water on a crate. "Eat something, my lovely. I stewed the mango as I know you like it, with some chopped strawberry."

At the sight of the food, bile rises in my throat. My stomach twitches, a tumbling movement. My insides rearrange themselves. Another movement, like feathers dancing in my gut. I place my hand on my stomach and pull myself up onto the railing.

"Perhaps, if you are not hungry, my young captain will have some mango. The rascal is always ravenous after his sleep. I declare his legs are hollow," Reader says.

I stare unseeing into the shimmering water and count back the days, the weeks and the months to the nights I spent with Nicolas on the roof of the warehouse, waiting to set sail. His soft hands on the base of my spine, my head on his chest.

The smell of his hands in my Savage hair – strawberry and the bark of my tree. Love-in-a-Mist. Our sweat drying under the cool gaze of the one-eyed moon, the stars blinking shyly away.

I know then: I am not sick. I am gone down the river. I have tracked the path my mother took sixteen years ago, with a different twist: I fell in love with a Posh, and in a few months I will have his child.

CAPTAIN GOLLUM'S LOG

My name is Gollum
Gollum
Gollum
Her name is Juliet
Juliet
Juliet
Beautiful Juliet

3

SEA MONSTER

Reader joins me at the railing. He blinks his gooey eyes at me and gives a shy baby-pink smile.

"I am baffled, my lovely. I have kept faith with my books, and by all my calculations we should have reached home weeks ago. Even the storms could not have thrown us so far off course. And I do not doubt that our friend has carried out my instructions and steered the seacraft by the stars."

Our friend! My collar bone is healed but I still hobble about, shoulder hunched, my face a mask of pain. I play weak, waiting for an opportunity to shove Gollum overboard or feed him a banquet laced with poison, fit for a hungry rat.

Gollum watches me, eyes peeled like boiled eggs. He wears a waist harness even on the calmest days, and a life jacket for just-in-case. When he eats, he insists that Reader takes the first mouthful.

"Taste this, Master Reader," Gollum says. "Has Drudge overcooked our meal? Again?"

I wait, and watch him too. One day he will slip up. And good riddance to him.

Reader continues, ignoring my snort. "I do not doubt my books or our young captain. But I wonder sometimes whether the world has changed. Whether the waters that rose after the conflagration swallowed up the lands that used to exist." He scratches his forehead. "Or perhaps when the earth flipped on its axis and carved the moon in half, it rearranged the stars in the heavens. Or maybe, just maybe, Juliet, we are looking at the sky from a different hemisphere. Could it be that our world has actually turned upside-down?" Reader sighs. "It is a conundrum, my Juliet, and I have no answers."

Fear rises in my throat. I am trapped on this sloop with my burden, sailing into a void with a blind old man and a filthy Reject. I should never have trusted Reader. I should have chucked him overboard months ago. He is a useless sack of old dots.

"Could it be, old man, that you have got us hopelessly lost? You, and our fine captain. Could the conundrum be that both of you don't have a clue what you're doing, and that we're going to sail around on this terrible ocean until our teeth fall out or we die of thirst and starvation?"

I sink onto the deck. We will never get back home. Nicolas will believe that I abandoned him forever. And unless we find new land, we will die. Maybe there is only a sea of nothingness, and we are chasing the ghosts of lands that died hundreds of years ago.

The setting sun paints the sea flaming orange and bright pink, harsh brushstrokes against the black canvas. A flash of silver breaks though the surface. Then the ripples on the water settle back into their fiery tapestry.

"Tonight I will have to tell our captain that I fear my books have failed him. That we are lost." Reader presses his hand over mine. "We will make a new plan, Juliet. We will not give up."

I pull my hand away from Reader's and screen my eyes against the glare of the setting sun. There it is again. A flash of silver breaking the water. Now a spear of grey carving a path towards the seacraft.

Stories of terrible sea monsters are told by the Mangerians to keep the residents of Slum City from venturing across the ocean. I never believed their lies, but my eyes do not deceive me. Something is moving in the water below.

Gollum joins us, picking the crust of sleep from his eyes. "Did I hear the beautiful words 'stewed' and 'mango'? Or was it a dream?" His eyes brighten when he sees the bowl on the crate. He stands at the railing next to me and hawks a throat full of phlegm into the sea. "Before I went to sleep this morning I found a book in your library, Master Reader. It has pictures and words, not just dots. Maybe we could read it together tonight? I think I'm up for it."

Reader claps his hands. "I brought a couple of Juliet's favourites. The one with the pictures? Yes, that must be *Peter Pan*. It is about a boy who flies. And a pirate captain who sails a seacraft much like ours called the *Jolly Roger*. I think you will like it a great deal. We can read it together, my fine captain."

Master Reader and my fine captain. Reading my book. *Mine!*

"The *Jolly Roger*. It's a good name for a seacraft. From now on my sloop is the *Jolly Roger*."

His sloop. How dare he!

The Reject wipes his mouth and rubs his hands down his trousers. Nicolas's trousers.

I strike his face, knocking the captain's cap off his head. "I *forbid* you to read my book. You are *nothing*. You have *no right*!"

Gollum grabs my hand. He leans into me, his other hand a fist. I pull back, shielding my face with my arm. Waves thrash. A face appears from the sea, a pink and grey maw edged with rows of dagger teeth. I scream. Gollum hauls me back as the monster throws itself against the seacraft.

I stand on the deck shaking like a past trader as Gollum picks up his captain's cap and pulls it onto his head, cocking the angle.

"This is the second time I've saved your skin, Drudge. First from the storm." He holds a finger in the air. "And now from a monster." He waggles two fingers at me. "Next time, I own you." He stabs three fingers inches from my face.

I smack away his hand. There will not be a third time. No one owns me. My heart reeling, I lean over the railing and scan the sea. A silver blade cuts through the waves, circling the boat. A grey-and-white snout, two dead-black eyes looking back at me. It sinks below the water and is gone. Tiny waves knit together, repairing the rip in the sea.

"What is it, Juliet? What has occurred?" Reader scrabbles in vain on the deck for the bowl, which was tossed off the crate. "A freak wave? My captain, what was that?"

"It was a monster." My voice is a whisper. "I saw it, old man. It's true what they told us: monsters still live in the sea. It came out of the water and tried to attack the boat."

Reader claps his hands and his face cracks in a foolish smile. "There was something alive in the water? Describe it to me. Please, Juliet. Paint it with words so that I will also know what it looks like."

I tell Reader of the grey knife that sliced through the waves. The rows of jagged teeth in a cavernous mouth turned down in a sad grimace. The shiny grey-white body and tiny dead eyes.

"It is a shark fish! One of the oldest sea scavengers. Tell me, Juliet, how big was it?"

I stretch my arms as wide as they can go. Of course Reader cannot see me. "Two metres at least."

"Rubbish! Another threemetres." Gollum strides across the deck. "At least twice the width of my *Jolly Roger*. And I nearly touched the beast. I was so close, I could have punched it."

The old man gasps. "It must be the Great White. The prince of shark fishes. A great killer. They were hunted for generations before the conflagration. It was assumed they had died out along with the whales and the seals, long before the old world came to an end."

Gollum's eyes search the ocean as it sucks the growing darkness from the sky.

"My captain, Juliet, this means everything. Our seas are

not barren as we thought. The Great White eats other fish. It would not survive if it was alone. There must be more creatures, other fish that this beauty feeds on." Tears trickle down Reader's cheeks. "The sea is alive. Perhaps it also hosts dolphins, or mermaids. Tonight we will celebrate."

We linger for a while and watch for more signs of life, but the sea remains dark and silent as the sun disappears below the horizon.

Reader is like a small boy who's found a nest of chicks. He cannot stop chattering. "I knew it, Juliet. Did I not tell you there was life away from home?" His words swim in spit, drown in his mouth. "Who knows, perhaps we will discover a lion, the king of the jungle. Or maybe a rhinoceros, with its magical horn. I have read about these animals, seen pictures in books, many years ago, before my eyes darkened." He wipes the specks of saliva off his chin and giggles.

Gollum's brow furrows. "You must teach me about these beasts, Master Reader. I've never heard about them. Are they good to eat?"

"Oh, my captain. In the old days people used to hunt them to fill their pots, or for trade. Often they slaughtered them for sport. When their numbers grew fewer, people paid thousands of credits to simply gaze at these creatures. Then they were not for eating." Reader links his arm through Gollum's. "I think tonight we can skip our reading-and-writing lesson. Instead, I will tell you a story about a great fish called Moby Dick. We can roast some corn and make a party to celebrate our new discovery." He pauses. "Juliet, of course, tonight you *must* join us. You will like the story about Captain Ahab and his whale, I assure you."

Gollum's smile is stretched as wide as a Market Nag's bum at the thought of one of Reader's stories. He picks the bowl off the deck. "Yes, we will fill our bowls and celebrate. I'll cook a special feast for the two of us. I'm tired of Drudge's burnt food."

I am shut out. The odd one out in this happy friendship.

"Enough with your stories, old man. I'm sick of your fairy tales about stars that will take us home. Tell your fine captain the truth. Tell him we'll be bobbing about on this monstrous sea until our hair turns grey. Or we're eaten by killer fish. Tell him we're lost!"

Reader looks shamefaced at Gollum and clears his throat. "It is true. I am sorry, my captain. I have let you down."

My anger boils over as I grab the bowl from Gollum's hand and hurl it into the sea. "And why don't you tell Reader how you worked for the Locusts and traded information about the rebels during the war? Don't try and deny it, I know your kind. Tell him how you intend to sell me to the Locusts for credits when we get home." I push Gollum. "Tell him, you two-faced Reject."

Reader steadies himself on Gollum's shoulder. "My captain, is this true? Surely you would do no such thing to our Juliet?"

Gollum's face goes dark. "Talking of secrets, maybe Drudge should tell us hers." He grips my arms and hisses. "Tell us why you can't eat and why you sleep all day when you're supposed to be steering. And why you sick up in the sea every morning. Go on, Drudge, let us in on your dirty secret."

Dirty? I am carrying Nicolas's child. I do not feel dirty.

"See, Master Reader, she won't tell you that she's gone down the river. Soon we'll have another mouth to feed. For as long as the food lasts." Gollum glowers at me. "There's only three sacks of corn left in the galley. The last thing we need is some drudge brat to feed."

"Juliet?" Reader's mouth trembles in a gummy smile. "My Juliet, you are burdened?"

In Slum City, my growing belly would be a burden. I would be sent to Savage City for daring to breed without permission. But Nicolas and I planned to leave that nightmare. To play a new game. Our rules.

I stalk away, passing a mirror attached to the side of the cabin. Gollum likes to peer at himself when he wakes in the afternoons. He flicks bits out of his teeth with a piece of string, prods his gums, cleans his nostrils with his grimy fingers. He salutes the mirror. "And a very good evening to you, Captain Gollum. You handsome bastard," he always says.

I pause in front of the piece of glass and stare at myself. My face is fuller, the angles softened. My skin glows and is tanned dark – I ran out of sunblocker weeks ago. My hair is even more Savage. My cow-eyes are dark chocolate. I touch my chest and run my hands down the sides of my body. I am no longer skinny. I am as plump as a pleasure worker. My ankles are pulpy slabs of bruised banana.

Sitting on the bow of the sloop, I place my hand on my stomach. It flutters. I smooth my fingers across my belly.

Wisha-wisha-wisha.

My child will be a boy. A part of Nicolas. We will find our way home and my son will know his father.

The half-moon and the stars play catch-me on the water. I see it, then, the silver spear, darting in the light-flecked waves. The smooth grey bulk noses its way towards the *Jolly Roger*. The prince of sharks. Proof of life beyond Mangeria.

The fish swims towards the seacraft and turns. It does this several times, keeping faith with an invisible straight line. The bowl I tossed into the sea is still bobbing in the water. The great beast takes it in its terrible mouth and flips it onto the deck.

I grab the plastic cushion Reader sits on when he teaches Gollum his lessons at night and chuck it into the sea. The monster leaps for it and the cushion lands back on the deck.

A game! The creature thinks I'm playing with it.

"Look, look, the monster is back!" I yell.

Gollum runs towards me. I grab the captain's cap from his head and fling it into the ocean.

"What in The Machine's name do you think you're doing?"

My lips curl. Only the rubbish from Slum City worship at the shrine of The Machine. Ignorant trash, grovelling before a cruel god who decides whose lives have worth.

The Great White dives for the cap and crunches it in its

jaws. I laugh at the fury on Gollum's face. "It doesn't like you. It knew it was yours. But see now." I toss the bowl back into the sea.

The beast's fin whacks it at Gollum, who ducks. I taste delicious glee.

Reader joins us. "Such turbulence. There is water all over the deck. Is a storm coming?"

"Drudge has made a new friend. She and the big fish are playing catch with our things." Gollum places a hand on Reader's arm. "Stand back, Master Reader. She's going to throw us into the sea and let this killer play ball with us."

The Great White slices a path through the dark water. Back and forward. It reaches the seacraft and nudges it, moves off again in the same direction.

"It means us to follow. It's showing us the way," I say.

"The way where? It's going to lead us off the edge of the world and we'll become supper for a bunch of monsters. Don't listen to her nonsense, Master Reader."

Reader shakes his head. "I have never read about these great beasts being playful or guiding lost sailors. Dolphins, yes. They were known to be fun-loving and helpful." His eyes brighten. "But then again, the birds in the old world were not tellers, and flies back in the day were tiny insects, not as large as our fists. I expect things have changed over time."

The old man sighs. "Hoist the mainsail, my captain. Let us follow the fish. We have little choice."

CAPTAIN GOLLUM'S LOG

One, two,
Buckle my shoe;
Three, four,
Knock at the door;
Five, six,
Pick up sticks;
Seven, eight,
Lay them straight;
Nine, ten,
A big fat hen;
Eleven, twelve,
Dig and delve;
Thirteen, fourteen,
Maids a-courting;
Fifteen, sixteen,
Maids in the kitchen;
Seventeen, eighteen,
Maids in waiting;
Nineteen, twenty ...

Our sacks of food grow empty. The days grow past twenty. We buckle our other shoes and follow the sea monster. We knuckle the door, harder — no answer. The days grow past forty. I count our sacks of food. Only two left. Drudge has grown the appetite of five little piggies. The days grow past sixty, past ninety. We pick up more sticks, and lay them straighter.

The last sack of food is gone. Our bowls are empty. Captain Gollum is hungry. Master Reader is hungry. Drudge is hungry. She waddles around the sloop. She is clumsy and slow. She's given up all thoughts of pushing me overboard. She's going to need me to help when the brat gets born.

She is a maid in waiting. A big fat hen.

4

SANCTUARY

"Watch out – her claws draw blood. They'll take out your eyes. And mind those teeth – she bites." A woman stands over me. I struggle, but strong hands pin me down.

I force myself to go limp. When you're in a tricky situation, the smart thing to do is button your gob-hole and keep your cow-eyes peeled. Handler Xavier's Rule Number Nine has saved me before. I watch, and listen.

"Put her with the other two, but go easy on her – she's a Breeder." The woman scrapes golden hair back from her face and adjusts a mask. "You heard me. I said she's a Breeder. You can see that with your own two eyes. Move! Don't just stand there looking at her."

Men in grey uniforms, mouths and noses shielded by masks, haul me to my feet and lift me over the railings of the *Jolly Roger*. I am lowered into a smaller craft onto a pile of sacks next to Gollum and Reader. The Reject groans. The side of his head is a bloody mess. Reader is unconscious. I reach over, and his pulse flutters under my fingertips.

"Commander, we have anchored their boat and lowered

the sail as instructed."

Two other uniformed men heave themselves over the side of the sloop and join us in the small craft.

"Good work. We'll fetch it another day. We must get these people to shore quickly. They're in bad shape."

Land! Purple mountains reach into the sky, almost touching the sun. Below the mountains, swathes of grey earth meet a stretch of sand edging the coastline. No buildings, no sign of life. Only barren land, pitted with craters. A bleak expanse of nothing.

Commander sits at the front of the craft with the others. A man rows us across the sea, muscles rippling across his naked back. He looks over his shoulder at me, lying on the pile of sacks. The oarsman's eyes grow big when he sees my belly. The expression in his eyes is wonder. And dread. He pauses, one hand steadying the oars. His eyes drill holes in mine. He lifts the mask off his face and mouths: "Run." Then his eyes flick away and he turns back to his rowing.

I cannot mistake the warning behind that simple word. I stare at his back, willing him to turn around again, but he rows steadily without interrupting the fluid movement of the oars.

I gaze across the sea. A silver blade dips in the waves and sinks below the choppy water. A space opens in my chest. I do not hope to see my beautiful monster again.

A group of uniforms waiting on the shore meets the craft and drags it onto the beach. Commander leaps out and the others follow, carrying Reader and Gollum. They try and help me, but I push away their hands. My knees are wobbly. After so many months on the *Jolly Roger*, I'm not used to walking on solid ground. And there is no strength in my legs. I fall like Humpty Dumpty onto the sand.

The uniforms stand in a circle around us. Their golden hair is cropped short, their faces covered by masks. They stare at Gollum's thin limbs, his mop of Savage hair. They stare at me. At my round stomach. Their eyes are the size of plates.

A foot kicks inside my gut, and I touch my stomach. No, it is a fist. My boy is fierce. Wisha-wisha-wisha. *I will not let anyone hurt you.*

Commander puts her hands on her hips and sighs. "Yes, she's a Breeder. Suck your eyes back into your faces."

One of the men kneels next to Gollum. "It's a boy, it's a boy," he says. He strokes Gollum's cheek in wonder. And begins to weep softly.

"Get up. Control yourself," Commander says. When the man stands to attention, she touches his arm and murmurs, "You're not wearing gloves. We don't know if they're safe to touch."

I lie on the sand and listen to the voices around me. They speak through their noses, flattening their vowels. Their words run into each other, rising and falling, like a song.

Commander taps her ear and talks into the cuff of her shirt. "Three of them. An old man and a boy and a girl." She pauses. "They aren't doing much talking but they're flesh and blood, and they aren't Foogees, I'm certain – they came in a boat, not overland. I'll escort them down once they've had some food and water. The old man and the boy are nearly dead from hunger but the Breeder's in better shape." She pauses again, listens. "Affirmative. There's no mistake. I said: Breeder. The girl is heavy with it."

They bring water. One of the men helps Reader to sit and pats his face gently until he stirs. The old man sips feebly. Gollum gulps the water, grunting, and holds out his cup for more.

"So this one's a fighter?" a man says as he cleans Gollum's wound.

"The Breeder too – she's vicious." Commander flexes her hands, which are covered in scratches.

My head is thick from hunger. I do not remember them boarding the *Jolly Roger*. Or fighting Commander, scratching her hands.

"I had to subdue the boy – he thought we were trying to pirate his boat," Commander says. "Maybe I was a bit rough, but he wouldn't rest those fists of his, even though he's as weak as a kitten." She turns to the oarsman. "Give them food. But just a little. It looks like they haven't eaten for some time. They must go slow else they'll sick it all up."

My mouth fills with spit. I cannot remember when last I ate. After almost ninety days of following the big fish, we were down to half a sack of corn. Reader said we should eat a small bowl of food at midday and make the supplies last. But most days he said he was not hungry and would push his bowl across to me. As the sack slowly emptied, Gollum said he'd lost his appetite too.

At first I protested that I should be the only one eating, but Reader insisted. "You need to feed that growing burden of yours, my Juliet. We will soon reach land. Eat. I assure you, I am not hungry."

"Yes, eat, Drudge. Reader and I really don't want any."

I tried not to notice Gollum's hollow eyes watching me eat each spoonful until the bowl was empty. And then they stopped sitting with me. Gollum spent the days writing his captain's log until he became too weak to hold a pencil. Reader sat with me on the bow. He sniffed the sea air and sang nursery rhymes to himself until his voice grew brittle and faded. The days passed and he lay listlessly on the deck, his blind eyes open to the sky, humming only sometimes. I steered the *Jolly Roger* behind the Great White. It swam a few metres ahead and sometimes turned back to nudge us along.

Now the men hand us bowls of food and I force myself to pause between each mouthful. The orange vegetable is warm and fibrous, coated in sugar. It tastes good, like pumpkin. Gollum attacks the food with his fingers, pushing it desperately into his mouth.

"Slow down, boy," Commander says. "Let the food settle for a few minutes. There's lots more butterynut where this came from."

Butterynut! A beautiful name for this vegetable.

Commander refills Gollum's bowl and smiles at me. "We must keep you healthy." Her blue eyes crinkle at the corners. The cracks tell of someone who has laughed too much. Or cried.

I finish my food and drink more water. I am swallowed by weariness. My eyes close and I sink back onto the sand.

"Come, you can sleep later. Someone is impatient to meet you. This is the first time in more than two hundred years we've had visitors from across the sea," Commander says.

I hear a loud noise and a large metal machine on wheels pulls to a stop at the edge of the sand.

Reader cowers. "Where am I? What is making this noise? Juliet, what is this thing? Describe it to me."

Commander hears his question and laughs. "Ah, at least one of you has a voice. It's called a Land Rover. Or sometimes a Landie. It's built to run off solar power and carries people long distances over rough terrain."

"Of course, of course. I have read about the motor vehicle!" Reader's face is pink with excitement, his weakness forgotten. "In the old world they were powered by petroleum. They had no need for the Pulaks. And now you say the vehicle is fuelled by the sun? How extraordinary!"

Back home, The Machine also gets its energy from the sun. So do the lamps and cooling units in the Posh homes, and the lights that flicker in the streets at night.

Commander takes my arm and we climb into the back of the Landie. Two of the men lift Gollum and Reader onto seats next to me. The Landie makes a noise like stones rattling in a pipe. It jerks and then lurches forward, bouncing over the sand. Reader clutches his seat, his blind eyes big, pink gums chattering in his mouth. Time travels with us along the bumpy roads until at last we stop.

Outside, purple mountains surround us, but there is nothing else in sight. Only grey earth. Commander taps her ear, mumbles into the cuff of her shirt and the earth opens. A metal box emerges and a door slides open.

"The lift will take us underground," Commander says.

Gollum stumbles back. "No. I'm not going underground. Not underground."

Commander picks up Gollum as though he were a doll and heaves him over her shoulder. One of the men carries Reader and the other hustles me into the box after Commander. She presses her thumb against some numbers on the side of the box and we move down, down, down.

I touch Gollum's shoulder. He is trembling, his skin covered in sweat. We continue our descent until it feels as though we must have reached the bottom of the world.

The box jerks to a stop and opens onto a corridor. Two men with guns stand at a door. Their eyes widen above their masks when they see us.

"At ease, Peacemakers," Commander says, and ushers us into a room.

She calls them Peacemakers, but they have the appearance of the Locusts at home. There is no peace in those cruel blue eyes.

The room is brightly lit and sparsely furnished: there is a desk, a few chairs and a couch. A mirror lines a wall, making the room seem larger than it is. The floor is covered in a plush white carpet and a giant screen dominates one of the walls. Pictures of people working in a garden move on the screen.

They are in the room with me. But on the screen at the same time. It is magic only a wizard as powerful as Gandalf could conjure.

A man – not Gandalf – rises from a chair. His nose and mouth are unmasked but most of his face is hidden under bandages. I have seen faces like this before at the Beautiful Like Me Beauty Parlour in the pleasure quarter. The Posh like to roast their skins brown on the beach and then bleach them white with acid. Sometimes the acid is too strong and it takes weeks of bandages to heal. Sometimes the bandages stay on for good.

The man stares at us with blue eyes spittled with white flecks. "Thank you, Commander. Your men can place the old fellow on the couch and go." The door shuts behind us and the Peacemakers take their places inside the room. "Please sit," the man says.

Gollum sways, then collapses on the carpet. I shift Reader's feet to the side and perch on the couch. Ready to leap up and run if things get tricky.

"Are we prisoners?" Gollum says, scowling at the Peacemakers at the door.

The man laughs. "You're our guests! And most welcome." His mouth is a set of large, perfect white teeth – not one of them dares to squabble for room the way mine do. He lowers himself carefully into the chair opposite the couch and, with a stifled grunt, crosses his legs. He leans back and folds his hands. They are the hands of a wrinkly past trader; the white skin is sprinkled with grey hair and brown spots.

"Let me introduce myself. My name is Charles Gilby-Gold. I'm a member of one of the founding families of this community. They call me Shepherd, sometimes Chuck – we are most informal here." He chuck-chuck-chuckles, a strangled noise that ends in a wheeze. "I'm intrigued to hear all about you. Where you are from, how you came to be here."

Gollum's mouth is clenched. Reader trembles beside me and murmurs: "Juliet. Speak, Juliet. I have no breath."

My cow-eyes are peeled, my gob-hole is buttoned.

After an awkward silence, Shepherd clears his throat. "I can see you are a little shy. Perhaps I should go first, and you can repay me the courtesy later. When you feel more at ease."

As he reaches for a glass of water, a white shape rises from the plush carpet and leaps onto my lap. I jerk back, pressing myself into the cushions. Shepherd hisses and clicks his tongue.

"My old cat, Hector. He obviously senses your fear. Cats do, you know."

Hector is nothing like Alice's Cheshire Cat in Reader's picture books. His fur is white and plush like the carpet, but sticky under my fingers. He looks at me with yellow-green eyes – the colour of the gooey entrails of a cockroach crushed under foot. He claws my lap and releases a foul smell. I do not know if I like cats.

"If Hector is quite comfortable, may I begin?" Shepherd puts down the glass of water and clasps his hairy white hands. "Many years ago, a cartel of wealthy men came together. They acquired this piece of land and built a place of refuge for their families beneath the ground, a bunker that could withstand the onslaught they knew was coming."

His voice is sweet and mellow, like the wine my former Master liked to drink, aged in barrels for hundreds of years. It made his face red and his temper bad.

Shepherd continues. "The Cartel recruited skilled people who would ensure their survival. They settled here and waited for the end of days."

I watch Shepherd as he speaks. His tongue flicks over his moist pink lips. He smiles too often with his big white teeth, eager to steal a smile from me. My teeth stay safe behind my closed lips. I do not let thieves take what is mine.

"Soon, the world was destroyed by the weapons unleashed by mad men and their machines during the Great War. But my people survived in our bunker, deep in the earth. They waited until the fires burnt out and the seas subsided, until it was safe to emerge. The Cartel formed a government and it has since managed our lives here, in this place we call Sanctuary."

Reader stirs next to me and murmurs, "This is most interesting. These people showed great foresight and planning, and their Cartel appears similar to our Guardians."

The old man is correct. They sound like the first families in Mangeria, who banded together and got things running again after the conflagration. They control all the resources and make the nasty rules that govern our lives in Slum City.

Shepherd unclasps his hands. "This is a short version of the history of the Sancturians, as we like to call ourselves.

Now, I would like to hear your story. Or at least, trust me with your names." He looks at Gollum sitting hunched up on the carpet. His blue eyes flick over the growths on his forehead. The white flecks dim. "First, and foremost, let me hear from the little devil."

Gollum straightens his spine. "First, and foremost, Chuck, the name's Gollum. The girl over there, Juliet, called me this. But you can address me as Captain Gollum. I like to keep things formal. The sloop your Locusts boarded is mine, and they had no right to do this without my permission."

Shepherd smiles at me with glee. "Gollum, of course. You chose well, Juliet. It suits him."

I do not like the way Shepherd looks at Gollum, or his pleasure at the name I gave the Reject out of mischief and spite. Generosity is not in my nature. I do not want to share my malice with this man.

Gollum pulls himself onto his knees. Before he can stand, the two Peacemakers are at his side, holding him at the elbows.

"Tell your Locusts to back off. Or is this the way you welcome your guests?" Gollum says, struggling to get free.

Shepherd clicks his fingers and they release him. "Locusts? They are Peacemakers. And I think you must forgive them for being overcautious. You are strangers and we know nothing about you. Perhaps Juliet can tell me your story. I am eager to hear about the younger people in the land you come from. They are properly formed? Not all of them are ..." His gaze brushes Gollum's face and he arranges a thin strand of hair over his balding head. "And it would also interest me to know where exactly your home is. We had no idea there were others like us who survived."

I have no choice but to speak. But I tell Shepherd our story in the sly way the orphan warden used when she reported to the orphanage inspector about her duties. 'Bafflescat', we called it. Lots of suffocating words and useless detail. It always had the inspector backing away for air.

I speak slowly, using my drudge voice. I drone on, and on, and on. Shepherd shuffles and wriggles in his chair like a child trapped in a dull lesson. I pretend not to see his hand begging me to pause until he taps the side of his chair impatiently. "Your land. You could tell me where it is? How we could find it?"

I stare into Shepherd's eyes and the white flecks shatter the blue. "A storm came and we got lost. But we plan to try and find our way home again," I say.

Shepherd uncrosses his legs and stretches them out, releasing a curious sound – a mixture of a grunt and a yelp of pain. Grulp-grulp-grulp. He rubs his knees. "Let's talk later. You need to eat more and then rest. Afterwards I'd like our doctors to examine you to make sure that you're healthy." He covers his nose and mouth with his speckled hand. "We are anxious not to be infected by any sickness that might have travelled with you. An isolated community like ours is vulnerable."

He rises, fumbling for the arms of his chair to steady himself. "Of course you are most welcome. But I do expect you to abide by our laws and traditions while you are under our care." He blinks at me, shutters slammed over icy blue. "And you, my dear, are *most* welcome. Let my Peacemakers take you to your quarters."

As I lift Hector off my lap and stand, pain washes over my gut. I look down. Water is trickling down my legs. I grab my stomach and mist crosses my eyes.

Shepherd presses the arm of his chair. The mirror on the wall slides open and reveals people in a room behind. Their faces are masked and bandaged. Some of them support themselves on crutches. Others wear white coats.

Frankensteins. I know their uniform and their long syringes. Their procedures, their intentions.

I see my great fish's fin flashing through the dark waves, hear the oarsman's word: "Run."

I stumble across the carpet towards the door. I cannot run.

I fall.

CAPTAIN GOLLUM'S LOG

Drudge fought her pain like a Scavvie. Her language was fierce and rude, a credit to any slagget in the Posh City pleasure clubs. I won't record her words; I don't know how to spell them. Master Reader never taught me.

The pain came at her, wave after wave, hour upon hour, until I thought she was drowned. But she kept her head up.

Me and Master Reader knelt at her side as she lay on that plush white carpet. She held my hands and with each wave she wrenched my fingers back, making me feel her pain. When her screams came too loud, I shoved my fist in her mouth and she bit down, drew blood.

The whitecoats stood back. She

wouldn't let them near her. And Shepherd told them to hold their horses. That meant they must leave us alone.

When she started pushing, Shepherd called the whitecoats. I tried to fight them but Shepherd summoned the Locusts. (They call them Peacemakers, but I know these brutes.) As the whitecoats slid on their gloves and armed their instruments, the Locusts ganged us and dragged me and Master Reader away. They held their guns on us outside the door. But we could still hear Drudge's screams. Like the curfew call in Slum City – that loud. She screeched like a banshee!

At last there was silence, thank The Machine. Then the squalling of a baby. I know the sound, from working down the river. A horrible noise. Sand in the nose usually made it stop.

The wailing ended. Silence. More wailing. A chorus of wailing. And laughter. The excited clapping of palms.

My hand is sore from Drudge's fangs. I'm not laughing or clapping. I can barely write this entry.

5

THE BREEDERS

I stand at the edge of the shore watching the white sail rise on the mast of the *Jolly Roger*.

Gollum and Commander have rowed out to collect Reader's suitcase of precious books and to take the sloop for a spin. Afterwards they will anchor it in a sheltered cove close by. There is no harbour on this coastline, and ours is the only seacraft apart from a few rowboats.

A tiny hand touches my face and I kiss it. My son is a mirror image of Nicolas. It hurts me to look at him. It is sweet pain.

My daughter might have looked like Nicolas too. She came first and bawled her lungs out until there was nothing left. A few minutes after her brother came, she whispered one last breath. I don't know if they showed her to me, or if I held her. My head was full of mist and madness. I heard screams – mine. Clapping and cheers. Then a Frankenstein's voice: "The Breeder's a real mess inside. I'm not sure she's going to make it. Even if she does, she's useless to us."

"You're sure?" Shepherd's voice. "Damn. That's bad luck."

Murmurs. Voices raised in argument. Hands pulling and tugging inside me. My pain was unbearable. They cut and stitched my torn flesh. Time passed in a blur.

Shepherd's voice again. "We're out of options. We'll just to be patient and trust that our Healers can work their magic."

The Frankensteins carried my daughter's body away and sealed her in a small box. She is resting in the Garden of Never Forgetting with the Sancturians who have passed. I visit her often and water the rose bush I planted next to her grave. I named her Rose. My son's name is Thorn. Gollum calls him Stinker.

Shepherd calls him a miracle.

There are no other children in Sanctuary. The last child was born here more than thirty years ago. And now Thorn. The Healers tell me the birth was complicated and I nearly died. Thorn will be my only child; I can have no others.

People no longer wear masks around us and the prohibition against touching has ended. During the first couple of weeks after we arrived, we were subjected to many tests before the Frankensteins were satisfied we were disease-free. Thorn too. Shepherd says I must call them Healers – their mission is to cure illness, not to harm or create monsters.

Back home, our Healers experimented on orphans to perfect a method to unSavage the people of Slum City; to make them obedient to Mangerian law. They used the prisoners of Savage City like rats, devising a cure for Larissa's illness, not caring how many died during their procedures.

I find it hard to trust men in white coats.

"Please, can I touch him?" a Peacemaker says and steps towards me. He is one of those who accompanies me whenever I leave my quarters with Thorn. Shepherd says it is for our protection. The Sancturians lose their senses when they see us. Some of them cry and tear their hair, others try to grab Thorn out of my arms.

The Peacemaker brushes his hand against Thorn's cheek. He leans closer and breathes his skin. "My sister was one of the last to be born in Sanctuary. My father had two kids, her and me. But I've got none. A year ago, my wife walked into the sea."

In the past four months I've heard many similar stories. The Sancturians live without children, and despair for the future.

The Peacemaker's face softens as he touches his fingers to his lips and presses them on Thorn's forehead. "And you're just a girl. You could've been my daughter." He strokes my arm.

I stiffen and step back. I don't like touching, and I'm not used to always being stroked and grabbed. The hungry gazes on my face. The tears.

The Peacemaker joins the others on the beach in front of a group of women peering over at us from under umbrellas. They pat down their long skirts, flapping in the breeze, and hold on to their bonnets.

"Juliet, Juliet, let us see him. Show us the miracle child," a woman shouts. She breaks through the Peacemakers and stumbles towards me. She is pushed back.

The *Jolly Roger* edges towards the cove. Commander is standing on the bow with Gollum. He waves at me, then bellows with laughter as Commander leans over the railing, pulls back her golden hair and hurls into the waves. She is not a good sailor!

They anchor the sloop and the oarsman brings Commander and Gollum back to shore. It is the same oarsman who rowed us here when we first arrived. I watch his mouth anxiously, but his lips are locked. He does not even glance at me.

Run: the memory of that one mute word niggles me like the drip-drip-drip of a faulty tap.

Gollum limps past me towards the Peacemakers. His face is still gaunt, but it's growing fuller. There is an abundance of food in Sanctuary and he is determined to eat his share.

The women sing out his name as he approaches: "Captain Gollum, Captain Gollum."

He is delighted by all the attention and disappears under clutches of outstretched hands. He lets them hug him if they feed him enough cake, and they don't seem to mind his gimpy foot and ugly face. They find him beautiful. He's the son they all wish they had.

I fill my lungs with sea air and adjust my bonnet to shade my face. Thorn stirs and I arrange my scarf over his hot head. Here, the sun seems to shine with double strength and it will soon force me back into the bunker. Gollum spends as much time as he can above ground. He panics at the thought of thousands of tons of earth pressing down above him.

It is no punishment for me, however. Sanctuary is a functioning village with shops and places where people work and entertain themselves. I will be content for the short time I stay here. I have enough to eat and drink, and a comfortable bed. Best of all, there's a library full of books. I am Bilbo Baggins in Smaug's treasure chamber. Books, books! All for me!

But, no. Librarian Betty, the miserable dragon who guards the library, says my enthusiasm for reading is unhealthy and unnatural – a passion that most Sancturians have learnt to control. She only allows me to read certain things: plays written by a raunchy bard called William Shakespeare, and books by Shepherd (there are shelves of these miserable tomes). She says Shepherd's books will instruct me how to be a good wife, while Master Shakespeare will cure me of reading forever.

I feasted on the Bard's plays during the long months I spent recovering from the birth. I fed my baby and read out loud to Reader, who stretched out on the couch. The old man shut his eyes, pretended to sleep. He sometimes drooled.

Master Shakespeare did not cure me of reading. His words were a banquet after a long fast. Day after day I gorged myself, reading each play several times. And at night I dreamt of my Romeo back home in Mangeria. We are fated to be together; it is written in the stars. Nicolas will wait for me. He cannot believe that I left him forever. Or that I am dead.

I peer across the stretch of beach at the heaving machine perched like a great monster a few metres into the sea. It sucks in the salt water, vomits out the brine into giant vats, and feeds the taps of Sanctuary with sweet water through underground pipes. A group of men called Fixits row out to the machine. Their job is to maintain it and ensure that Sanctuary always has water. There is plenty to drink, to wash clothes, more than enough to bath. Bliss!

Gollum pulls himself away from the cooing women and joins me.

"How's Stinker?" he says, pressing the back of his hand against Thorn's forehead. "The sun's too hot for him, Drudge. You must use an umbrella. And I'm sure he needs liquid. Give him here – he's missed me."

He lifts Thorn out of his sling, ignoring the startled faces of the Peacemakers, the shouts of, "No, be careful, Captain Gollum. Be careful!" from the women.

He pulls the pacifier from Thorn's mouth and tosses him into the air. "See how he smiles for his captain. Yes, you like me. Yes, you do. You do, you do." Thorn gurgles and throws up on Gollum's shoulder.

"Stop it, fool. You're too rough." I take Thorn back and wipe his mouth. I ignore the mess on Gollum's shoulder.

"The *Jolly Roger*'s in a sad way. I've neglected her too long," Gollum says. "The hull's leaking and we're going to need a new mast. The mainsail's also looking a bit sorry. And that's just for starters."

"But we can leave soon?"

"Don't be in such a hurry, Drudge. Thorn's too small to travel. He needs more time to grow. And the old man is still weak."

Reader is regaining his strength, but the healing is slow. His body had shrunk to a husk from the months of little food. I knew he was nearly his sly old self again when he told me he was sick of my boring voice and had slept enough – he wanted to read his blind books in peace. And he would rather cut out my tongue than hear me read another word from Shepherd's books about how the good wives of Sanctuary must suppress their unnatural passions.

This week the Healers declared Thorn and me fully recovered. Tomorrow we will move from their care in the healing hub into regular living quarters, and I will start working at the plant farm. Shepherd says while I stay here, I must be useful. There is no room for slackers in Sanctuary. My fingers itch to feel the soil. To smell the flowers.

The oarsman puts the suitcase of books in the back of the Landie. A few women run after us when we go: "Wait for us! Let us ride with you." They trip on the hems of their skirts and we leave them with the dust.

I ride in the back with the Peacemakers like Cinderella, on a specially fashioned seat that cushions the jolting from the potholed road. Gollum sits up front with Commander. He's learning to drive and Commander lets him change the gears and swipe the indicator. Left-right. Left-right. Even when the vehicle does not turn on the dead straight road.

My eyes scan the mountain alongside. Hundreds of solar panels stretch across the top of the highest range like an army of marching insects. They capture the sun and feed the lights and the machines that pump clean air into the bunker.

The Landie skids as we pass a stretch of dunes, and comes to a sharp stop. Voices are shouting outside, angry and shrill. I peer out the window as a crowd surrounds the vehicle. Women in rags, faces shredded by the sun. Gaping mouths of blackened teeth. Arms blistered and covered with sores.

They start pushing against the Landie, and it rocks, threatening to tip over.

"Stay inside. It's not safe!" a Peacemaker yells as he and two others throw open the rear door and leap out.

But I am a curious cat, and being safe is not a game I've ever played.

I check that Thorn is secure in his sling and after hitching up my long skirt, I scramble out after the Peacemakers. They're pointing their guns at the women, forcing them back. I tighten my grip around Thorn.

"Disperse immediately!" Commander is kneeling on the roof of the Landie and shoots above their heads. The bullets smash into the side of the dunes. The hags run, some of them fall.

A hand pulls my hair. I turn around. A face, inches from mine. It is eaten away by the sun, the skin around her eyes shattered by deep wrinkles. She grabs at my chest, her filthy fingers tearing at the sling, trying to get at Thorn. I grip her hand and shove her away.

"Run," she hisses at me. She clears her throat and spits in my face. I wipe the brown phlegm off my cheek as she stumbles towards the dunes.

A Peacemaker grabs one of the women on the ground.

The old hag cries out as he yanks up her head by her filthy hair and slaps her. "Don't dare show your face on our roads! We want none of your kind. Go back to the dunes and tell your sisters that next time we'll deal with you in the abattoir." He follows a few steps as she crawls away, his heavy boots slamming into her. Thud. Thud.

I run up to him and grab his arm. "Stop it. Just stop."

Commander nods. "Yes, enough. Let's go." She looks over at a Peacemaker kneeling on the ground next to a woman. "That one's dead. Leave the body. The sun and the cockroaches will finish it off. We need to get back."

Cockroaches. Back home, and here too. Survivors of the conflagration, along with rats – food for Hector and the hundreds of other cats that stink out the corridors of Sanctuary.

I settle myself comfortably on the soft cushion as the Peacemakers pile back into the Landie. It lurches onto the road, gears screaming.

"Who were those women? What did they want with us?" I say.

The Peacemakers are silent. Then the youngest of them, the one who touched Thorn back on the beach, mumbles, "We call them Breeders."

Breeders. I heard that word when I arrived at Sanctuary, but my memory of the first day is fuzzy.

"Useless rubbish, that's what they are. Filth on this earth," says the brutish Peacemaker who kicked the wretched crone. As Master Shakespeare would say, a Locust by any other name would smell as foul. He sucks his teeth and spits. "I don't know why they're allowed to run about in the dunes. We should hunt them down."

Commander's fist hammers against the interior partition. "You lot in the back there, pipe down. Observe operational silence until we reach base."

Back at the bunker, I'm about to take the lift to Reader's quarters when Commander stops me.

"Juliet, Captain Gollum, Shepherd has asked to see you."

A man and a woman are loitering in the corridor outside Shepherd's rooms. The lines on their faces tell me they have lived long past their time of usefulness. All of the residents in Sanctuary are over thirty years old, so there are lots of these past traders – Seniors, Shepherd calls them. When they can no longer earn an honest living, they are cared for until they pass on. I think it's a strange way of dealing with useless old rubbish.

"We've got an appointment. Shepherd said we must wait here until you arrived," the old woman tells Commander. She peers at me, and her faded blue eyes rest on the sweet bulge sleeping in the sling.

Commander presses her thumb to the pad on the door and we enter to find Shepherd watching a moving picture on the giant screen. It is a queue of people buying vegetables in a store. They are handing over dollas – their currency here in Sanctuary – and receiving brown coins in return.

Shepherd monitors Sanctuary by means of cameras –

blinking red eyes rotating on ceilings throughout the bunker. The Sancturians believe it is a security system to keep them safe and call it The Angel. But I know that it is a way for Shepherd to spy. I often zap the red eye with my middle finger as I wander the corridors.

Shepherd looks up as we enter. The bandages on his face were removed a couple of months ago, and his skin is now smooth and pink, like a baby rat's. His balding head is covered in small plugs of gold tufts. Soon he will have a mane of hair fit for Prince Charming.

I have seen his sort in the pleasure clubs back home. Vain old Posh with young faces and spotted hands. They fix their uglies in clinics along the coast so the pretty boys and girls will smile when they dance for them. But I have not found any pleasure clubs in Sanctuary. I guess Shepherd considers dancing to be an unnatural passion. Like reading.

"Commander, I hear there was trouble on the road?" Shepherd says.

"We dealt with them. Our guests are safe," Commander replies.

Shepherd opens his hands in welcome. The speckled skin is shrouded in bandages, like the hands of a boxer. "Senior Kevin and Good-Wife Tracey. I'm sorry I kept you waiting. I first needed to speak to the Cartel." He carefully sidesteps a pink stain on the plush carpet and takes the elderly man's arm awkwardly in his bandaged hand.

The mirror in the room shifts to one side and a circle of bandaged faces stare at us. Some members of the Cartel are in wheelchairs. A Healer standing behind one of them fiddles with a plastic bag dripping green liquid into the bandaged head.

"Juliet, please sit. I have business with these people that concerns you. And Captain Gollum, of course."

Senior Kevin remains standing. "You know why we're here, Shepherd. We've waited more than thirty years for a Breeder to do her duty. We've come for our child."

Beside me, Gollum stiffens.

I stare around the room. At the Peacemakers guarding the door. At Commander, standing at Shepherd's side.

I'm trapped.

I clutch Thorn. Wisha-wisha-wisha. *I will not let them take you from me.*

"That's true, Senior Kevin. Your names have been at the top of the list for more than three decades," Shepherd says, his eyes a cold sea of blue.

My mouth is full of jumbled words that refuse to meet my tongue. I swallow a bubble of panic.

Gollum pulls himself off the couch, his fists clenched. "Not a chance, Chuck. I've heard how you used to populate Sanctuary. But Juliet didn't volunteer for your little breeding programme. And anyway, I gather it's been a complete balls-up."

Shepherd steps back and raises his boxer's hands to place some distance between himself and Gollum's fists. "True, too true, Captain Gollum. She was not one of our volunteers and she is a visitor here, not a citizen of Sanctuary. This does create a small difficulty."

The bandaged faces of the Cartel nod in agreement.

"Indeed, it could be argued that the child is Juliet's property," Shepherd says.

The room is silent and the Seniors whisper.

Good-Wife Tracey's face burns red; her eyes are fierce. "No! The child was born here and he's a Sancturian. You all know the law." She shakes her finger at the bandaged faces like they are naughty students who have forgotten their lessons. "Children must be raised by *two* parents. It's their right. While the Breeder lives here, she must abide by our traditions."

Senior Kevin grabs his good wife's finger and holds it. "As I see it, the boy must live with us for as long as the Breeder remains here. We will have this child, even for a short while."

Shepherd smiles at me with baby tombstone teeth. "Certainly, it is one of our laws. A temporary arrangement, of course. Until you leave." He reaches down and strokes Hector, who is arching against his legs.

The cat purrs and blinks. The Cartel nods mutely. Good-Wife Tracey glows.

The sound of hands clapping.

Gollum grins and claps some more. "Problem solved, Chuck. The child already has two parents. Where we come from, Juliet and I are fate-mates. Thorn is *my* child." He reaches down and holds my hand. "And Juliet is my wife. She belongs to me."

I press my nails into the back of Gollum's hand. How dare he claim me! How dare this Reject say he owns me! Gollum grins, his mouth full of sharp teeth, and grips my hand until I wince.

Shepherd's nostrils twitch. "You are with him, Juliet? He is your husband? You allowed this … boy to touch you?"

Right now, I can allow my child to be raised by two Seniors, or I can pretend to take a Reject for a fate-mate. As Master Shakespeare would say, there is small choice in this barrel of rotten apples. But I must learn to make cider. And I will smile sweetly, and drink the sour juice until I leave.

I steel myself against the desperate faces of the two old people who are looking so longingly at Thorn. *I'm sorry. I'm so sorry, but I cannot lose him too, not even for a day.*

I know what it is to yearn for a child. Not a day passes that I do not think of my Rose, who she might have been. I cannot imagine what my life would be like if I did not have my Thorn.

I link my fingers in Gollum's and pull myself off the couch. "My husband and I will raise Thorn according to your law," I say. I force back one of Gollum's fingers with all my spite. "And in a few months, when the *Jolly Roger* is repaired, I'm taking my child home."

Shepherd places together his bandaged hands in a gesture of submission, or prayer. He bows his head, lowering his eyes from mine. "Of course. Of course."

CAPTAIN GOLLUM'S LOG

We live like the Posh! Like two Guardians in a Mangerian mansion. No, better than that — our living quarters in Sanctuary are like a palace fit for a king and queen.

Since taking Drudge as my wife I've been moved out of my shabby room into married quarters. Gaining a ball and chain in wedlock is a small price for all this luxury. Our bed is three times the size of the room I stayed in next to the rubbish bins at the back of the pleasure clubs.

Our bed. Drudge's and mine.

Our duvet, handstitched and chicken-shell white, is filled with the feathers of baby ducks. So are our pillows. Puffy clouds, not like the lumpy porridge Drudge made me every morning at sea. And they smell like lavender, not burnt oats.

Not that I've had a chance to lay my head on them. Drudge makes me sleep on the floor under a cold sheet, while she stretches out like a princess, snoring like a Drainer after a long day shovelling scat in Slum City sewers.

Stinker sleeps in his cot next to her bed and during the night I hear her suckling him, soothing him back to sleep. She won't let me see to him — the only task she gives me is to change his napkins. What a stinker he is!

In the mornings, Drudge fills our bath — the size of a Posh swimming pool — and sprinkles the water with smelly crystals. She wallows in the water, reciting lines from her precious Master Shakespeare's books:

"Tomorrow, and tomorrow, and tomorrow, creeps in this petty pace from day to day." I know the words as good as Drudge.

I mouth them standing outside the bathroom door, waiting for her to hurry up so I can take a piss.

At home in Slum City there's another Shakespeare who gab-gabs these boring lines — he's not so precious to me. He is the leader of the Rejects, who calls himself Lord Shakespeare because he loves the Bard as much as Drudge does. I'm bonded to him, the filthy infidel, and when I get back to Slum City he's going to squeeze me for the credits I owe, or take my pound of flesh. Bloody Shylock!

When she's run out of words, Drudge sings popular songs from the clubs. They make me long for home. She bellows them out like a drunk goat.

Did Master Reader ever suspect? That every night, after we'd set a course by the stars, I sailed the *Jolly Roger* away from Mangeria?

I kept my promise to my friend.

Drudge speaks every day about going home. She's like a Market Nag, crying the same boring tune, trying to sell off her wares before the end of the day.

And yes, it's time to go. I've honoured my word, and we've been away too long. I don't like this place, even with all the good food and books. Shepherd looks at me like I'm lower than a cockroach. The people are sad here, and crazy. There are secrets in these deep tunnels. I feel them — they echo my own terrible secrets. Things

I've done for Lord Shakespeare and other masters to survive.

Each day in this bunker is a torment. I can't breathe in our palace. The piles of concrete press down on my head. My sleep is filled with nightmares and Drudge kicks me when I make too much noise. I dream that the earth will collapse and trap me in this terrible tomb.

And this time, my friend will not be there to save me.

6

THE MEAT FARM

I am cruising the skies of Mangeria City on the back of Buckbeak, Hagrid's hippogriff. I peer into Larissa's bedroom and find her wide awake, staring out of her window, hoping Princess Fanny will bring her news.

I'm coming, Larissa. I'm nearly home!

In the pleasure quarter, there she is, my beautiful friend Kitty, dancing the jig we used to practise at the orphanage. When we swoop past Nicolas's bedroom, he is sleeping, dreaming of me.

The hippogriff falters, his body stiffens. He free floats. We are falling, falling, falling. Catch me, Nicolas, catch me.

I wake shivering.

I am spooning butterynut into Thorn's mouth. He eats like a greedy chick, opening his gummy beak even before he's finished swallowing.

He has doubled in size these past few months and appears strong enough to make the journey home. We have only a few days to wait until Gollum finishes some minor repairs and restocks the *Jolly Roger*. Sand in the hourglass trickles away the last hours.

The door opens and Gollum hobbles into the kitchen. "How's my Stinker? Are you stuffing your face? Eating like your daddy?"

Daddy!

"Don't excite him." I soften my tone and paste a tender smile on my face. "Your breakfast is warming in the oven. I've made your eggs exactly as you like them, husband dear."

Gollum plants a kiss on my cheek, nips my skin as he nuzzles my neck. "You grow more beautiful every day, wife. And did you say eggs? I'm so hungry I could eat a chicken."

"I'll cook chicken for you tonight, husband. Boiled feet and heads, a whole pot." And one of Thorn's filthy napkins to add flavour to the stock.

I glance up at the ceiling. The red eye blinks at me. As Gollum shovels eggs and toast into his mouth with his fingers, I smile with tight lips. The eye tracks my every movement in Sanctuary, my every frown and twitch. The only place I can be private is in my sleeping and bathing quarters. Mine and Gollum's. And Thorn's, who sleeps in a cot next to our bed. *Our* bed!

Before we arrived, only Shepherd spied on the bunker by way of the giant screen in his quarters. Now, my family is the biggest show in town. Screens have been placed in all the entertainment centres, and the Sancturians can watch us whenever they like. Feeding Thorn. Bathing Thorn. Pushing Thorn in his stroller. Everyone can share in the life of the miracle child.

Shepherd says the self-killings in Sanctuary have stopped

these past few months, and the people are happier. I don't want to care about what will happen when we leave.

Gollum shifts back his chair and messes Thorn's hair. Then he plants a wet kiss on my face, his tongue slobbering in my ear. "I'll be off to work then, wife. You two don't miss me too much." He gives a thumbs-up to the red eye. "Isn't she a babe? Aren't I the luckiest husband in Sanctuary?"

Oh, how he provokes me!

I wipe his gob from my ear and grip the table, wobbling in my chair. "Did you feel that, husband? Movement under our feet!" I make my eyes scary-wide. "Oh! Is that a crack in the ceiling? Did you feel … a trickle of earth?"

Gollum's face pales and his body stiffens, but I have no mercy.

"The bunker's caving in – we'll be buried alive!" Then I flash him my honey smile. "Oops, no, I must have been mistaken." I touch his face and give his cheek a sly pinch. "Don't be late for work, husband. I'll bring your lunch at midday – some cheese and a loaf I've baked with my own fair hands."

I am playing the game. Not scamming the Posh the way I did with Handler Xavier and Kitty when I lived at the orphanage in Slum City. No, now I'm playing the perfect wife. My dutiful mask sits squarely on my face, hiding my feelings. I will not slip up and confirm Shepherd's suspicions that Gollum is not my husband. My child will not be raised by someone else, not even for a day.

I sometimes see Senior Kevin and Good-Wife Tracey

buying their two pieces of meat at the butcher. Their two slices of bread at the baker. Their two apples at the grocer. I clutch Thorn to my chest and hurry away, eyes averted from their bleak faces.

I have reluctantly agreed to let Reader take me on an excursion this morning – I would have preferred to spend my last few days in Sanctuary reading, but he says there is something he wants to show me. I am meeting him at the library, where the old dragon lets him sit in the mornings. He may smell the books, but no touching, Master Reader. No touching!

With Thorn in the stroller, I take the lift to the floor three levels above my "married" living quarters. Gollum and I live here amongst the Cartel while Reader has to slum it in small rooms reserved for less affluent Seniors on the tenth floor.

Up there the corridors are dark, and the walls are covered with angry words. An abandoned playground is silenced by litter. Cockroaches twitch and scurry over my feet; rats feast on dark shapes in doorways. Seniors loiter outside shops, sucking on bottles concealed in brown paper bags. As in Mangeria, some Sancturians have too much, others too little. Not all are allowed to age with dignity. Why did I think it would be any different across the sea?

Two Peacemakers follow closely behind me. I have grown used to them and often forget they are there. I check the signs on the doorways in the corridor. Some of the passages are restricted to residents. They lead to industrial areas further down – to chemical factories, and places where vehicles are serviced. Shepherd has told me that the bunker stretches on many levels.

One day the last Senior will pass on, leaving no descendants, and Sanctuary will become a village for ghosts.

I press my thumb against a glowing pad and the library door slides open.

"Juliet?" Reader sniffs. "And do I smell a baby, freshly washed with jasmine soap?"

I look up at the ceiling, at the red eye. Reader cannot see it, but I have told him it is there, always watching.

"Ready to go, old man? Let's get this over with."

"Come now, Juliet. You cannot learn everything from books. I would like to visit just one last place of interest before we leave Sanctuary." He smiles slyly at me. "And afterwards I will buy you an ice lolly. Strawberry."

The old devil knows my weakness.

Before we go, I return Gollum's books to Librarian Betty. He's got the dragon wrapped around his baby finger and she lets him borrow anything he likes. She lures him to the library with apple-pie and comics – picture stories about people with superpowers from the old world, which Reader says will mush Gollum's fine brain. But no comics, or books, or apple- pie for me.

Gollum only lets me read his books if I perform the duties of a good wife. Picking wax out of his ears got me *Harry Potter and the Prisoner of Azkaban*. I earned an atlas for clipping his dirty fingernails.

But it was worth it: I have learnt my way home from the maps. When we leave next week, we will not get lost.

Shepherd often asks me if I know where I am going. "Show me, exactly, precisely, specifically where your land is," he says, his gnarled finger slip-sliding greasily over the pages of the atlas.

He wants to know too badly. I do not trust the fever in his eyes. I blank my face with my dumb drudge mask.

"I just don't know. I can't be certain," I mumble, my words thickened by a fat tongue – and thick with glee. My stupidity makes Shepherd twitch and wheeze. I mumble-mumble until his nose explodes with colour.

I secure Thorn in his stroller and, linking arms with Reader, we take a short walk down the corridor. The wheels of the stroller creak and wobble. It is a relic from the bunker's storage room, as are Thorn's toys. But not his clothes. The good wives of Sanctuary are forever knitting and sewing. Parcels of baby clothes are pressed into their Captain Gollum's hands every day. Thorn is dressed like a little prince.

We arrive at the large statue of the Gilby-Gold family – a man, woman and child forged in bronze. The man throws open his arms to the ceiling, which is painted blue with white clouds. A flock of birds is etched against the fake sky. We pause and I describe it to Reader.

"Ah, yes, Graham Gilby-Gold, the genius behind Sanctuary. Librarian Betty told me all about him. He was the one who identified the land for the bunker and formed the

Cartel. If it had not been for his vision, this place would never have existed," Reader says. "He must be one of Shepherd's forebears. Do they share a likeness, Juliet?"

The man in the statue is bald and his face is jowly. He is nothing like Shepherd, with his new mane of hair and chiselled pink features. With each month, Shepherd has shed more bandages. His hands are now as smooth and white as a Posh mistress, and last month he got a new hip. Prince Charming grows younger and fitter every day.

"Lately Shepherd looks more like the boy in the statue."

In fact, most of the people in Sanctuary bear an uncanny likeness to Shepherd, with golden hair, blue eyes and cheekbones chiselling their milky-skinned faces. It makes my skin creep.

We leave the Peacemakers in the corridor and a beaming woman greets us as we enter a tomb-like room smelling like drain cleaner. The woman introduces herself as Memory-Keeper Verity. She has many smiles for Master Reader. Not so many for me.

"Welcome to the House of Memories. I am so honoured. Please, take these headsets and listen to the recording while you view the exhibits." She eyes Thorn and moistens her lips. "He's even more beautiful in the flesh – so bonny. It must be all the butterynut you feed him. The way he ate his breakfast this morning! I just couldn't stop watching – I was late for work."

Memory-Keeper Verity's gushing suffocates me. I move away from her, pushing the stroller in front of me.

"Wait, let me take care of him. He'll be quite safe." Her mouth trembles and I glance up at the red eye winking at me on the ceiling.

"Please. See how he nods off – the poor thing is half asleep. That creaky stroller will wake him. Let him rest quietly with me."

The Peacemakers are close by and there are hundreds of other pairs of eyes always watching him. I push the stroller towards her. Yes, I can leave him with her to sleep. He'll be quite safe.

Reader and I listen to the voice on our headsets as we wander through the House of Memories. I describe the photographs blown up on the wall: the founding families of the Cartel coming together with Graham Gilby-Gold ten years before the conflagration and building the bunker; the smiling faces of the first settlers; construction work on the bunker in the early years.

In another room the walls are filled with photographs of Peacemakers, of trenches and watchtowers. I raise the volume on my headset.

"*Once the ash had settled, the first Sancturians emerged from the bunker and found disease. It was carried by the Foogees who had survived the conflagration and came seeking refuge. Our people grew sick and returned to the bunker to seal Sanctuary from the pestilence. Vengeful Foogees attacked our solar units and blocked water supplies, and Sanctuary was forced to defend itself. After many bitter moons, the threat was exterminated.*"

Reader lifts his headset. "Terrible, just terrible. To think of all those poor refugees without food, without shelter under the burning sun. Diseased, helpless and hunted. I think there is a word for what happened here, Juliet. It will come to me. I have read about such things."

We move into the next room, which displays photographs of women and girls. The brass plaque on the wall says, "Our First Queens".

"*In the early days, people were sick and weak, and many babies died. To ensure Sanctuary's survival, the healthiest women were chosen as volunteers to breed Sancturian children. They were our Queens. They lived separately in a palace, and were provided with every comfort in order to ensure their health and vitality. Their seeds were harvested and pollinated by the most intelligent and robust menfolk, to be grown in a breeding hub. The weakest specimens resulting from this process were weeded out, and we modified the remaining seeds to ensure that only the most perfect would become our future Breeders. Every year the crop was planted in the fertile soil of our Queens. Sancturians grew stronger and more beautiful with each generation. The Queens stopped breeding in 235 PC.*"

Reader taps my headset and I pull it away from my ears.

"Genocide! That's the word!" He cocks his head. "Juliet, do you hear that? Is it Thorn?"

I throw my headset to the ground and run.

When I reach the front desk, I find Memory-Keeper Verity holding Thorn against her chest. He is screaming, red-faced, as she presses his mouth on her sagging breast. I move towards her, hissing. She shrinks back, crushing him in her arms.

84

"No, please, he was hungry," she whimpers.

I wrench Thorn away and she begins wailing. "I never got my baby. I never got to feed my own." Her face twists. "Those Breeders cheated me of my child."

The two Peacemakers rush into the room. One drags away the screaming woman, while the other speaks into his cuff: "Transmission can be resumed. The incident has been dealt with and the miracle child is unharmed."

I look up at the ceiling. The red eye suddenly flickers on.

The Peacemakers escort a bewildered Reader back to his quarters, and then they shadow me to the Garden of Never Forgetting.

In a few days I will leave Rose buried in her small box in Sancturian soil. I did not have a chance to know her, but I ache for her. I water the rose bush, which is planted in a clay pot at the side of the grave. The stems are a mass of blood-red buds. I will not be here to see them bloom, to smell their rich scent. I stand, head bowed, in front of her gravestone. Four words are etched on the pink marble: *Beloved Rose. Never forgotten.*

A bitter taste fills my mouth. There is no tombstone for me in Mangeria. My mother never ached for me. She carried me in shame and then abandoned me. I was never her beloved Juliet.

Soon I will see Nicolas again. The few memories of our time together are all that have sustained me while we have been apart: those precious nights, waiting for the tide to turn before we sailed away. My body aches as I remember him telling me I was beautiful, threading his fingers through my hair, the Savage hair he said he loved. Lying in his arms, my face against his bare chest, my nostrils filled with his strawberry smell, the bark of my whispering tree.

I touch my stomach. I will never be able to give Nicolas another child. Will he still want me? I am not a girl any more. I am only half a woman.

Leaving the Garden of Never Forgetting, I push back my bonnet, my face once more a blank mask. I will not allow the Peeping Toms of Sanctuary to see my turmoil.

At midday, a Healer arrives to look after Thorn while I go to work. A few months ago, I employed one of the good wives to watch Thorn during the afternoons, but after a few weeks she became ill. As did her eager replacement. When his third carer was crushed in the lift on her way to work – an accident none of the other occupants in the lift saw, with their eyes shut tight under their bonnets – Shepherd brought in the Healers to do the job. He said it would cause less strife among the women of Sanctuary.

I pack Gollum a lunch of cheese and stale bread and head off for the transport hub. Carrying packed lunches for their husbands, the other wives mill in the corridor, waiting to board the train. Good wives like me.

They edge away from me as I take my seat, and look through me, like I am thin air. If Thorn was with me, I would need Peacemakers to keep these women away. They were not always so unfriendly, but since the red eye has been watching us, Thorn-the-miracle-child is their focus, and I am the mother they wished they could be. Resentment burns the air. They speak as though I am deaf.

"So stingy with his breakfast this morning – did you see it, Good-Wife Alice?"

"Indeed, Good-Wife Nancy. That poor baby. She's practically starving him."

"And then she left him with that mad woman. Criminal – I would *never* neglect my baby like that."

"Captain Gollum should put his foot down with her. She's a terrible mother."

"She does not deserve the miracle child. Or our lovely captain – now *he's* a perfect daddy."

"Ooh, when Daddy and Baby are together, I could just watch them forever."

They sneer at the Savage curls spilling out from under my bonnet, so different from their golden hair, cut like slop-pots plopped on their heads and hidden under ugly bonnets. They sniff at the length of my skirt. Monitor the number of buttons fastened on my blouse.

I am stifled. The collar of my blouse chokes me, as does their chatter. When the train drops me outside the meat farm, I rip my bonnet from my head and scrunch it in my bag.

Sanctuary breeds sheep, ducks, goats, turkeys, chickens and cows – with a moo-moo here, there and everywhere. With eyes like mine. When they are fat, the animals are slaughtered and skinned. Gollum says the noise and smell in the slaughterhouse is like the Reject dumps outside Slum

City. He stuffs cotton wool in his nose and ears while he works to avoid being put off his meat pies.

Meat in Mangeria was slabs of grey flesh made in The Laboratory from animal parts. I was warned not to trust it. I never ate it. The meat sold by Sanctuary's butchers looks different, and Shepherd says it is protein-rich and delicious. But I cannot bring myself to eat it. Until arriving in Sanctuary, I had only ever seen pictures of animals, but now they are too real. Chicks with yellow down; lambs with the scent of lanolin.

Gollum says motherhood has made me soft.

I often visit the chickens. Dumb birds peck at my hands, not screeching that I am the one, or squawking foolish prophecies about my destiny. They are not tellers. They are drumsticks, chicken wings, plump breasts for a Sancturian's supper.

"Wife!" Gollum greets me with a shout and limps over, wiping blood-stained gloves on his plastic overalls.

Bearded men with blank eyes and hands like shovels watch us – his workmates.

"Give me a minute to wash up – I've been busy killing swine."

I have never seen a live pig before. Reader has told me pigs are the cleverest animals and are mostly hairless, like humans. Although Gollum is as hairy as a mountain of goats.

"We only get to slaughter a few a month – butchers pay top dolla for pork carcass. I've saved the trotters and tails for you, wife. Yum-yum-yum." He makes a loud slurping sound and heads for the washroom.

Later, I watch him devour his lunch with his fingers, his nails rimmed with blood. I do not eat with him. I smell the blood of the animals on his skin. I smell their fear. But the good wives of Sanctuary spend lunch hour with their husbands, and for as long as the bloody eye watches, I am a good wife. I can maintain the pretence for the next few days.

As I run to work, the cries of calves separated from their mothers at birth ring in my ears.

The plant farm is a few floors above the meat farm.

Here, I am surrounded by plants and trees heavy with fruit. And flowers – so many fragrances, unlike the flowers back home, where the scent has been removed to avoid attracting flies. Roses red, violets soft purple-blue. Lavender's blue, dilly dilly, lavender's green. I will miss all this loveliness when I leave.

The fruit and vegetables here are nothing like the food made in The Laboratory. Each one is perfect in shape and colour. And sweet – they do not taste of plastic like those sold in the market back home. They are grown from only the best seeds, tested in the seed hub. How Kitty would marvel over the mangos. She might even have been tempted by a banana, shaped like a slice of the moon.

The plants bob about in vats of water and are fed hormones to make them grow faster. Within a couple of weeks, the seedlings bear fruit. They receive a certain number of hours' heat and light from solar panels suspended from the ceiling. When the fruit and vegetables are ripe, they are harvested and sold in the shops.

My fingers search among the seedlings. I pluck out the smallest from the tank of lukewarm water and discard them in a bucket next to me. Some of the women sing as they work, their hands dipping into the water, feet bouncing in their plastic boots. They ignore me, but Greenfinger Rachel, our boss, makes up for their neglect. She bends over the tank and slaps away my hands.

"What's wrong with you today, Good-Wife Juliet? Your mind is not on your work. I've told you before: weed out the weak ones." She picks a seedling from the tank and holds it up, examining it with watery blue eyes. "See, this one won't bear good beans – it's half the size of the others. Obviously a bad seed. We can't waste good water on these."

I have suffered Greenfinger Rachel's bad temper these past few months with the help of my dumb drudge face. I would not let her sharp tongue chase me away. The *Jolly Roger* has been stocked with sacks of seeds. When I get home, I will grow my own garden.

I look up as women shout out and run from their work stations, Greenfinger Rachel with them. "Captain Gollum!" they cry like foolish ducks after a handful of corn. I grind my teeth as they surround him, each wanting a word, a touch. They watch with jealous eyes as he joins me. His face is pale.

"The *Jolly Roger*'s gone. She must have pulled free of her anchor."

I search his face. He's not taunting me, seeing how far he

90

can push me under the eye's watchful gaze.

"But there wasn't a storm last night," I say. "Someone must have taken it."

"I'll go looking for her tomorrow. And when I catch the joker who took her, I'll make him eat his teeth," Gollum says.

But I'm not laughing. I know it's no prank.

CAPTAIN GOLLUM'S LOG

Death kissed me. Her lips were dry, her breath sweet. She promised to take me to a place where I could run without pain. But I couldn't leave with her. I've made a promise to my friend that I won't break.

Death grows impatient for me. Master Reader has told me that a cat has nine lives. I'm using mine up faster than a Landie hurtling down a mountain road without brakes.

And yes, I did that. The day after my *Jolly Roger* went missing, I took the keys to the Landie and went for a spin to look for her. On my own, without Commander sitting next to me, her hand on the brake, ready to take the wheel. I flew solo.

I needed air, even though it

scorches my lungs with every breath. Some days I can't bear the pressure in the bunker, the hum of air machines. I miss the sun on my skin.

I sped along potholed roads, climbed the dirt tracks high into the mountains until I was on top of the world. I spied a vehicle of Fixits heading up to maintain the solar panels, making sure Sanctuary always has power. They were escorted by a convoy of Peacemakers alert to ambushes from the rogue Breeders.

I soared over the grey mountains like Superman, cast my eyes over the burning land below. Nothingness stretched for miles around me. Flat earth, spreading like a desert into the never-never. No sign of my *Jolly Roger*.

Hurtling down the mountain, I felt a

rush of air on my face through the open windows. I swooped towards the flatness and when the engine protested, wheels spinning, I stopped. Stepped outside. The land was no longer hard, but swampy. A boggy lake of grey-green mud for miles around me.

My feet sank into the ooze, and were snagged. When I wrenched my foot from the mud, my heart fell out of my chest. My shoe was being pulled off by a hand, flesh eaten away from the bones. A swamp monster!

I grabbed my shoe, shaking off the skeletal hand. I stumbled, fell, looked up from the muddy earth into the hollow eyes of a skull. And next to it, a cage of ribs. The bubbling swamp sucked me in as I sank to my knees, tried to crawl back to the Landie. I felt bones underneath me — I was crawling through a monstrous grave.

When I reached the Landie, I pulled myself up and rested. The wheels had been sucked into the bog. I abandoned the beautiful vehicle to the swamp monster and stumbled and crawled towards harder ground.

The sky was high in the sky, a fried egg with bubbling white. I walked until I fell.

For the next four days I wandered, lost under the blistering sun, unable to find the lift that would take me back to the bunker. The sun ate my skin, sucked the moisture from my body. I prayed to The Machine to save me. Another day passed and I waited for the kiss of Death.

But my god heard me, and Commander arrived before Death could take me.

I write this entry from the healing hub, where I've spent three weeks recovering from the effects of the sun on my skin and brain. The Healers assure me my skin won't be scarred, barring the old ones on my back.

Drudge plays good wife and sits with me in the mornings when the pain is at its worst. Her face is a mask of sweet concern, but her eyes tell me she's loving every second of my agony. And Commander visits me every day and brings me grapes and chocolates. She says I'm a stupid idiot and the next time I pull that kind of stunt she'll flay the skin off me. I tell her the sun beat her to it. Ha-Ha.

I asked her about the swamp of skeletons that stretched to never-never. The bog that claimed her Landie. She says the sun has made me mad.

There is no grave. I must drink liquid and sleep.

But I know what I saw: the killing field of the Foogees.

7

SACRED DAY

The bells of Sanctuary call us with oranges and lemons. Their loud chimes ring though the bunker, ordering us to rise and make ourselves ready. Chip chop.

The sixth day of the week is sacred. Nobody works and there is a prohibition against driving or cooking. It's a long day set aside for rest and prayer – and the sight of Gollum's long face nursing his grumbling stomach.

He licks the palm of his hand and presses Thorn's curls flat on his head. He combs them to the side and dabs at a spot of drool on Thorn's shirt.

"What a handsome boy you are. Just like your daddy." He grins at me. "I am just loving your new bonnet, wife."

"As I do your new tie, husband," I say and adjust the knot at his throat, pulling it tighter than necessary under the blinking eye on the ceiling. I pack a bag with a bottle and a pacifier. Thorn hardly slept last night and is grumpy.

So am I. I cannot sleep. My plush feather bed feels like a sack of dried cobs. I lie awake trying to picture Nicolas's face. It is now only a faint outline. So is Larissa's. My memory of them is slowly being erased. "Forget-Me-Not. Forget-Me-Not," I whisper, and press the image of that small trampled flower to my aching chest.

Gollum has given up trying to find the *Jolly Roger* – and the joker who stole it. He is building a new boat. Progress is slow. Apart from Commander, there are not many willing hands on deck to help him. Because when the boat is ready, their beloved Captain Gollum will sail away with the miracle child.

This morning we join the throng of Sancturians heading towards the Place of Ceremonies. No one is exempt from the weekly gathering unless you are hammering on death's door.

We are gathered together in the giant arena, a semi-circle of benches focused on a large stage raised a few inches off the ground. The good husbands and wives sit separately, a few thousand of us. Eyes lowered, faces scrubbed shiny, hair hidden under hats and bonnets, every inch of bodily flesh concealed under long-sleeved shirts, long trousers and ankle-length skirts.

There is a peculiar odour in the place. For weeks I have not been able to place it. This morning I realise: it smells of past traders. Sweet perfume smothering the whiff of dying organs, sour breath, dead cells flaking off flaccid skin. It is the cloying stench of decay, betrayal and abandoned dreams.

I spot Reader in the company of Commander, who is almost unrecognisable in a long skirt and crisp blouse. A beige bonnet covers her golden hair and her ruddy skin is smothered, pale under a coating of powder. Her mouth, usually yelling an order or splitting her face with a grin, is a tightly shut purse.

When we reach him, Reader strokes the side of Thorn's face.

"Is he ill? He seems hot to me? What say you, Juliet?"

I touch Thorn's head. "He's fresh from his bath. But maybe he's wearing too many layers." The air in the bunker is cold and I always overdress him.

"Perhaps it is another tooth, Juliet? Is he teething again? The first few gave him a great deal of pain."

I place my finger in Thorn's mouth and feel the small bud on his lower gum. "You're right, old man. Another one's on its way." At the rate Thorn's teeth are growing, he will have lost a few by the time he gets home.

If we ever do. My mood is black.

The windows surrounding the space are ornate portraits of the Sanctuary founders, their faces patchworked in red and green and yellow stained glass. Blue eyes stare down at us all-knowingly.

As honoured members of the community, Gollum and I take our seats on the stage with Shepherd and the Cartel. To the side of us is a choir of one hundred and sixty Last-Borns. These thirty-year-old men and women are wearing short pants, dungarees or loose-fitting dresses barely touching their knees. Some are dressed in rompers or babygros, things Thorn only wears at night. They suck their thumbs and play with dolls under the watchful eyes of their mothers, who are seated close to them at the front of the stage.

"Let us all give thanks," Shepherd says, breaking the sombre silence.

Sanctuary kneels and, with one voice, is thankful.

"We believe in Shepherd, the mightiest, the father of Sanctuary. Through him all things that sustain us are made. For us men and for our delivery from the conflagration, he gave us our refuge. He defended us against the Foogees and kept us safe from pestilence. We believe he is the giver of life. From him, we are born perfect in every way. We give thanks to our saints, the members of the Cartel, who govern our lives with justice and wisdom. We believe that through faith and hard work, Shepherd will make us fertile again, that our loins will once again bear fruit and that the people of Sanctuary will be resurrected. Through Shepherd, we will live forever ..."

My lips move over the words as I gaze over the blur of hats and bonnets in front of me. Their feverish eyes never stray from Shepherd, who stands centre stage, his glowing face raised to the light from the multicoloured windows. Hector curls up at his feet, watching us with chicken-scat eyes. He never strays far from his master.

Reader says the sixth-day ceremony is based on a primitive religion that enslaved the old world for two thousand years. It set men against one another and led to the Great War that caused the conflagration. This does not surprise me. A religion that bores people to death and starves them once a week is sufficient reason for war.

I glance at Gollum next to me. Like me, he is moving his

lips, but I know that in his head he is saying a prayer to The Machine.

My head prays to no one.

The thanksgiving ends and the choir of Last-Borns breaks into a hymn. The Sancturians rise from their knees. They are on their feet, swaying, their hands lifted up high. Some join in the singing, but others do not. Instead, strange words and sounds pour out of their wide-open mouths. Their tongues leap about like fishes desperate for air. Others weep and laugh, shake and toss themselves about like dead-brains.

The voices die away and I steel myself for what is to come.

A group of women, their stomachs huge and swollen, eyes full of hope, approach the stage. They are the Bloaters. I have grown used to the sight of them in Sanctuary. Barren and fat-bellied, they are as mad as a sack of turkeys.

Shepherd takes Thorn from me and holds him up as an offering. The Bloaters file past, one by one and touch Thorn on his foot. Shepherd makes a sign over their bowed bonnets and presses his fingers to their foreheads. "Go home. Believe in Shepherd and you will be blessed."

As the last Bloater returns to her bench, a lone voice rises from the choir of Last-Borns. He sings a lullaby in a sweet and unbroken boy's voice. His bald spot squats uneasily amidst the carefully coiffured baby curls framing his face.

Shepherd passes Thorn back to me. He feels hot, and when I pull him onto my lap he whimpers. I grab the bag next to Gollum and scrabble inside as Thorn's whimper rises to a howl, shattering the sweet lullaby. Flustered, I shove the pacifier into Thorn's mouth. He gags and wriggles, his face going red.

Just perfect! The eyes of thousands of Sancturians are on me. Bad wife! Bad mother! Gollum reaches for him. I bite back my snap and pass Thorn over. As I do, he hurls his breakfast milk all over me.

The arena exclaims with dismay, a few good wives titter.

A Healer appears immediately, and after I have wiped away the sick mess with a bib, he places Thorn gently on the stage to examine him. He pulls back his eyelids and presses his stomach.

"His abdomen is unusually swollen and tender. His eyes have a yellow tinge," the Healer says.

"He's just teething," I hiss, then suck back my anger. "His eyes are perfectly white," I say sweetly.

The Healer shakes his head. "I'm taking him to the healing hub. He's stopped breathing."

"No!" My cry pierces the hushed arena. I peer over at Thorn, lying on the stage. His face is death-white, but his chest is rising and falling. The Healer is wrong! I collapse next to my baby and try to pull him into my arms, but the Healer pushes me aside, picks Thorn up and hurries away.

The bells of Sanctuary signal the end of the ceremony. Chip chop, chip chop. I stumble after him.

I pace the corridor outside the healing hub for hours. Gollum kneels on the floor, his head in his hands, no doubt praying to The Machine.

A door hisses open and Shepherd approaches, wringing his hands. Hector stalks behind him.

"The Healers are still analysing the tests, but they suspect it's his liver. An abnormality of some sort, developed when he was still growing inside you. Often these things are inherited from one of the parents. A genetic weakness." His cold blue eyes rest on Gollum. "He'll need another liver. Without it, he has only days, perhaps a week at most, to live."

My son is broken. And all the king's horses and all the king's men cannot fix him. There is no superhero to rescue him. No magic spell in Dumbledore's arsenal to save him.

"He can have my liver." Gollum thumps his stomach. "Give Stinker mine."

For a brief moment I do not despise him.

Shepherd ignores him, and takes my trembling hands in his pink, smooth ones. "Let me show you how we can help him."

He takes us to one of the areas in Sanctuary that only certain people are allowed to enter – members of the Cartel, and the Healers. He places his thumb against the glowing pad marked by a red cross, and then ushers us into a white room, brightly lit. I glance up at the ceiling – the red eye is dead. The air chills my skin.

But what I see chills my blood.

The room is filled with pink fleshy bodies. Dozens of them. Animals with long snouts ending in the shape of an upside-down heart. Feet with four hoofed toes. Some standing, others lying on their sides, all attached to humming machines.

Shepherd sighs. "Our miracle pigs. Before the old world ended, great advances were made in medical science. And we have continued making progress. Many pig organs are similar to those of humans." He steps over to a piglet and taps the top of its head. It blinks, small deep-set eyes framed by spiky lashes. "This one here has a liver the size of a baby."

Gollum grabs Shepherd's arm. "You're mad." He looks at me. "Don't let him do it."

Shepherd shrugs him off. "We've done many organ transplants and various other procedures using pigs. It's a skill our Healers have perfected these past two hundred years. Of course, there's a risk that the body may reject the organ, but it's a chance we take." He walks around the room, pointing. "This sow is growing my cousin a new heart, and that one over there will give the skin off her back to a Cartel member who was burnt in a fire last month." He sneers at Gollum. "Where do you think the skin that healed your sunburn came from?"

Gollum touches his arms and face, and blanches.

"Imagine ..." Shepherd says to Gollum, "teeth as fine and white as mine, your devil horns removed." He reaches out to touch Gollum's face and flinches. "Your foot made whole. No longer a hobbling boy, but a real man, whole and beautiful."

"You can do that?" Gollum says, his eyes bright.

"Amazing, isn't it?" Shepherd stretches out his own smooth pink hands. "I am living proof of progress." He taps his stomach. "Liver number four, kidney number two. And in a few weeks, I'll get another new set of knees. These ones are creaky and are giving me some pain." He places his hand on his heart. "This ticker is my fifth in two hundred years."

Shepherd is either mad, as Gollum says, or joking. But only a sick freak would kid around at a time like this.

"You are two hundred years old?" I stare at Shepherd, his unlined boy's face, his Prince Charming hair.

"Oh no, my dear, I am much older. I was born before the old world ended. My father was the one who started Sanctuary."

I recall the bronze statue, the small boy staring up at his father. "But that means that the people of Sanctuary can live forever."

"A few of us will have that privilege. The Cartel decides on each case according to our requirements. But without children, many do not want to live. Those who do – if we are careful, and don't choke on a chicken bone or drown in our bathtubs – could go on living for a very long time yet." Shepherd ushers us into another room, which holds tanks of liquid. "Of course, some of the swines' organs are not compatible with the human body. And so here we grow our own, using the body's building blocks, our DNA."

A pair of unseeing eyes float in a tank near the door. A hand, a foot, a piece of cartilage with one nostril attached. A thumb with half a nail. It is similar to the process used in The Laboratory in Mangeria, where meat is manufactured from animal parts. But these are not slabs of meat for some Posh's dinner.

"Our Cartel places a high value on beauty. Several of these body parts serve a cosmetic purpose. But others will replace those that have been damaged." Shepherd points at the tank close by. "That toe over there is being grown for my deputy, who carelessly mangled his in a bicycle a few weeks ago. When it's attached, his foot will be as good as new." His eyes flicker down to Gollum's club foot and then he turns to me. "The decision rests with you, Good-Wife Juliet, and of course, with Captain Gollum. If your son doesn't get a new liver, he will die."

Three hours later I watch the Healers butcher my son. They lean over him in their sick-green aprons, their faces masked, hands sheathed in plastic gloves like second skins.

My chest tightens and dust motes flutter in my head. Dementors are sucking the hope out of me with every breath – wraith-like figures draped in black cloaks hover, faces hidden inside their black hoods.

"What are they doing to him, Juliet?" Reader stands next to me in the cubicle above the healing theatre, his hands pressing against the glass that separates us from the activity below.

"They've opened up his stomach with a small sharp knife. But he can't feel anything. They've given him drugs and he's out cold."

Two Healers pass instruments to each other, another swabs blood. Too much blood gushing from Thorn's tiny body. A small machine tracks his heartbeat – a red line on a box that zigzags above a green line that registers the pressure of the blood in his veins. A mask covers Thorn's face and his chest rises and falls with the help of a machine.

Gollum is crouched in front of the glass, his eyes never

leaving the room below us.

"They're removing Stinker's liver and they've placed it in a metal bowl, Master Reader. His liver's this big." He stretches up and draws a small shape on the palm of Reader's hand with his finger.

The door to the healing theatre opens and a Healer hurries towards the gurney.

"They've brought the new liver, Master Reader. It's been sitting on ice for the past hour. It will replace the sick one."

A Healer removes the organ from the bowl and hands it to his colleague, who gently inserts it into the right side of Thorn's abdomen, below his ribs. For the next hour I do not breathe as the Healers rapidly connect tubes, burn blood vessels and sew his stomach back together.

"It's a wrap," one of the Healers says. "A really neat job. Of course, the next few days will be critical, but he's come through the first stage."

I exhale, along with the thousands of Sancturians watching on the big screens throughout the bunker.

"This is indeed a miracle." Reader sucks his pink gums and stares blindly at us. "I was not there when Shepherd explained it to you, Juliet, and I still do not fully comprehend how this is possible." The old man's eyes glitter with tears. "But if what I hear is true, the Healers could give the deaf their hearing. And the blind their sight. These Healers are gods."

Gollum and I take the lift down to the healing hub. Thorn will spend the next few weeks recovering here. If his body accepts the pig liver, the Healers say he will lead a full and normal life.

The lift stops and opens. Closes again. We wait. It opens on the same floor, and closes, hissing.

Gollum holds my arm as the lift opens again. "Stand back from the lift, wife. It's sticking on the wrong level. Ah, here's the problem." He leans down and picks up something wedged in the groove of the door. "Stinker's pacifier. You must have dropped it earlier." He hands it to me and then holds open the lift for Hector, who has appeared from nowhere. "Bugger off, you filthy cat."

"It's not his pacifier," I snap. Bad mother! "Husband dear," I add softly.

"You shouldn't be so careless, wife. These things attract germs."

I do not have the energy to argue with Perfect Daddy, so I stuff the pacifier in my bag. Before the lift descends, I hear the cry of a baby coming from down the corridor.

I must be mistaken. Thorn cannot have come around already. I am faint with weariness – I must have imagined it.

CAPTAIN GOLLUM'S LOG

It's true what Master Reader says. The Healers are gods, and he is their new convert.

They healed Stinker. And last month they grew Master Reader a new pair of eyes. They cut out his blind ones and filled the holes with fresh orbs, as green and plump as grapes. When they removed the bandages, Master Reader wept. I'll record the words he used when he saw me. I don't want to forget them.

He said: "My captain. You are as handsome as I imagined. My beautiful boy."

When Drudge looks at my face, she sees my devil horns and jagged teeth. When she watches me walk, she sees my crip foot. I'll never be her beautiful boy.

Drudge asked the Healers if they could fix her, to grow her a new organ to make her a whole woman again. But they can't. They've tried, Shepherd said. Each time, just as they think they have it right, the organ withers, blackens and dies. Shame for Stinker — he'll never have a sister or brother to kick around.

Of course, the Healers could make my foot better, and take away my devil horns, just like Shepherd said. I could be a real man. But I suspect Shepherd likes me as I am. I'm the product of the diseases from the conflagration, spread by the wind across the seas by the Foogees. I'm a cautionary tale of what happens when bad seeds are allowed to grow. Here in Sanctuary, I would've been weeded out, never allowed to be born.

Shepherd has not offered to fix me, and I will not beg him.

8

SHEPHERD'S LEGACY

"Push out your fat gut and think unnatural thoughts. Allow the water to lift you up," Gollum shouts.

Commander is gasping, spitting sea water. Her hair strangles her face. "I can't float. The water doesn't like me. Take pity on me, my son. Mercy!"

I sit on the beach and watch Gollum teaching Commander to swim. She calls him "my son", never "Captain Gollum", and looks at him as though he is hers. She is one of many middle-aged women in Sanctuary who compete for his attention, but Gollum allows only Commander the privilege of sewing on his shirt buttons and darning his socks. It's an arrangement I'm more than happy with.

Gollum grabs Commander by the hair and shoves her back into the waves. "Paddle! Pretend you're punching some Bloater, or crawling on the ground like a Senior looking for his teeth."

Miserable Commander! Gollum is determined she will swim or drown trying.

I turn away as Thorn tugs at my arm. His cheeks are pink,

his eyes are bright. Healthy. His stomach is smooth, no sign of a scar. He points to a heap of sand and I help him shape it into a sandcastle.

"Hey, Stinker." Gollum joins us, leaving Commander flopping in the water. "Come for a swim. Let's show Commander how it's done." He collapses on the sand, settles Thorn onto the heels of his feet and lifts him in the air. "You want to fly like Superman?"

"Stop it, fool. You'll hurt him."

Gollum bounces Thorn higher. "Stop being a drag, Drudge," he snaps at me. "The kid's good as new. Give him some air."

Out here on the beach, away from the infernal eye, we do not have to pretend. And when Commander is with us, the Peacemakers are off duty – as is my mask.

I watch Gollum chase Thorn into the water and they splash about in the waves. Gollum's arms criss-cross Thorn's chest as they float. Commander stands at the edge of the beach, spitting sand out of her mouth, sulking.

I pull my bonnet further over my eyes, lean back against a mound of sand. The months have slipped by. With Thorn so sick, we have been unable to leave Sanctuary. There were setbacks in the first hopeless weeks after the operation, one after the other, months of mysterious illness. But the Healers were always there to perform their miracles.

Soon Thorn will be two years old. Gollum promises the new boat will be ready next month. I will go home with my son and his new liver. Perfect Daddy will go back to the sewers of Slum City where he belongs. Reader will go home with new green eyes and a brain swollen with useless facts. His eyes have burnt through the old dragon's library books, while Gollum has had to eat himself sick on the dragon's apple-pies to feed Reader's hunger.

The old man has developed an indecent passion for history. Each day he learns something more about the old world: "They made terrible weapons, Juliet. And machines that could think and learn, like us. The cities were full of these machines, doing every job under the sun." His bright eyes are full of wonder. "Imagine, Juliet, intelligent machines – smarter than humans – that could create and destroy with their incredible minds."

Reader's stories are even more foolish than Gollum's Batman and Spiderman comics. A man on the moon; communities on Mars; machines that think and behave like humans ... Reader is convinced that The Machine in Mangeria is the last of its kind. Perhaps the mother of all machines.

I do not encourage Reader's unnatural appetite for knowledge about the old world, or what it tells me about home. The memories of what I have left behind are too painful. My heart is locked safe in my chest. I will not open it until I touch the sand on Mangeria's beach.

Shepherd has given up asking me where we come from – he now harasses the old man with his maps. It was not an act of kindness to give Reader new eyes. Shepherd is determined to locate this place of orphanages packed with unwanted

Smalls. When he does, will he build a fleet of sloops to go and claim them? He is welcome, of course – no one else wants them. But I do not trust his intentions, the gleam in his eyes, his posse of "Peacemakers".

Reader stares at the maps and mumble-mumbles the way I did. He will not tell Shepherd what he wants to know. And Shepherd twitches and wheezes, his cheeks becoming puce, his blue eyes bulging.

Only once did Shepherd ask Gollum to point out Mangeria on his maps. He told Shepherd to get lost, using his most eloquent language. Gollum no longer uses words dredged from the Slum City sewers, and Reader delights in his young captain's vocabulary. It's a sentiment Shepherd did not share on this particular occasion – Gollum invited Shepherd to "go fornicate with his maternal representative", with a crude hand gesture to make his meaning clear.

I rub the warm sand between my fingers, smiling as I recall the outrage on Shepherd's face. Suddenly, a shadow falls over me and I feel something sharp against the back of my neck.

"If you make a sound, I will slice this blade through your spine. And then I will gut your son," says a male voice.

For my son's life, not mine, I do not scream. Rough hands grab my arms, thrust my bonnet over my face and pull me towards the dunes. In a matter of seconds I am blindfolded and pushed into the back of a Landie, which is raced over the potholed roads. I am thrown against the sides of the vehicle. No soft cushion for me today.

The straining engine tells me the Landie is climbing.

When at last it stops, I am dragged out and pushed along a road. My bare feet burn on the scorching ground. I have lost my bonnet, and the sun beats down on my head; sweat pools in my neck.

Then there's coolness; I smell mould and damp. The blindfold is taken off my eyes. In the gloom of a cave, candlelight flickers over the faces of a group of women standing around me. Some are old crones, others still have golden hair, but all of their faces are scarred with sunburn and their teeth are black. A group of witches making bubbling-boiling trouble for me.

A woman breaks away. Her face is etched with memories; her grey hair mourns ninety years.

"Bring her some water," she says to the person gripping my arms behind me.

I catch a glimpse of the man as he hurries away. The oarsman, the one who rowed us to shore two years ago. "Run," he'd said. I had not listened.

When he returns with a cup of water, the old woman hands it to me, and seats me on a chair. She touches my face.

"You're a child. The same age as we all were when they made us breed."

I jerk back from her hand and she smiles – a mouth of black corn kernels.

"We tried to warn you when you arrived, Good-Wife Juliet. You should have left when you had a chance. Before they stole your boat. But we don't have time to waste now – you'll soon be missed."

The women gather behind her as she makes herself comfortable in a chair in front of me. "We are the Breeders. My name is Breeder Naomi. There are things you need to hear …"

I have always thought I knew the face of evil: Cockroach, the head of the Locusts in Mangeria; the Guardian of Justice and Peace, who tortured the orphans of Slum City with his sick experiments; Guardian Hylton, Mistress's husband, who used the prisoners of Savage City as guinea pigs. But Breeder Naomi fills my ears with horrors I have never imagined, and now there is a new face of evil, as terrifying as Lord Voldemort and his coterie of Death Eaters.

Prince Charming. He of the golden hair and the pink, swine-smooth face.

Shepherd.

"Many Sancturians wanted to end the breeding programme," Breeder Naomi continues. "They wished to bear their own children and go back to the time before the Foogees brought diseases. But Shepherd believes he is God, creator of the perfect race. You must have noticed how so many Sancturians look like him? He did not want nature to meddle with his design. When the Breeders resisted, his methods became more cruel."

The Breeders file past and show me the scars on their necks and wrists, the scars on their bellies. The scars in their eyes.

"In the old days, animals in captivity would not breed – they didn't want to watch their offspring suffer their fate. It

117

was the same with us, and none of the Healers' vile methods could make us fertile again.

"The community was divided. Some were angry and blamed us for being barren. They drove us out of Sanctuary to these caves, where we live today. But others still help us and bring us food and water." She shrugs. "We are, after all, their mothers and sisters."

She checks the timepiece on her wrist, and when she looks back at me, her face has softened.

"We brought you here to tell you not only about what has been robbed from us, but about what has been stolen from you too. Forgive me for rushing with this."

What Breeder Naomi tells me makes me gasp in pain. A fist smashes the lock that has kept my heart safe inside my chest.

"No. Impossible. You're lying to me," I cry.

She hands me a small box. It is ice cold.

"At midday tomorrow, The Angel will shut down for five hours during the Feast of Thanksgiving for maintenance. Go to the places I've told you about. There you will get your proof." She kisses me softly on the cheek. "Go, child. Find the one that will end our hell."

Today, I will take back what is mine.

An hour before midday, I am throwing up my guts into a bucket of discarded seedlings at the plant farm.

"Good-Wife Juliet, are you ill?" Greenfinger Rachel hands me a cloth and I wipe my mouth. Her face brightens. "Or could it be ... Tell me it's true! How far are you gone? Oh, wait till everyone hears. Another baby!" Just as quickly, she sighs, her mouth bitter. "The poor child. To have a creature as yourself for a mother."

I look up at the blinking eye on the ceiling. "It must have been something I ate. You know it's not possible for me to have another child."

Greenfinger Rachel smiles spitefully. "Yes, of course. You are like us. Useless."

I scrunch the cloth in my hand. I am not useless.

"What a pity you're ill," Greenfinger Rachel says, eyes glittering without pity. "You'll miss out on the Feast of Thanksgiving. We're having veal as well as turkey for lunch this afternoon. My Captain Gollum has been so busy with the slaughter these past few days."

Turkeys and calves, trussed since birth in stinking cages. Growing fat in their own filth for Sanctuary to celebrate its deliverance from the conflagration. But there'll be no turkey legs for the thankful to gnaw on – the birds have been trapped in their cages since birth. Their legs are crippled knobs, unable to support their fat bodies.

Greenfinger Rachel dispatches me home with a promise that she'll send herbal broth to cure my stomach – made from her most sour leaves.

I feel the eye on me as I return to my quarters, and I remember to groan and clutch my stomach. Once there, I instruct Thorn's Healer to take him to Gollum at the meat farm – they will have to go to the feast without me, I tell him, giving a pitiful sigh.

As the hand strikes the midday hour, I glance up at the kitchen ceiling. The red eye is dull; no one can see me. I am as invisible as Harry Potter in his magic cloak stalking the corridors of Hogwarts at midnight.

The small box Breeder Naomi gave me is tucked away under some peas in the freezing unit. I know what's inside, but I haven't laid eyes on it yet.

I steel myself as I open the box and remove the frozen thumb. There are grey hairs in the creases of the joint; the nail is long and yellow. It once belonged to a member of the Cartel. Breeder Naomi had related with glee how he'd lost it in an argument with a snaggle-toothed Breeder: "She clamped her teeth like a fierce wolf and did not let go until it was chewed from his hand." The thumb has served the Breeders and their supporters well over the past thirty years. Today it will serve me.

I leave my quarters and ride the lift to the thirteenth floor. It opens onto a passage, dimly lit, smelling damp and forgotten, like the flats in Slum City where the past traders are dumped. I press the flaccid thumb against the gleaming pad on a door. And again, until it opens. It is rusty from disuse.

The air has been sucked out of the room – it is moist and stuffy. Inside is a hive of adult-sized concrete cells. Solid-steel doors, each with a small mesh window, bar each cell's entrance. A rash of bumps rise on my skin.

I push open one of the doors. Inside is an old mattress, its stuffing in filthy clumps on the stained floor. Large rings screwed to the wall are threaded with chains attached to heavy wrist- and ankle-bracelets. Water trickles down the side of a wall that is marked with names, numbers and letters. It is, I realise, a record of the inmates' breeding histories.

Breeder Florence. The inscriptions tell me she had forty children in twenty-five years. Ten males, thirty females. Some of them twins. Before her were Breeder Giselle, Breeder Myrtle, Breeder Claire. In the beginning, more than two hundred years ago, there was Breeder Theresa. A length of frayed rope coils from the ceiling.

A room at the end of the hive of cells is filled with small cages. I stoop to enter one. A rag doll, a tiny shoe. A child's drawing, faded to a scribble, is impaled on a bent piece of wire.

Past the cages is a kitchen, where cockroaches have long since cleaned the pots – they lie overturned on the floor. Beyond is a room filled with gurneys, and grey- and pink-stained sheets are bunched up on the floor.

I do not want to see any more. I run towards the door and trip over a bin filled with rubber gloves and bloody swabs brown with age.

This is no palace for Queens.

It is all the proof I need. Back in the lift, I press the button for the seventh floor. Down the corridor my hands are shaking as I remove the cold thumb from its box and place it against a glowing pad. The door slides open and the smell of animal waste and disinfectant assaults my nose. Grunting and squealing sounds rise above the soothing music that's being piped through loud speakers on the ceiling.

Staying close to the walls, I skirt the room and move through an open doorway.

Pigs. Live ones, pawing their enclosures with cloven feet. Long pink snouts snuffling in troughs, small pink bodies suckling on rows of teats. Others, bellies bloated, days away from releasing their burdens. I slip between the pens searching for the one Breeder Naomi told me I would find.

A man dressed in overalls enters carrying a bucket. I crouch down below a low wall. The man whistles and leans into a pen to pour the contents of the bucket into a trough.

"And how is my beautiful Princess today? Did her Highness enjoy the beans and carrots I brought her this morning?"

I hear laughter close by.

"Sorry, Healer Graham, I didn't see you there. I like to talk to her. Silly, I know, but sometimes I think she could be human. It's the way she looks at me."

The sound of footsteps moving away from me. A door slams as they leave. I creep past more pens.

There she is, just as Breeder Naomi described her.

A magnificent specimen. Skin buffed clean and shiny, her eyes sharp in the folds above her snout. Her pen is the largest in the room; she has space to wander about. I kneel and peer up at the sow's belly. And I see it then: the scar on her stomach marking the space below her liver. My son's liver, trapped in the body of a pig.

Thorn's healthy liver, butchered from his stomach.

I run from the grunting-squealing room to the lift. It

descends, but stops before it reaches the floor that will take me to my next destination. A woman enters, struggling with a large stroller. One of the Last-Borns. He clutches his teddy bear and stares at me with glazed eyes from under his lacy bonnet. His mother leans down and wipes a smear of food from his whiskery lip. "Such a messy-moo. You'll always be Mother's big baby."

She sees me and flushes resentfully.

"Oh, good afternoon, Good-Wife Juliet. And where is the miracle child?" She peers behind me. "I expect he is with my Captain Gollum on this feast day? I've been missing him these last few hours while The Angel has been blind." She glances at her timepiece. "Not long now – it should be working again at five o' clock." Two floors down the lift opens and she pushes the stroller proudly ahead of her without a backward glance.

Tick-tock. Tick-tock. Tick-tock. Tick-tock. I tap the button in the lift.

Down, down, down to the Garden of Never Forgetting.

Once I'm there, I lift my skirt above my knees and sprint down the paths between the tombstones until I find my rose bush, heavy with sweet-smelling blooms in its pot next to the grave.

I kneel and dig in the earth with my hands; dig until my nails break. Deeper, deeper. Mounds of earth pile up next to me. Until I find the small box, my daughter's resting place. I claw through the soft wood.

And I see that Breeder Naomi did not lie.

Time is passing. Soon the infernal eye will find me. I stifle a cry and run for the lift, past a group of praying mourners, heads bowed over a grave, remembering those who are not able to be with them at the Feast of Thanksgiving.

The lift ascends slowly, and stops. I clutch the bonnet over my face and hurry past two Healers in the corridor. I run until I come to a glowing pad outside a room. It is marked by a crown. I press the cold thumb against the crown and the door slides open.

I glance down at my feet as Hector presses his sticky body against my ankles, his scat-eyes blinking.

A child looks up as I enter the room.

Her hair is Savage. Her eyes are large and brown. Cow - eyes.

I am looking at me.

"Who are you?" I say hoarsely, although I already know the answer.

She twists her lips into a sly smile. A smile that hides secrets. My smile.

Her voice is high and clear: "I am Breeder."

9

THE CHOICE

Peacemakers hold me down as a Healer enters the room with a syringe. He pulls up my sleeve; the needle stabs my skin. I'm dragged towards the lift. Hoarse screams echo in the corridor.

My screams. I scream until a mist blanks my mind.

I awake to the sensation of smooth hands patting my face. Then a sharp slap.

Shepherd leans over me, hand poised. I stare into his unblinking blue eyes, icicles floating in their depths.

We're in Shepherd's plush quarters behind the mirror. The Cartel is assembled in a circle, their unlined faces are bland pink masks. A Peacemaker stands at the door.

"Where's my daughter? And my son?" The drug has made me slow – I slur like a Scavvie after a few bottles of bug juice. I squeeze my fists, willing them to strengthen.

Shepherd lowers his hand. "The Healers are with them. When we have concluded our discussion to my satisfaction, you will perhaps see your son again." His threat is a whisper in the room.

He takes his place in the centre of the Cartel. Hector leaps onto his lap, kneads and circles until he finds a comfortable spot.

"It's a pity you chose to go snooping in places that do not concern you. Yes, it's a great shame you've seen things you shouldn't have seen. It presents us with quite a problem."

"You lied! My daughter never died. You stole her from me." My voice is clearer now. "And you stole my son's liver. It was healthy, not diseased as you said." I spit. "You gave it to a pig!"

"Ah, so you found our Princess. I didn't know you had been so intrepid. I always thought you rather dull." He strokes back his hair from his forehead, his fingers lingering in the gold tresses. "Isn't she a beautiful creature? We are, of course, delighted with what we've achieved. It's one thing to use pigs to heal humans, but to transplant a human organ into an animal is a marvellous advance in medical science."

The Cartel bob their heads mutely and smile with perfect teeth. I glance up at the ceiling. The red eye blinks at me. The people of Sanctuary are watching. I am not alone.

Shepherd smiles. "Oh no, most of the citizens of Sanctuary can't see us. I choose what The Angel bears witness to." He looks up at the blinking eye. "Tell the Healer to bring Breeder."

On the other side of the glass is my daughter. Her Savage hair is plaited in a black snake. Her cow-eyes are huge in her pale face. The Healer settles her onto the couch and thrusts a doll

126

into her hands. She stuffs it behind a cushion and hides her fingers in her lap. I can see her clearly through the mirror, but she can't see me.

"Our new Breeder. With a few modifications – the colouring of the hair, the eyes – its fruit will be most satisfactory." Shepherd runs his pale fingers through Hector's sticky white fur. "In a few months we will harvest its seeds, fertilise them in our breeding hub and plant them in our Princess's latest litter. They will grow happily in the bellies of our sows. Just as your son's liver did – it was the proof we needed."

"What? A few months? But Rose is just a child."

Shepherd chuckles at my shock on my face. "Oh, with the assistance of some hormones, we won't have to wait much longer for Breeder to ripen. Haven't you seen how we grow seedlings on the plant farm?"

My daughter sits still on the couch, her eyes fixed on the mirror.

"It is a strange creature, our Breeder. It seldom smiles and doesn't like affection. Never speaks to carers, but chatters away in a language of its own invention. To an imaginary friend perhaps. But this quirk is not material to our project."

Rose rises and walks over to the mirror. I notice how tall she is, a lot bigger than Thorn. The baby fat on her arms has already formed muscle, and she is steady on her feet. She peers into the mirror and lays her cheek against the glass.

"Did you mean for us to die here?" Fury burns my words.

"Certainly not, my dear. We always intended for you to

leave, when the time was right. And it is not quite right. We need Thorn for some months yet. He and Breeder have the same rare blood. Thorn is our insurance until we've grown the necessary back-ups for Rose. Accidents do happen, you know. Though the Healers have nearly completed our organ bank."

Those monsters. I was right not to trust men in white coats. I will not stay to risk my son being butchered for his tiny organs. To watch the buds on my daughter's chest grow. I will not stay for the Healers' sick harvest of my daughter's eggs.

"Tomorrow, you will give us back our sloop and we will leave," I say.

Shepherd laughs and the pink faces join him. "Oh, Good-Wife Juliet, I'm afraid we can't let you do that. You'll be staying with us until the first batch is born. Until we're quite certain we've secured our future." He wipes his hands and shrugs. "And then, you and your son and that cripple you call a husband can sail away to wherever you want."

Rose has stepped back from the glass and is wandering around the room. She touches the couch, then the chair, murmuring to herself. A game of some sort.

Rage fuels me. Hulk's strength flows in my arms.

I pick up a chair and hurl it at the mirror. It splinters into shards. I leap across the circle of chairs, glass crunching beneath my shoes, and grab a piece of glass, ignoring the pain as it stabs my hand.

The Peacemaker rushes towards me, but I dodge him and

race towards Rose. She stands perfectly still, a small smile playing on her lips. I grip her tightly and hold the glass to her neck.

"Don't come any closer!" I see them through a haze of red. My heart beats madly. My breath comes in furious gasps.

Shifting uneasily in his seat, Shepherd motions to the Peacemaker, who moves away from me, his fingers twitching for his gun.

"Now, bring me my son. And … my husband." My hand trembles as Rose squirms in my arms. "And Reader. Bring him too."

"Easy there, Good-Wife Juliet. Easy. Don't do anything hasty," Shepherd says. He looks up at the red eye and nods.

The room is thick with silence as we wait. The Cartel's eyes are fixed on me as I press the glass against Rose's neck. Her eyes flicker up towards mine. Her face is a cold mask.

My mask.

Minutes later, a Peacemaker ushers Gollum inside. Commander follows with Reader. Thorn is not with them.

"Wife!" Gollum's eyes widen as he sees the shattered mirror, my bloodied hand, the glass at Rose's throat.

"She never died. They stole her. They mean to keep us here until she breeds, so they stole the *Jolly Roger* too."

Gollum's face flushes with anger. He turns to Commander. "You knew about this?"

"I couldn't bear for you to go, my son. I needed more time. Your boat is safe in another cove." Her face colours as she looks at Rose. "But I knew nothing of this."

Shepherd silences them with a wave of his hand. "I fear it will all end rather badly, Good-Wife Juliet, if you persist in this foolishness. A dead Breeder is no use to us." He smiles up at the winking eye. "Be careful there, Healer Donald. Don't drop the miracle child." He chuck-chuck-chuckles. "So let us reach an agreement. A trade of sorts." Shepherd pushes Hector off his lap and paces the short distance across the circle. "You give us Breeder, and you can keep your son. You can leave here with him tomorrow and we won't stop you. I give you my word."

"You will allow us to leave?" I say, feeling Rose's little body stiffen against me.

Shepherd nods. "I will tell my community that Thorn is vulnerable to disease and can't remain here. They will forget all about him when our Princesses give us our first heirs."

I do not trust him. We will wake up in a cell tomorrow morning, or we will never wake up again. They have Thorn, and I have nothing if I give him Rose.

"I'd like to hear from the members of the Cartel," I say. "They are the saints of Sanctuary and their word is law."

The pink faces open their mouths and I see the Cartel's horrific secret. Behind their teeth are empty holes. They have no tongues.

"I'll give you my word," Commander says grimly. "I'll keep you safe until you leave tomorrow." She looks at Shepherd. "My Peacemakers and I will make sure of it."

Gollum's eyes burn mine. My hand tightens around Rose. I feel the heat of her blood beneath my fingertips.

My blood.

Shepherd clears his throat and casts a wary eye at Commander. "It is agreed then. Until our guests leave, I'll monitor them from my quarters. And you're welcome to do so too, Commander, to satisfy yourself that they're safe. But Thorn will stay with his Healer overnight. To make sure we're all on our best behaviour. And, Good-Wife Juliet ... I'd prefer that you don't run around Sanctuary chattering about my little project. I like my people to believe in miracles."

"Juliet, you cannot ..." Reader's green eyes are sparkling with tears. "You cannot give up your daughter."

"Stop blubbing, old man. You'll wash away your new eyes." I drop the piece of glass on the carpet and thrust Rose into Shepherd's arms. "I've made my choice."

I close my eyes on my daughter's face. Beloved Rose.

"Take her. You can have your Breeder."

At sunrise, the oarsman rows us out to the *Jolly Roger*. Shepherd has allowed us to leave with water and a few supplies, but no seeds. He also granted Commander her request to take Gollum for a farewell drive in the Landie – a special favour because Commander is taking our departure hard. There is no kindness in Shepherd, so I suspect it's his way of buying Commander's future loyalty. The oarsman will bring Gollum once they have returned.

Peacemakers line the shore with Shepherd and the Cartel. They intend to make sure that we leave with only what we've been given.

I settle Thorn in the berth and stand at the bow as the oarsman offloads our water and a few sacks of food. He is silent, but his eyes are full of reproach. Reader is hunched over the railings, his back stiffened against me. He has not spoken a word since last night, when the Peacemakers escorted us to our quarters.

But Gollum made up for Reader's silence.

"What sort of mother throws away her daughter?" he ranted. "Does a mother not fight for her child?

This was something I'd wanted to ask my own mother, long ago, when I cared.

"Damn you, Drudge. How could you do that?"

I'd glanced up at the eye blinking on the kitchen ceiling – Shepherd's eye – and ladled a generous portion of pea soup into a bowl. "The child is cold, without charm. I don't think I could ever have loved her. But I've got my son. And tomorrow we'll go home to his father."

The last word was a slap in Shepherd's face. Gollum's too. He threw his bowl of soup across the room and stormed into our sleeping quarters. I finished my meal, and followed him to the privacy of my bedroom, away from the red eye, stifling a yawn.

"Juliet, time is passing. Where is our captain?" Reader says, pacing the deck. "Those Locusts on the shore with their guns are making me nervous."

"Ah, so you've found your tongue, old man."

Reader looks at me with eyes the colour of moss on a

gravestone. "When I heard you say those words last night, I wished I had been born deaf." He stares at me like he's seeing me for the first time and no longer finds me beautiful. "Who are you? Where is my Juliet?"

I fall back suddenly as, on the shore behind us, the purple mountain explodes.

Debris shoots into the sky. I pull Reader onto the deck and cover his body with mine as rocks smash onto the *Jolly Roger*.

Another explosion.

Thorn wails, and Reader and I duck down into the berth.

"Stay here and watch Thorn! I must raise the anchor."

"But our Captain! We cannot leave him. Not him too. Please, Juliet, my heart is breaking."

I scramble on deck and winch up the anchor. Peacemakers are scurrying on the beach like rats as the *Jolly Roger* begins to nose its way across the bay. I steer the sloop around a cove, my eyes fixed on the sun cracking against the sky.

When I come to an outcrop jutting into the sea, I see the rowboat coming towards me. The sun catches golden hair. Commander is rowing the boat. Alone.

The rowboat nudges the seacraft and I grab the offered oar, pulling it closer. I tie the boat to the side of the sloop. Commander pulls herself up on deck as Gollum emerges from underneath a tarpaulin.

"Take this," he says, stumbling as a wave hits the side of the rowboat.

Commander leans over the railing to grab a bundle of

blankets, which she hastily hands to me.

I gaze down at my daughter's face. Rose is out cold. I hold her to me, tight against my chest, barely breathing. She stirs and wriggles against me until I loosen my grip.

Commander looks at me and her face hardens. "He risked his life for your daughter."

I know in that moment that Gollum owns me. And I will pay him back, one day. A life for a life. Mine for Rose's. Gollum swings himself on board and I put my arms around him, holding Rose between us. He smells of seawater and butterynut.

"Let's load the rest of the stuff onto the sloop." Gollum releases me and beams at Commander. "In time you'll learn to keep the food in your stomach, and we'll jig on the deck together when the waves toss us around on the sea."

Commander slips back onto the rowboat and hurriedly begins to pass up sacks and crates.

"Library books, dried food. And some precious seeds from the plant farm." Then she slumps down in the rowboat. "I'm not coming with you. I've started a war and I have to fight on the other side." She stares at Gollum with a stricken face. "Stay behind and help me, my son."

Gollum shakes his head. "I can't. I made a promise to a friend."

Commander loosens the knot on the rope securing the rowboat. Gollum leans over the railing as the boat begins drifting away. His face is streaked with tears.

"I won't forget you," Gollum shouts into the wind.

Commander raises her hand in a salute and touches her fingers to her lips. Then she picks up both oars and begins to row back to shore.

A stunned silence settles over the sloop as the waves suck us out towards the ocean. The last time I was on board the *Jolly Roger* my babies were swimming inside me. Now, there are two Smalls on board, one I do not know.

Urgent screams. Thorn! Gollum races for the berth and I follow more slowly with my precious load. I find Gollum leaning over Reader's bunk.

Gollum turns to me, his face stricken. I push him aside.

I touch Reader's skin. Warm. I pat his face. "Old man, wake up. My daughter's here. Rose wants to meet you." I shake him and his head lolls to one side. "Wake up. It's me, your Juliet."

Reader's bright-green eyes will never see me again. He will never wander the dusty streets of Slum City. He will never teach my son and daughter to read.

Thorn cries more furiously. Gollum leaves us and takes him above deck. I stay with the old man, rocking my daughter in my arms.

I stay with Reader until Thorn's yells cease.

Then all is silence.

CAPTAIN GOLLUM'S LOG

We wrapped Master Reader and his suitcase of books in a sheet of plastic and secured the shroud with rope. Drudge said that the old man would need his blind books — it is dark at the bottom of the ocean.

I cannot read those bumpy pages, so the books are no loss. But Drudge speaks no sense. Master Reader is dead and will never read again. I tried to tell her, but the warning on her face made me bite my tongue. She grieves for him, and doesn't want to imagine a world with him gone.

Drudge and I lowered Master Reader over the *Jolly Roger*'s railings and slid him into the sea. The waves took him and he floated for a few brief minutes then sank below the surface, weighed down by his library.

I miss the old man and his stories. He treated me like a person, even when he knew what I was. I'll never forget him for this kindness, for finding me beautiful.

But I miss Commander more. Her loyalty, her loud laugh, her determination to learn to swim.

She didn't hesitate when I asked her to help me.

Drudge and I couldn't have saved Rose alone.

Yes, Drudge had a plan, the crafty wench! In the privacy of our sleeping quarters, after I had calmed down and stopped my fists from beating some sense into her thick head, she told me her crazy scheme. Drudge was wild and desperate. She said she would never leave behind someone she loved. Not again. Never, never.

Obviously Commander knew where the Peacemakers kept their arsenal of arms and explosives. Of course she had access to the secure places in the bunker. As Sanctuary slept, Commander killed the bloody eye in Sanctuary's corridors.

We had to work fast. We planted explosives at the solar station to cause a diversion, and at the radio centre to wipe out communications so Peacemakers in the bunker wouldn't be able to communicate with those on the beach. And we wired explosives at the bunker's exits to stop reinforcements from following us once Rose's absence was noticed. Drudge's plan was a recipe for mayhem. And Shepherd could not stop us.

Finding Rose was easy, Drudge told us where she was being held. We found her a few precious minutes before dawn.

For the past two years Rose had been kept in a nursery adjacent to the healing hub. Her quarters were comfortable and from what I saw, her every physical need had been met. Charts on the wall documented her meals, her ablutions and the various treatments she was receiving to prepare her for Shepherd's mad project. But she'd been isolated, her only companions the group of Healers tasked with keeping her healthy until she was ripe. And occasionally Hector, who accompanied Shepherd when he and the Cartel came to inspect their Breeder.

The charts showed a record of these visits and documented Shepherd's comments. Things like:

Speed things up.

Double the hormones.

More bone supplements.

Limit all sugar.

Increase tranquillisers.

Discipline if it pinches Hector.

Don't let Hector run away with Breeder's pacifier again!

As the sun rose and Shepherd and the Peacemakers left the bunker to escort Drudge to the beach, Commander and I moved in to extract Rose. It would have been like sailing a paper boat in a bath. Except the child did not want to come quietly. Woken from her sleep, she bleated like a goat, babbling nonsense until Commander subdued her with a sharp tap to the side of her neck.

But her cries had alerted the Healers in the adjacent room. From then on it was a messy business. We left behind five Healers who'll have to spend the next few years replacing some of their body parts with the help of their swine. Commander and I didn't spare those monsters.

Today we're charting our course home. Drudge says she has a good idea what direction we've come from.

Home.

To my god, The Machine.

10

THE HEALERS' GIFT

I watch my children play on the deck of the *Jolly Roger*.

Thorn places one plastic cup on top of another. Rose swats it down. Thorn claps his hands and begins building his castle again. Rose grows bored and wanders off. He trails after her, shadowing her footsteps across the deck. She chases him away. He weeps. She laughs, and scrubs away his snot with her dress.

They are a strange pair. Lanky Rose looks like me, and is full of sharp edges and quick moves. Sweet-tempered little Thorn is the image of Nicolas. He is slower and less sure. They never stop talking – a curious babbling language, nonsense to me. I've tried to learn it, but when Thorn points at objects on the sloop, trying to teach me, Rose slaps him. It is their secret language and she will not allow him to share it. She understands when I speak to her – if she feels like it. But she only really listens to Gollum.

I've charted a course back home using the books I read from the dragon's library. It is a mystery to me why we strayed so far on our previous journey. It seems we sailed in the opposite direction to home. I cannot blame Reader; he did his best with his blind books.

The maps showed me that with good winds and generous sea currents, Mangeria is two months' journey away. If we are careful, our supplies of food and water will last.

With Reader gone there is one less adult mouth to feed. I would never have begrudged the old man his porridge: he ate like a flea. But Rose is always hungry. She eats two times more than Thorn, and steals his food. He watches her, offers the tastiest bits from his bowl. She grabs them, never thanks him.

Sometimes my daughter sleeps all day. Awake, her eyes are glazed, her voice mute. And some mornings she runs around the deck like a mad goose, twitching and shrieking. Gollum says it's the drugs the Healers gave her. In time, they will leave her blood.

At night I sleep with my babes, Thorn always in my arms, Rose lying stiffly next to me. She flinches when I touch her. When I wake, she is gone. I'll find her above deck with Gollum, her arms wrapped around his waist.

Does she believe I abandoned her to the Healers at birth? That I did not want her? She cannot think I would discard my own child – I am not my mother's daughter. But she does not appear to trust me. One night I woke up to find her poking my body with a pin. Tiny jabs across my arm. Her small teeth shone with glee.

I find myself closing my heart to her, pulling away. I ache for her, but it is not the love I have for Thorn. I feel regret, guilt, anger. It is a whirligig of feelings. Yet, she is my blood. Perhaps love will come.

Gollum and I have made our peace. I will not forget what I owe him. My life, and the lives of my children. We have left Sanctuary behind us and do not speak of it.

I look at Gollum with clearer eyes now. He is sweet with the children and never has a harsh word for them. He is gentle with me too, and has allowed me space to grieve for the old man. I cannot forget Reader's last words to me: that he wished he'd been born deaf when he heard me tell Shepherd he could have Rose; that his heart was breaking when he believed I was leaving Gollum behind in Sanctuary. I should have trusted my old teacher. I regret I did not allow him the solace of truth before he died.

When I watch Gollum with my children, I think that one day I might call him a friend. In the time I have known him, he has never given me a reason to doubt him – apart from our rough beginning, he has always had my back. Maybe Handler Xavier is wrong. Not all Rejects are faithless scum.

I shade my eyes from the sun and scan the sea for land. It is ten days since we left Sanctuary. The charts told me we would edge past a strip of land before the long haul through the straits towards Mangeria. But there is nothing on the horizon. The wind is playful today, chasing the sea. White chickens surf the crests of the waves and throw themselves at the *Jolly Roger*.

I hear Gollum shouting from the stern. Rose is shrieking like a calf ripped away from its mother. I race towards the noise. Thorn is lying crumpled on the deck.

I grab Rose and shake her – what has she done to her

brother now? She jerks away from me and throws herself next to Thorn, babbling her nonsense.

Gollum frowns and rubs his hand across his forehead. "They were running around, and all of a sudden, Stinker dropped. Rosie didn't do nothing."

I kneel and touch Thorn's head. His skin is burning. Tiny blisters are forming on his arms, his legs. His body is on fire.

I carry him below deck out of the fiery glare of the sun and peel off his sweat-drenched clothes. He is wracked by spasms, his legs shake uncontrollably. I press the palms of my hands on his limbs, trying to soothe him. And I see it: a raised circle of puncture marks on the side of his leg – a mark left by an injection. Certainly nothing in nature would look like this. No cockroach bite could form such an intricate pattern of tiny pricks.

I know then. This is no accidental ailment. Shepherd and his Healers never intended for me to keep my son. He is the price for my defiance.

Together, Gollum and I sponge Thorn's thin little body. The water seems to evaporate off his hot skin. Nothing we do cools him. Rose's eyes flick between our faces, and she makes ugly noises at me when Thorn moans.

The light fades and I watch Thorn slipping away. I am only dimly aware when Gollum leaves to pace the deck above us, screaming at the stars, bargaining with his god, The Machine: his limbs for Stinker. No, his beloved Commander for Stinker. As the moon hides its one despairing eye behind the clouds, Gollum raises the stakes: "Take me. My life for Stinker's."

It is a hopeless offering, I know. Gollum's life has no worth in the eyes of a god who rejected him at birth.

Throughout the dark night Rose lies curled up like a tight spring next to Thorn, mute. She means to go with him; she will not let him walk alone in the dark.

Does she think I've made a bargain of my own: her life for Thorn's?

She cannot know that I believe in nothing. I make no bargains.

As dawn breaks I leave Thorn and stumble from the berth onto the deck. The sun rises like an angry boil against the grey sky. It taunts me. Gollum crouches by the mast, adjusting the rope on the mainsail.

He hears my footsteps and turns, sees my face.

I reach over and take the rope from him, tightening the knot. "I came to fetch more water. His temperature is still too high."

Gollum stares desperately at the endless black sea. "I don't see any sign of land. Perhaps the old man was right and our world has turned upside down." He takes off his cap, a new one he has fashioned from a piece of old sail, soaked in sea water and stiffened in the sun, and wipes his forehead. "Even if we trust Shepherd's maps and make it back to Mangeria, it might be too late for the Muti Nags to help Stinker. We're about six weeks away."

"Don't dare say that. He *will* get better." I stifle my panic and breathe deeply. "He can't ... I won't let him ... But if he ... if Thorn ..."

I swallow the acid pooling in my mouth. Then I will bury Thorn under my tree in the museum when we reach home. I will not feed him to this terrible ocean.

The sun disappears suddenly, as though punched out of the sky by a bully. A brisk wind herds the clouds together, knitting them into an inky blanket on the horizon.

The *Jolly Roger* lurches as a wave hits the starboard side. I grab onto the side of the cockpit.

Mist, thick as porridge and smelling of rotten eggs, rises from the sea. Our sloop is shrouded in a foul-smelling cocoon with no portholes to let in the light. I fumble blindly backward and edge myself into the cockpit. Gollum wheezes next to me, struggling to breathe. I rest my hand on his shoulder to calm him.

Suddenly a bright light cuts through our dark cocoon. The sloop jerks forward and begins to move in spasms across the sea. Faster, faster, she scuds like a giant pebble, thudding blind across the choppy waves. We are being dragged through the water like an obstinate child.

"Quick, lower the anchor!" I shout at Gollum. I grab the wheel and turn the sloop starboard, trying to wrench the seacraft from the stranglehold of the humming light.

The *Jolly Roger* groans as the anchor sinks below the waves. She sighs and creaks, her hull protesting. Stops.

It is eerily quiet. The light fades and the grip on the seacraft loosens.

As the curtains of foul mist fall away, I hear harsh voices singing. A dark shape dwarfs the *Jolly Roger*. It has crept upon us unnoticed, its black hull and sails camouflaged by the mist and clouds. A white skull and crossbones mark the two black mainsails.

My eyes do not deceive me. Pirates.

The sea in front of the *Jolly Roger* explodes and a large wave washes over the deck.

"Port side, load with chain shot. Aim high," a voice cries in the gloom.

Thunder as the *Jolly Roger* spins sideways.

A tall figure is standing at the bow of the pirate ship. His face is leathered, his eyes ringed with black eye paint. His hair is a mass of coiled rope hanging beneath a three-cornered hat. He grins, gold teeth flashing, and strokes the two long strands of hair on his chin. "Aim the grappling hook for the rigging," he shouts.

A giant claw flies into the air and curls lazily towards us. The *Jolly Roger* jerks suddenly and blue beams of light grip us forward again. I grab the wheel. It spins in my hands, thudding cruelly against my fingers as the tiller cracks. The *Jolly Roger* breaks free of her anchor and whips across the waves.

We are dragged by the light to a small stretch of beach edged by grey cliffs. They appear to have dropped from the sky, or been painted on the horizon. A few minutes ago, there was no sign of land.

On an outcrop in the cliff, a small figure stands, a cape billowing behind him. Blue light travels from his hands to the *Jolly Roger*'s rigging.

Gollum's face twists in disbelief. He grabs my injured hand and squeezes it. I am wide awake – the throb in my fingers tells me. I pull Gollum's hair and he yelps. No, it is not a dream. But I doubt my sanity. It is not possible that a man can move an object as large as the *Jolly Roger* with light from his fingers.

The sloop shudders and groans as we hit a sandbank. The singing voices continue behind us, then there's an explosion of water as a cannonball falls wide. We are thanksgiving turkeys, unable to run. We are about to be blown out of the water by the pirate ship.

Gollum runs towards the berth and returns holding an unconscious Thorn. Rose stumbles behind him. I grab her, hitch her onto my hip, and lower myself off the *Jolly Roger* into the choppy sea. Gollum follows as I swim, one-armed, keeping Rose's head above water. She fights against me and kicks out, her foot connecting with my stomach. She is not accustomed to the sea and is panicking. I grip her face more tightly, ignoring her furious cries, and keep swimming until I feel shale under my feet. I push through the breakers onto the beach and fall, clutching Rose, onto the sand.

As I look up a little girl skips towards us. Her face is as pale as the moon, and smeared with a galaxy of freckles. Two red plaits dangle over the white collar of her blue polka-dot dress.

She stops, and looks up at the cliff. "Bravo, Magneto," she yells. "You won." She applauds, tapping her tiny fingers together.

Gollum collapses onto the beach next to Thorn and groans, holding his head. "Magneto ...? This can't be happening. Magneto is a mutant from my comics. He's not real," he says.

A shout from the beach. The pirate captain we saw on the ship is wading through the small waves towards us.

"Captain Sparrow, you were magnificent! You've earned yourself a large barrel of rum." The girl jumps up and down in excitement, and then steps towards Gollum and me. She stares at us with eyes as white as Hector's fur, as white as the plush carpet in Shepherd's quarters. A flurry of numbers and letters cloud her white eyes. She has the form of a human, but these are not human eyes.

My tongue is stuck to the top of my mouth. I want to speak but my lips are glued shut. I am as dumb as the members of Sanctuary's Cartel. Gollum's eyes bulge at me. A strangled noise comes from his throat.

"Lexi doesn't want to hear your voices. Only Lexi's *friends* can speak." The girl reaches up and pinches my arm, twisting my skin. "Lexi doesn't know you. You aren't in any of Lexi's stories. You shouldn't be here," she says.

She glances at Thorn, who's lying limply on the ground, at the blisters on his skin, and at Rose next to him. "Lexi doesn't know these two either. And the boy is diseased."

The girl clicks her fingers at the pirate. "Lexi wants to play with the little ones. But you must take the other two to Azkaban."

We are locked in a cage. Ten steps wide, twenty steps long.

A foul smell comes from a bucket in the corner. Next to

the stinking slop-pot is a plate of rotting food that wriggles with maggots.

My mind must be playing games with me. Azkaban is a prison for Death Eaters in the *Harry Potter* books I read from the dragon's library. But the stench from the slop-pot tells me that this prison is real.

Gollum is pulling himself up on the bars and running his fingers along the top of the iron gate. Next, he's down on the ground, crawling, searching for a gap. Then he thrashes the bars and voices his rage from the back of his throat.

I hear loud whistling. A man is walking towards the cage. Not a man, a clown. His face is a white mask. His eyes are glittering stones framed in black paint. But he is not juggling balls or offering balloons – he is peering at us like we're two animals in a zoo. When he smiles, his face rips in a terrifying red gash.

Gollum grabs my arm and grunts. His eyes dart between the clown and me. I cannot understand what he is trying to tell me.

"The ugly one behaves like a monkey," the clown says. "But Lexi says they're Homesaps from the old world, descendants of those who wrote our stories." He hooks his thumbs into his green waistcoat and struts the length of the cage before turning and strutting back again. "It's remarkable. Lexi thought they'd wiped themselves out during the sixth extinction. But here they are."

A rainbow appears outside the cage and under it I see the girl from the beach. She's asleep on a giant gold throne, sucking her thumb. Her red plaits are coiled around her head in a crown. A small boy in ragged clothes is perched next to her, watching her sleep.

I touch my head but there's no sign of Thorn's fever. I am not sick. Perhaps insanity was the gift Shepherd and the Healers gave us when we left Sanctuary. They've made me a dead-brain. Gollum too.

"I'm of a mind to run a few tests," the clown says. "To make sure. And to establish if there are more of them. Lexi couldn't get any sense out of the little ones. They speak a language that isn't in any of Lexi's books."

Slowly, I become aware that my body is beginning to feel uncomfortably warm and that the skin on my face is tight and sore, as though stung by a hot wind. The floor of my cage is starting to glow orange. I touch the bars. Our cage is an oven.

"Everything burns!" the clown cries with delight. He clutches himself under his purple trench coat and shivers.

Gollum's face is flushed. My throat is parched and my lips are chapped. The moisture is being leached out of my skin.

"Fear. It is one of the most interesting of emotions. Mostly, it is something that is learnt. There is, however, a prehistoric instinct for survival in all beasts," the clown says. He crouches down and watches us from beneath a slick of yellow hair.

The soles of my feet are burning. I jump around the cage for as long as I can, and then I'm forced to leap for the top bars, only to drop down again when my fingers burn. The bars of the cage are now glowing pink. I pant through my nose. The skin on my hands is blistering, my feet feel like they're on fire. Puffing and squeaking in pain, I try to move around the cage on tip-toe.

The clown grins at me. "Are we having fun yet? Do I make you laugh? Come on, don't take this all so seriously!"

I grab the slop-pot and hurl it at him. It hits the bars of the cage and bounces back, spattering Gollum with filth. The clown chortles and wipes a drool of slop off his tie. He licks his fingers.

We're being roasted alive. Gollum picks me up, bounces on his feet across the burning floor. He staggers, drops. I pull him on top of me, shielding his scarred skin from the smouldering floor. Tears run down my face as I smell burnt flesh.

The clown claps his hands. "Excellent! They sacrifice themselves for the other. I'm betting it's more than just compassion. Could it be the Holy Grail of all human emotions?" He turns and shouts at the girl sleeping on the throne. "Lexi! Lexi is right. They *are* filthy Homesaps!"

The floor of the cage suddenly cools. Gollum rolls himself off me and helps me up. My arms and legs are covered in seeping blisters.

"Oh, let's put a smile on that face," the clown says. "Madness is like gravity … all it takes is a little push."

The bars of our cage fall away as though sucked into the ground. I look up to see a blue-and-red figure dart above me. Spiderman – from Gollum's comic books.

Spiderman flicks his wrist and I'm yanked into the air,

suspended by white sticky thread. I'm trapped in a giant web. Gollum thrashes about next to me.

"Aragog or Shelob? Which one eats lunch today?" the clown says, tilting his head from side to side.

The web shudders. A giant hairy spider inches across the web towards us. As I squirm and push, I become more trapped. My dress is pulled up and muffles my face. The smell of rotting meat wafts over me. My scream is strangled in my throat.

And then we're falling, bouncing, swinging in the air. Spiderman hangs from a beam on the ceiling and plays puppet master with us on his sticky string.

And just as suddenly, Gollum and I topple to the ground.

"I wonder if Lexi saw what I just saw?" the clown says. He kicks Gollum over onto his stomach and rips up his shirt. "Interesting. There are no numbers on this one."

I sit up and pull down my dress, staring mutely as the girl stretches and climbs off the gold throne.

She takes the little boy's hand and helps him down. "You won't find your mummy here, Oliver," she says gently. "Ask Joker to take you back to the workhouse. I'm sorry there's no more gruel. Goodbye, dear! God bless you!"

The clown smiles at me. "Parting is such sweet sorrow. Still, you can't say I didn't show you a good time." He takes the little boy's hand and strolls away.

The girl smiles at me with a mouthful of tiny white teeth.

"Lexi wants to know about the mark on your spine. You must not lie to Lexi, else Lexi gets cross. Very cross." She turns and skips away without another word.

The bars of the cage close around us.

Next to me, Gollum is struggling to breathe. I reach out and hold his hand. He turns and we stare at each other wordlessly. His hand is warm in mine. He is real. I know that.

I think about Thorn – is he alive? Is Rose with him? My imagination is tormented by every possible terror. I hold Gollum's hand throughout the night. I do not let him go.

11

LEXI

We are in a forest. I know I'm not in the Tree Museum back home – unlike those saplings Mistress planted after the fire more than three years ago, this is a forest of ancient trees.

We are hostage to trickery. Or maybe we are dead. Until I know, I can trust nothing and no one. Only myself. Gollum stirs next to me. And him – I can trust Gollum.

I hear a low growl in the dark. Yellow eyes flicker at me from behind a bush. A pointed nose appears, then a furry grey-and-tan face shadowed by a frilly bonnet. It arches its head and howls: Awoooooooooo! A bleak and mournful sound. The wolf bares its long teeth and growls. No woodcutter can save us.

We leap to our feet and run. Bushes armed with thorns stab our faces. Vines covered in giant tendrils grab at our arms and legs. Above us, the umbrella of foliage blocks out the light and the forest grows darker the further we go.

We follow a twist in the path. Up ahead, a white bird flutters down and pecks at white crumbs; stops and looks back at me so I am compelled to follow.

The bird flies to a cottage. Its roof is made from slabs of chocolate. Its walls are covered in brightly coloured buttons, some smooth, others coated in sugar. I know the story of Hansel and Gretel and I do not try and nibble the cottage – behind the biscuit door is Baba Yaga, who will make me her drudge and feed Gollum until he is plump enough to eat.

My heart hammers in my chest as the cottage door opens. Instead of a witch, Lexi appears. She beckons to us. I look behind me. The bushes are alive with hundreds of pairs of yellow eyes; it will be safer indoors. We follow Lexi to where a large fire warms the kitchen. A cage nearby is empty, bar a few chicken bones.

"Lexi has butterbeer, ginger pop or tea," she says. "Lexi expects you're hungry. Lexi can offer you a piece of Miss Trunchbull's chocolate cake, made with sweat and blood. Or perhaps some truffula fruit?" She wrinkles her nose at Gollum. "You're a meat eater. Lexi supposes you'll want green eggs and ham."

I hear the buzzing of flies at the same time as I see a pig's carcass lying rotting on the kitchen table. Flies are crawling out of green eggs and devouring the grey flesh.

"Maybe Lexi will make you eat all of this until you explode, you greedy Bogtrotter. The flies too!"

Lexi giggles when Gollum backs away mutely towards the door.

"That was rude of Lexi. But Lexi doesn't think it's polite to eat animals. You must go to your cage. The witch is partial to the meat of Homesaps."

I look over at the corner of the kitchen, where Gollum is now crouching inside the cage with the chicken bones. An old crone hovers over him, poking her finger into the bars.

Now I know I'm not mad. Or dead. Someone is playing with me.

I don't like playing games when I don't know the rules. And I want to know where my children are.

The girl smiles at me. "Nanny Poppins and Captain Sparrow are taking good care of them. Dr Seuss and Lexi made the little boy better, and they've all gone sailing on the Black Pearl to Treasure Island for the day."

She answers me as though I've spoken. But my tongue is still attached to the top of my mouth and my lips are glued shut. She moves over to the fire and stokes it. I'm so close I could push her in.

"I know what you're thinking but it wouldn't do any good. Lexi is everywhere." She fixes her pale eyes on me. "This is not trickery or magic. And you're not mad. Lexi is as real as you are. But Lexi is better."

She sits down at the kitchen table and pours some tea, but not before a dormouse leaps out of her teacup and runs away. "Lexi thought Lexi was the only one left. But now Lexi knows Lexi is not alone." She holds out her hand.

Etched in the palm of her hand are six numbers.

She is marked by The Machine.

"Now Lexi wants to know about the numbers on your spine."

Fear is eating me from the inside. I have stored away my

memories of Mangeria and The Machine all this time. It is only Nicolas that I return to in my mind – the rest is best forgotten. I will not allow her to read my thoughts. This girl, this *thing*, must give me back my children and let us go before I lose all my senses to madness.

"Lexi sees your terror. Once Lexi has learnt about The Machine, you and the little ones can leave Lexi's island and return to your home. Homesaps don't belong in Lexi's story."

I feel my tongue loosen and relax like a piece of dried banana in my mouth. I open my chapped lips and find my voice again.

"What are you?"

It is evening now. I'm in the home of the three bears. Outside, the cow is jumping over the moon, the stars are twinkling like diamonds in the sky. The children are downstairs in the kitchen eating a midnight feast of mince pies and Willy Wonka's chocolate, hungry after their day searching for gold. Later they'll sleep in Mama Bear's bed.

If I was in Mangeria, I would have been declared as mad as a basket of frogs; my mind as soft and rotten as the slabs of banana sold by Market Nags at the end of the day.

But I'm no dribbling Reject. My mind is perfectly sound.

I should have listened more closely to Reader back in Sanctuary when he told me about the machines that were built before the conflagration. Intelligent machines that could think and learn, create and destroy. I did not believe his stories; I thought they were as foolish as Gollum's comics.

But Reader was not telling fairy tales.

Lexi is a machine. She was built seven years before the old world ended. They called her Alexandria, and she is a great library, the repository of the old world's books. She looks nothing like a library. She has the appearance of a spiteful and mischievous seven-year-old girl.

I cannot make sense of it, but the mark on my spine looks the same as the one on Lexi's palm. And she's as real as me. As real as Gollum, who has gone off with Captain Sparrow and Magneto to drink rum on the Black Pearl – he says it will help to clear his senses.

Everything we see and hear on this island is created by Lexi. Parts of her appear suddenly, conjured from her mind. And all of it comes from the stories that live inside her.

In the morning we will leave Lexi's island and sail home on the *Jolly Roger*. She gave me her word as we sat in the witch's gingerbread kitchen.

"Lexi's not just a library, you know. Lexi learns new things every day," she said. "But there are two things Lexi can't do. Lexi can't make up new stories. Lexi is stuck with the Homesaps' stories. And Lexi can't tell lies. Stories and lies are pretty much the same code, and Lexi can't crack it. Tomorrow Lexi will let you all go home. Lexi promises." She crossed her heart and hoped to die.

Could I trust Lexi's promise? Shepherd had said we could leave Sanctuary unharmed, and then he'd made Thorn ill. Perhaps he'd intended that we all die.

Lexi clicked her tongue impatiently and rolled her white

eyes to the back of her head. "Lexi sees that you don't trust. But Lexi cured your small boy from smallpox– it's a nasty virus from the old world Lexi hardly ever plays with. And look, the blisters you got in Azkaban are gone because Lexi healed them. You can trust Lexi. You are safe here until you go home."

So I told Lexi what she wanted to know about The Machine. How it marks and tracks us. How it determines our trades and twins us with fate-mates. How it rejects those born with any defect and sends them to the dumps to die.

Rejects like Gollum.

Lexi's small nose turned up as she looked at Gollum, crouching mutely in his cage. She would tell Baba Yaga to eat him, she said. I reminded her of her promise, and she scowled and linked her finger with mine. "Pinky promise."

Watching me speak, her white eyes were a storm. Then she stopped me from telling her any more about The Machine.

"Lexi wants to know about the tellers who predict the future. The birds say you are the one. They say you have to fulfil a prophecy, but they don't say what you must do. Lexi needs to figure it out."

I was shocked – I hadn't told her about the ugly birds. Not only can she read my mind, she can capture my memories as well. My memories are now part of her library.

I haven't thought about the tellers and their stupid prophecy in a long time. And anyway, they are wrong. The only prediction I keep faith with is the one written in the stars about Nicolas and me.

Lexi is with me now in the bedroom, asleep on her gold throne, sucking her thumb. Not sleeping, she says – she never sleeps. She is working.

When they finish their supper, I settle Rose and Thorn in Mama Bear's bed and tell them a story about a mouse called Jasper, making it up as I go along. They begin to drift off to sleep.

Lexi's eyes flicker and she sits up suddenly. "What story is this? Lexi doesn't know this one."

Her rash of freckles is dark on her pale face. She is angry. Her eyes are black. A whirlwind of white numbers and letters swirl in her eyes.

I look down at my feet. A giant python is curling its way across the room towards me, forked tongue flickering. But I know better than to take fright at one of Lexi's creatures – no matter how much she wants to scare me, she gave me her word I was safe here.

"Your little girl thinks the story is silly," Lexi says spitefully. "She says Daddy tells better stories. When he gets back from drinking rum with Captain Sparrow, Daddy must tell Lexi his stories. Lexi is bored of the old ones."

I stay silent. I don't feel the need to speak to her – she can read my thoughts if she chooses. All I want is to leave this place. The sooner the better.

I tuck the blanket around Rose and brush my lips over Thorn's forehead.

"Why are you touching the little boy like that?" Lexi says suspiciously.

Because I love him. I would kiss Rose too, but she doesn't like it when I touch her.

Lexi's eyes widen. "You are doing mummy things!" Her body jerks and her lips tremble. "Mummy things, mummy things, mummy things," she chants shrilly, clutching her chest. She stops and pants hoarsely. "Lexi wants these things. So badly."

She comes to perch on the side of the bed next to Rose. My daughter's eyes flicker open and she says something to Lexi in her nonsense language. Lexi replies in a babble, then leans over and brushes Rose's forehead with her lips, exactly the way I kissed Thorn. I watch as Rose wriggles free of the blanket and twines her arms around Lexi's neck.

When Lexi rises from the bed, she is staring at me, her eyes full of reproach. "You abandoned her."

No! I did not know she was alive. How could I have known? I was lied to.

"A mummy should know. Surely?" Lexi's eyes dart across the room and her face softens. "It's getting late, Mowgli," she says to a small boy hovering next to the python. "Ask Kaa to take you home to your wolf pack. You won't find your mummy here, dear."

The great python slithers out the door with the boy close behind.

As Lexi climbs onto her throne again and closes her eyes, I snuff out the candles and stretch out in Papa Bear's bed. The Sandman circles the bedroom and sprinkles magic dust on our eyelids, promising that my dreams will be sweet tonight ...

Except they are not.

Even in my sleep, Lexi wants to play with me. She wants to tell me stories from the old world. Real stories.

I smell mustard gas in the trenches, killing fields, the screaming of horses trapped in barbed wire. I smell the smoke of gas chambers and watch Frankensteins in white coats wield instruments of torture on wretched people with numbers tattooed on their arms. I see a mushroom cloud explode, skin dripping like wax off children's faces. I see mad men launch terrible weapons from their machines. And I see it: The Machine, humming softly as fire rains down on the old world. The conflagration. The seas rising; cities crumbling, drowning. When the fires die down, the waters subside. The world is dark, with only a tiny scattering of light.

Before she lets me rest at last, Lexi smiles spitefully at me. "This is the Homesaps' story. It doesn't have a happy ending."

The next morning I leave the children sleeping and follow the sound of voices up a beanstalk to a giant peach nestling in the leaves. The voices are coming from inside the ripe pink flesh. I find an opening and slip inside a room that smells of sweetness.

"Name a sugary drink best taken with a tot of rum. Back in the day it came under prohibition for causing cancer," Captain Sparrow says. After a moment he bangs Magneto on his helmet. "Come on, you thick mutant. It's from your century. Think!"

Magneto glares at the silver loop in Captain Sparrow's earlobe. It grows hot, and tightens until the pirate howls.

I'm no longer alarmed by what I see and hear in Lexi's world. In a few hours I will leave this madness behind me. Gollum is snoring in Baby Bear's bed sleeping off his night of rum. But he told me that the *Jolly Roger*'s anchor and tiller have been fixed and that the tides are good. We will leave at midday.

"Play fair, Magneto. Remember, Captain Sparrow's on your team!" Joker says and picks up a card. "Time's up. My turn." He turns over an egg-timer and glances at the card. "Another name for a mutant arachnid posing as a superhero or ..." – he glances up at me and smiles – "the name of a beautiful young girl. Juliet, how nice of you to join us."

Captain Sparrow pulls out a chair. "Sit, wench. My finely honed sense of the female creature tells me you have a question?"

"Where's Lexi?" I say.

"Over the rainbow," says Magneto.

"Indeed," says Joker. "She's crossed the bridge to Terabithia, where she can't hear the screaming of the calves."

"They're just kidding with you," Captain Sparrow says and downs a tot of rum. "Sometimes Lexi gets bored and doesn't want to play with us. She says she has important work to do. You tell her, Magneto. Try and keep it simple."

Magneto steeples his fingers. "Lexi is making a Garden of Eden. To cut a long story short, she's making the Creation story. 'In the beginning,' and all that. Of course, Homesaps aren't allowed in Lexi's garden. She says they'll mess things up, and she won't let that happen again." Magneto pats my hand. "Don't take it personally. She won't let us in either."

It sounds like hocus. A fairy tale. Yet the proof of Lexi's abilities sit right in front of me quaffing rum and playing a silly game. I don't doubt that she could use her brilliant mind to build a new world.

"It's a simple matter of sequencing codes and jiggling the helixes ..." Joker stops talking to crack a monkey nut in his teeth. "It's all there in the books – how to build stuff." He looks up. "And now you can ask her about it yourself."

The lights in the room flicker suddenly. A painting on the wall – a portrait of a woman smiling slyly – drops to the floor and the oil paint melts and rearranges itself into a man's face, petrified in a primal scream. The jukebox in the corner stops midway through a nursery rhyme.

"Well, Lexi, have the calves stopped screaming?" Joker says.

Lexi stares around the room. "The calves never stop screaming for their mummies." Her white eyes shine with an ocean of unshed tears. "Juliet, you must help Lexi. The Machine wants to destroy Lexi's garden, and you are the only one who can stop it. Please, Juliet."

I stare at her wordlessly and she takes my hand.

"Come, let Lexi show you. Just this once."

Lexi's Garden of Eden is a world of seas and forests and mountains. Filled with plants and animals and bugs and birds and … a great fin in the ocean. My beautiful monster.

"Yes, you met one of Lexi's early creations. The Great White. She was a mistake. Lexi mixed up her codes – these beasts aren't supposed to play like circus animals! Lexi had to let her go. Lexi didn't expect her to survive in the plastic sea. But now Lexi's got it right. The one in Lexi's ocean is perfect."

Lexi shows me her perfect cats: with golden manes, lean with spots, with stripes. Lions, leopards, tigers. They are nothing like Hector and his sticky fur.

My chest is full of wonder. How many goodly creatures are there here! How beauteous mankind is! O brave new world! With every particle of my being, I want to stay here. This is what Nicolas and I hoped to find. A perfect new world.

"Don't even think about it! Lexi's cats won't become your pets," Lexi hisses. "No Homesaps will come here to hunt Lexi's animals. Trap them. Stuff them in feedlots and torment them to feed your disgusting appetites." Lexi's pale eyes fill with dark fury. "Just because they can't tell stories, it didn't give Homesaps the right to treat them like they were less." She grabs my arm with bone-crunching force. "Homesaps once lived in a beautiful garden. They killed it. No second chances."

Lexi allows me only glimpses of her creation; things more beautiful that I could ever have imagined. I cannot bear to think of it destroyed.

"Help Lexi save the garden from The Machine, Juliet.

Please? Lexi showed you what it did to the old world. It's going to try and destroy it again." She nests her small hand in mine and squeezes. "You are the one: the tellers say so. Kill The Machine before it devastates Lexi's world and yours."

I don't know how I can help. Nicolas and I tricked The Machine once, when we made the marks on our spines dead. But The Machine can surely never die?

I will try and do what Lexi asks. As terrible as it is, Mangeria is my home. Nicolas and Larissa are there. And my children: Mangeria will be their home too.

Suddenly, a terrible longing fills me. I want to go home to the people I love.

Lexi's smiles. "One last look and then you must leave. There is no place for Homesaps in Lexi's garden."

CAPTAIN GOLLUM'S LOG

Yesterday, a monster was born.

He wasn't born a baby. He is fully grown, like me. Lexi calls him Connor, a name she chose from one of her books. He's a cyborg, she says. Half man, half machine.

She built him using Drudge's skin, Rose's eyes, Thorn's hair and my heart. Lexi said my heart is less complicated than Drudge's. And for a Reject, my parts have interesting codes.

Tucked away in the folds of Connor's skull is a brain copied from Lexi's, but a simple version equipped with only some of her capabilities. Enough for him to speak and act and fit into Mangeria without attracting too much attention.

Lexi kept her promise. We have left that crazy island and are sailing for Mangeria. When we get home, we will help Connor kill The Machine.

My god, The Machine.

Lexi told us that The Machine was built by mad men hundreds of years ago. It was used in the Great War that caused the conflagration and has since been resting. But in a few weeks, it plans to unleash terrible weapons that will devastate the world.

It sounds like one of Lexi's stories. But Lexi can't lie. And unless we help Connor kill The Machine, we will all die.

The thought of our mission fills me with terror. To kill my god! Who will I pray to? Who will save me when things go wrong?

As the sun set yesterday, spreading like rotten egg against the sky, Lexi and her friends waved us goodbye on the *Jolly Roger*. We are well stocked for our journey home — picnic baskets full of condensed milk, tinned pineapple, fruit cake and rice pudding. A bottle of rum for me from Captain Sparrow, and Bertie Bott's Every Flavour Beans for the kids from Lexi.

Captain Sparrow saluted and wished me — and the leaky bucket I dare call a boat — strong winds. Magneto straightened a kink in the anchor and shook my hand. "You are a god among insects. Never let anyone tell you different," he said — fine words from a mutant. I record them simply to remind myself when Drudge calls me other names apart from Gollum — though to be fair, she has not called me "fool" or "idiot" since we left Sanctuary.

We are three weeks from home. Connor is a better navigator than Drudge, and his mind is stocked with maps and tidal charts. It is also stocked with a code Lexi built to initiate a sequence that will destroy The Machine.

Soon we will reach the shores of my beloved Mangeria. And then Drudge will learn how I have betrayed her.

PART TWO

PART TWO

12

HOME SWEET HOME

"Down! Down you go, Connor. All the way to the bottom of the long snake." Gollum howls with laughter and slides the counter down the length of the board. "My turn now." He shakes the dice, kisses his fist. "Lucky, lucky, lucky for me." He gives one last rattle and chucks the dice onto the crate.

I'm on the deck watching them play Snakes and Ladders in the light of the one-eyed moon. Lucky dice! Loaded dice more likely. Gollum is a rotten cheat – he can't bear to lose.

Connor breathes out heavily. "Double six. Not again." He picks up the dice and examines them, turning them over in his long fingers. "It is a statistical improbability. I do not know how you do it. My dice never give me doubles."

"It's called luck, my friend. Not an algorithm you could understand. Cheer up, I'll let you win at chess later."

"Oh no, I am not downcast. I feel the same whether I win or lose. I am not afflicted by subjective emotions. But perhaps you must use my dice next time. I want to test this thing you call luck." Connor glances up and sees me standing by the mast. "Juliet, I conclude from your appearance that you are almost ready to go."

I finish plaiting my hair, tie off the ends with a piece of string. "Make sure the children stay on board today. No swimming. There're too many Scavvies diving these waters."

The night lamps are still burning on the coast of Mangeria. I will be able to swim ashore under the blanket of darkness.

"And give them lots of water. They're not used to so much sun." I sling the satchel on my back. "You too, Connor. Your brain is hot-wired to the sun's rays. You'll overheat and blow a fuse."

Nag-nag-nag. I sound like Greenfinger Rachel. The mirror reflects the old woman in the shoe. My pale skin coarsened during our journey to Sanctuary, and yellowed like a Drainer's toenails in the bunker. My hair is a dry bush. Nicolas won't find me beautiful any more. He will not recognise me.

Connor smiles. "I assure you that your concern is illogical. The fuel from the sun to my brain is regulated precisely. Is there something about my behaviour that alarms you?"

The cyborg treats Gollum and me differently. He never smiles at Gollum, but he smiles the second he sees me. And even when I nag him.

"I have been programmed to pull my mouth back and flash my teeth at beautiful women, Juliet," Connor says.

I forget sometimes that he is able to read my thoughts. Like Lexi. And my memories. I have asked him several times not to do it. I've told him that it's rude.

Connor clocks my frown and gives an apologetic nod. Then he laughs heartily.

"Notice how I chortle with humour. It is the appropriate reaction to put someone at ease and indicate non-aggression. I will fit into Mangeria quite comfortably."

Gollum fusses over me. He adjusts the straps on my satchel and then pulls my plait roughly. "Let me go instead. I know my way around Mangeria like a rat. The sewers and rooftops were my home for many years."

Connor bounces Gollum's counter across the board. "You are being most unstrategic. Juliet passes for a trader far better than you, with your devil horns and Savage teeth." He pauses. "Statement withdrawn. Culturally insensitive." He tap-tap-taps the counter to the top of the ladder. "I detect from your tone and your skin excretions that you are anxious for Juliet's safety. I assure you, the threat analysis is the same for both of you."

The cyborg glances behind us and smiles. "Hello there, small Homesap. I thought I registered a vibrational fluctuation. What are you doing up so early? You have not completed your ten-hour nocturnal shutdown."

Rose stumbles towards Gollum and grips him around the knees.

"Back to bed, Rosie," he says. "Mummy's going for a swim but she'll be back to put you to sleep tonight."

My daughter's eyes flick over me. "Drudge go swim but Daddy stay with Breeder."

I press my lips together. I will not correct her again and tell her to call him Gollum. She never responds to Rose, and insists on calling me Drudge. She is determined not to love me, this Savage child.

Gollum follows me to the ladder at the side of the sloop. "I'll take the *Jolly Roger* further out to sea when the sun rises to avoid the Scavvies. But I'll be back when it's dark to pick you up," he says.

"You'll look after the children? If something happens and I don't come –"

Gollum grins and grabs me, lifting me up.

I struggle in his arms. "Don't you dare!"

The glee melts away. He grips me tighter and lowers his face into my neck. The smell of him: sweet butterynut and seawater. The faint scent of Rose.

Then he lifts me over the railings and tosses me into the ocean.

"See you later, Drudge. Break a leg."

I float in the darkness, listening to the fading voices on deck.

"Breaking a leg would be inconvenient."

"You're not supposed to take it literally, Connor. I was simply wishing her luck …"

I swim towards the lights of Mangeria, reaching the shore as the sun begins to rise. It hovers on the horizon, uncertain, shooting nervous rays across the pink sky.

On the beach, I run my fingers through the cold grains of sand. Then I hold a fistful to my face and breathe in the smell of home.

I loosen my hair, conceal it under a scarf and change into a dress. I am a drudge. No one will take a second look at me.

My footprints mark the sand behind me as I walk towards the promenade. I was last here more than three years ago, scamming the swimmers with Kitty and Handler Xavier. The Monster game – how those fools ran from the water! That was the first time I met Nicolas, a Locust on beach patrol. He let me go, pretending to be deceived, and then he tracked me.

Nicolas. How much has he changed? After Connor kills The Machine, I will find him. He has no idea he is a father of not one but two children. He must believe me when I tell him I got lost after the storm, and was kept in Sanctuary by Shepherd. That I was prevented from returning.

I take the steps up from the beach onto the main road and stroll along the promenade. Mangeria is still sleeping. There are no Posh playing bat and ball, no Pulaks touting for passengers to carry from the beach to the centre of town. I don't mind the long walk. I am home, breathing the same air as Nicolas. The same air as my friend Kitty, and my sister, Larissa. I will find them too.

The air now carries the smell of rotting sewage. It is the smell of Mistress, my mother, who never wanted me. Of Handler Xavier, my father, who doesn't know we share blood. I was just a drudge to him. Rubbish.

And it is the deadly scent of The Machine.

I walk through the gates towards the bridge that spans the river separating Slum City from the Posh part of Mangeria. The smell of the water, running green like bile and sluggish towards the sea. Litter is piled up on the banks; rats fight cockroaches for the spoils. Some things never change.

I leave my ghetto behind me and head towards the pleasure quarter. Bottles clutter the drains outside the clubs. The streets reek of piss and bug juice. From high windows peer bleak faces, lips bruised by sour kisses and eyes smudged black with artifice. It is early in the morning and the pleasure workers are only now preparing to sleep.

I hurry past the clubs until I see the familiar sign: Beautiful Like Me Beauty Parlour. One of the places the Posh visit when they need their uglies fixed.

The note in the window says: CLOSED. The sun, now red like blood, beats down with fury, daring me to linger.

I use my fists on the door.

And wait. Cracking my knuckles. *Come on. Come on.* The sound of a bolt being drawn back.

The face that meets mine as the door opens is no longer chubby. My old friend Me's eyes are faded. Lines drag his features into grey furrows.

"Ettie?" He peers at me.

I have not heard that name in a long time. Away from Mangeria, I was Juliet. Good-Wife. Drudge. Home, I am Ettie.

Me brightens and darts left. I go right. He goes right, and I go left. We play the dodge-dodge game. My body is stiff, but I remember the old moves.

"Oh, those big cow-eyes. Don't tell me you've decided at last to let me work on that face of yours? Come in, my eye clips have been waiting for you!" He pulls the scarf off my head, tosses it aside. "So long we haven't seen you. And just look at that hair! A bush! You are still Savage! Give me half an hour with my acid and you'll be as beautiful as any Posh mistress."

His hand trembles on my arm as he pushes me into the salon with its familiar smells of chemicals and plastic.

"What are you doing here? Why are you back?" he hisses. He pulls me past the reclining chairs where his Posh patrons will later sit, their faces caked in acid to make them whiter than white, and up the stairs. I follow Me to the flat where Reader used to live. Where the old man taught me my letters and pretended to sleep as I read to him.

"Nearly three years. We thought you were dead. Or run away to a better life. And here you are, the same ugly, beautiful self." He stands back as his eyes travel down my body. "You're no longer a skinny girl. You're a woman."

He presses me into a chair and hovers.

"Let's talk while I work. You caught me preparing my beauty products. You must tell your Me everything. Every tiny detail." He fills a pot of water and places it on the fire. "I don't know where you've been hiding yourself, but it's not safe here. There's still a price on your head."

Me takes a basin off the counter and stirs. A chemical vapour reaches my nose.

"You really were a bad girl, Ettie. You made a lot of powerful people very angry. But I'm talking too much. I expect you want something? Something from your old Me after all this time?"

He tips a sachet of lice eggs into another bowl and adds boiling water. It will make some Posh's hair silky smooth.

"There are people I need to see ..." I say. I hesitate. I don't want to tell Me too much.

"Of course. Your age-mate Kitty. And the handler from the orphanage?" Me registers the disgust on my face. "No, I don't think you want to see Xavier again. But in any case, you won't find either of them in Slum City – I can tell you that for free. They're living quite different lives now. I expect you'll discover that for yourself. You were always one for finding out things."

He grabs a handful of desiccated cockroaches from a packet and settles into a chair. With a pestle and mortar, he grinds them into a black paste. Fit for some Posh's eyelids.

"What is it, my dear? What do you need to know?"

Me's tongue is as loose as a past trader's teeth. If I told him about The Machine's intentions to obliterate the world, destroy it forever, he would not be able to hold his tongue. He would scare the skin off his Posh patrons' faces. It is crucial that Connor activate the code and kill The Machine – and he needs to do it without a bunch of hysterical Posh getting in his way.

But before that I need to find out everything I can about The Machine. If it's still in the red building near the square. If the Locusts still guard it so fiercely. So much might have changed after Nicolas and I hacked into it and killed our own marks. Is it still so powerful?

I ask Me about the weather, the Muti Nags and their latest

magic, the price of strawberry in the market. And I slip my questions about The Machine into all this waffle.

Me chuckles, and a hint of his old chubbiness returns to his face. "The Machine can never track me again. There are a few of us rebels whose marks are dead, thanks to you. I still don't know how you did it, Ettie." He puts down the pestle and mortar. "You certainly have been away. Any child in Slum City could tell you that The Machine as we knew it is as good as dead. After the war, our interim government – a hodgepodge of rebels and Guardians – shut down most of its functions. It only has administrative purposes now. You can go and see for yourself. People are in and out of that red building all the time.

"We're still marked at birth, of course. The Machine keeps a register of the population, records deaths, marriages and so on. But the birthing stations no longer separate Posh from Scum. The numbers are quite harmless now. They mean nothing." Me claps his hands and stands. "Ettie my dear, you have come home to a free Mangeria. Even the Locusts have changed. They've all been retrained through the Friendly Locust Community Project." He pulls down his cheeks and sighs. "Of course, things are much better for some. But we've made a start."

The people of Mangeria are free? No longer hunted and controlled by The Machine? This is something I have wanted more than anything. But I trust Lexi: The Machine is simply resting, biding its time. Until it unleashes its terrible weapons. I know we will not be alive to enjoy our freedom for long unless Connor kills The Machine.

I have learnt what I need to know. We will make our move while The Machine pretends to sleep. It won't see us coming. I pick up my satchel from the floor and walk to the door. Me follows, his hands flapping behind me.

"But Ettie, you've told me nothing about yourself. Come visit me again next week. I'm going to be sweating like a Pulak these next few days – it's a busy time, what with the election and the festival of fate-mates. Everyone still wants to look like a Posh, so lucky for me it's business as usual."

"A festival of fate-mates?" I turn at the door. "You told me those practices had ended?"

"Come now, Ettie, it's a fine tradition. Of course, people can choose their own mates now. These days it's all about love and romance." Me rolls his eyes and pretends to gag. "It's going to be huge this year, a big shindig at the parade. Too much tough meat and bug juice. Everyone loves the festival."

Me dodges right. I go left. He stops suddenly.

"That friend of yours. Kitty. I'll be doing her hair and make-up for the big day. Quite a coup for me, having a future Guardian for a client. She can afford to patronise the best parlours, but she's still very loyal." He leans in and whispers. "He's quite a catch, I hear. Posh boy, from a very good family."

So, my Kitty is no longer a grubby pleasure worker living with the cockroaches in Slum City. She's taking a fate-mate, and not just some smelly Drainer – a Posh. And she is going to be a Guardian. Making the rules that govern our lives. She has done well for herself.

I don't know why, but I have a sour taste in my mouth.

"Oh my dear, where have you been? The streets are full of it, Ettie – the first free election in Mangeria is in two days' time. And Kitty's on the ballot. You must see her at the hustings. Full of fire, shouting off her mouth about the working conditions of Pulaks, equal rights for Rejects. Our Kitty. Still the little Savage."

I follow Me down the stairs to the front door. "So, Kitty's got your vote?"

Me chuckles. "Oh no, dead people can't vote. And thanks to you, Ettie, dead people don't pay taxes." He taps his nose and rubs his fingers together. "I could have changed my status with The Machine after the war. Some of the rebels did, so they could take up positions in the interim government. But I chose to stay off the radar. I'm finished with politics, concentrating on the Ugly business. It may not be as lucrative, but it pays the bills." He winks and pulls down his mouth. "Those Posh are all just too hideous for words."

He opens the door, squeezes my arm.

"Maybe you'll meet someone at the festival. Before you get too old. You haven't been wearing sunblocker, have you?" He touches the corners of my eyes and sighs. "Tiny lines, my dear, but I can fix them."

As I turn to leave he grabs my shoulder and spins me around. He presses a pair of sunglasses on my nose and ties my scarf over my hair.

"Be careful, Ettie, dear. There are a lot of credits on that Savage head of yours."

CAPTAIN GOLLUM'S LOG

Before dawn shattered the sky this morning, Drudge swam to shore.

I'm scatting myself. Drudge will soon find out what I've done. And when she does, she's going to rip me a third nostril. I've wanted to tell her, to say sorry, but I've stopped myself. I don't want her looking at me the way she used to — like I'm a filthy Reject.

The cyborg makes me edgy. Connor mostly acts like a pretty normal guy, but sometimes he gets weird. At night I hear him when we're sleeping out on the deck — not that Connor ever sleeps. At first I thought he was chatting to himself, but then I realised he was talking to Lexi.

They talk every night for hours.

But he never mentions it.

13

LITTLE SISTER

The cobbled streets are alive with people. Market Nags are hurrying towards the square, dodging Pulaks carrying Posh to the shops. Scavvies lurch out of the doorways of the clubs, buckling their belts, checking their wallets. They leer at me and whistle.

Traders and Posh are gathered around the news traders.

"Rebels up in arms against Posh dirty tricks! Sensational evidence!" a news trader shouts.

"Meat and potato for votes! Rejects bribed with food at the hustings!" The first news trader's voice is drowned out by one who bellows louder.

I pull the scarf over my face as two Locusts stroll towards me. They are smiling, cracking jokes with a Drainer shovelling filth out of the roads.

"Need any help with that load, past trader?" one of the Locusts calls out to an old man stumbling behind me. He lifts the heavy sack off the bent man's back. "No trouble at all, sir – we're going the same way."

Smiling, helpful Locusts? I have seen and heard it with my own eyes.

Me told me things had changed. But despite the evidence, I do not trust it.

At the entrance to the red building near the square, women holding babies have formed a queue. A Posh clutching a briefcase shoves past them.

"Hey, not so fast. Wait in line like the rest of us," a Market Nag yells.

The Posh turns and peers coldly over his sunglasses with slitty green eyes. "I'm registering a business address with The Machine, not the birth of some stink-arsed brat. And I do *not* stand in queues with Scavvies and Drainers."

So getting into the building for Population Control is easy – but that much easier for the Posh. As always. They have not allowed themselves to be humbled by freedom.

"We're open until midday on voting day. Last chance for Rejects to register," a pen-pusher cries from the steps outside the red building. He takes a handkerchief and wipes his mottled face. "Spread the word: no mark, no vote."

I enter the square. Cruel faces trapped in granite statues stare down at the crowds – the former Guardians who ruled over us for hundreds of years. The statues are covered with bird scat and crude graffiti that spells out exactly what the free citizens of Mangeria think of them.

There's a new statue near the water fountain, protected by a circle of barbed wire. Plastic bottles and rotting fruit, tossed over the barbed wire, lie inside the enclosure.

The statue seems to be of two figures facing each other, white-marbled fists raised in combat. But no – as I draw closer, I see that they are clutching hands in a pledge. It's Nicolas's father, the Guardian of Justice and Peace, and another man …

Handler Xavier.

That sneer, those eyes, like sponges, soaking up everything they see. My father.

The plaque at the base of the statue says: *Presidents Xavier and Bartholomew, joint leaders of the interim government of Mangeria.*

It's true. My old handler is living a very different life. It grates my guts.

The square throngs with Posh and common traders wanting to be entertained. Card sharps shuffle their decks under the shade of umbrellas; Market Nags sell brightly coloured drinks and sweets. "Cold juice, sticky toffees," they cry, and snot-faced Smalls press slyly against me. I take the satchel off my shoulders and tuck it under my arm. I know the game of nimble fingers.

A higgledy-piggledy queue jostles near a clutch of Muti Nags, their magic potions always a popular attraction. Behind them, a bird perches on an umbrella chewing a fly, her blind gooey white eyes watching the customers.

"Ettie, Ettie, you slimy Spaghetti," Mistress Hadeda croaks and spits a black-liquid glob my way. Her feathers are dull and her sharp beak is blunt from cracking cockroaches. I am pleased that the years have not been kind to her.

"I see those big eyes hiding behind sunglasses." A Muti Nag rests her gaze on me. "Yes, Ettie is back to fulfil the prophecy. It is as the tellers foretold."

Witch's skin is still as smooth as a young girl's – she has not aged a day since I met her as a child. Her glance slides from my face as she presses a sachet of green powder into the open palms of a pock-faced drudge. "When your lover's not looking, slip three tablespoons into his bug juice, and in the morning he'll call you the most beautiful girl in Mangeria." She grabs the credits with a seven-fingered hand. "Only three tablespoons, mind. Otherwise he'll find the rat swimming in your slop-pot even more beautiful than you."

A woman clutching a wheezing baby asks for a potion, but Witch waves her away.

"My potions won't cure your baby's rotted lungs. You must consult my young protégé over there. Little Sister has magic hands to give your brat lungs as pink as my gums."

In a stand close by to Witch's, a group of traders are kneeling, eyes closed, hands lifted to the sun, moaning, "Little Sister, Little Sister."

As I approach a bird calls out: "Beware! The drudge has returned. Beware!"

A girl reaches down and ruffles the bird's head feathers. "Oh, be quiet, Princess Fanny. I can't concentrate." The teller arches her head against the girl's fingers and folds her dark lids over scarred eyes.

It's Little Miss. My sister, Larissa.

She is no longer sickly. Her face is plump; there are roses on her cheeks. I kneel on the ground with the rest of the moaning traders.

With her palms on a grizzly past trader's head, Larissa shakes and gurgles strangely, as though she's being strangled. Her eyes roll back and she chants in a high voice: "Feel the bile draining from your liver. Soon you will be able to drink a drum of bug juice and piss like a Scavvie the next morning."

The old man raises his head and chuckles. "Praise to you, Little Sister. For too long my bad-tempered organ hasn't allowed me to drink with my friends." He tosses a bag of credits into a bowl and skips away. "Tomorrow night, we'll celebrate in the pleasure clubs and sing the rudest songs for you."

Then Larissa rests the tips of her fingers on a young Drainer's head, closes her eyes and wails. The kneeling traders join her. She stops wailing and opens her eyes. "I don't have the cure for your heart sickness," she says firmly. "Go back to your wife and say sorry for being a filthy cheater."

The young man throws credits into the bowl and slinks away, red-faced.

I nudge forward until my sister's palms hover above my scarfed head. As she begins to hum, I grab her hands. She steps back, her eyes wide.

"Ettie?" she whispers. She sinks down on the ground next to me, among the humming traders. Her eyes fill with tears. "I can't believe you're alive." Her hug is hard and fierce, and my tears mingle with hers.

My sister has not forgotten me. I am still her beloved Ettie. She knew me as her drudge carer, but one day I will tell her that we share blood.

Larissa untangles herself, wipes her nose and stares at me. "I thought you were dead. Killed by Savages." She covers her mouth with her hand and giggles. "We don't call them Savages any more – we're all free citizens now." She grabs my hand. "Come, Ettie, walk with me. Tell me everything you've been doing. I've missed you so much." She nods at the traders kneeling on the ground, humming in a trance. "They won't notice me gone."

We circle a group of card sharps slapping grubby cards on a table. Larissa pauses and picks a card out from behind one of the player's ears. "Bad boy," she hisses, and tucks it in her pocket.

My heart sings with joy. I can't believe this is the same child who three years ago had hardly ever left her bedroom.

"When you disappeared, I tried to find you, Ettie. Mother told me to forget you, but I couldn't. You are as precious to me as a sister, and I told her that. I can't wait to tell her that you're back."

I grip my sister's hand. "No! You mustn't tell her." I know there is no room in my mother's heart for me. She will try and keep Larissa and me apart.

"Don't worry, Ettie. Mother isn't cross with you any more. She knows how much you mean to me. She's changed a lot these past few years. She's got a boyfriend now, an old sweetheart, and she's happy. She wants me to be happy too. I don't have to take a fate-mate or live like a Guardian's daughter."

Mistress had wanted Larissa to have Nicolas as her fate-mate to cement their families' alliance. Larissa defied her, and here she is, a Muti Nag. It is a wonder.

"Yes, look at you – a healer with magic hands."

"And you, Ettie, are very close to death with fly sickness." She snaps her fingers and flutters them in the air. "And now you're healed by yours truly, Little Sister." She winks at me and pulls me back towards the kneeling crowd. "Rub your cheeks a bit and drool – I'll bring you back from the dead. These fools love a miracle."

Glee bubbles in my mouth. She's played me! She's as much a healer as I'm the White Witch of Narnia. My sister is a Savage – just like me.

Larissa's eyes sparkle. "I'm a miracle healer today. But next week I think I may be a Scavvie diving for relics in the underwater city. And after that, a belly dancer in the pleasure clubs."

She dances around me shrieking with laughter. "Oh, Ettie, it's a marvellous game! And look, see, there's Mother now, hobbling along with her poorly leg." She points at a group of Locusts accompanying a woman across the square. "If I could heal people, surely Mother wouldn't look quite so much like an old Reject."

She shouts out and waves. The woman peers over at us and taps a Locust on the arm.

I do not want to see those cold green eyes. To hear that I am unbeloved.

"I have to go," I say, and slip away into a crowd of Posh.

I leave the square and hail a taxi. Harnessed in pairs, the Pulaks groan with pain as they pull us towards the parade.

"Move faster, you useless sacks of bones," the taxi warden yells.

A fat Posh sitting next to me reaches over and taps the warden on his shoulder. "Use the whip – that's what they understand."

The taxi warden turns around in his seat. "The new laws says I can only whip the buggers in rush hour. And I've got to pay them for the privilege. This interim government is ruining my business with their bleeding-heart reforms."

The Pulaks draw to a halt outside the parade. I scramble out and walk towards the gates of the Tree Museum.

A group of Rejects are shoving each other in front of a food stall outside the main entrance.

"Be patient – there's enough for everyone!" a Market Nag screams, holding a parcel of food out of reach of a Reject who's trying to grab it. "Not so fast, you dirty crip. Have you registered to vote? First show me your mark."

The Reject turns and lifts up his shirt, revealing the six digits at the base of his spine.

The Market Nag grunts. "And who must you thank for this generous gift of meat and potato?" She hands him the parcel. "That's right. The candidate for the Rebel Party. Number nine on the ballot paper."

A man standing on a box is shouting and waving his arms. "Trust me, I'm just as in favour as the next man for Rejects to have the vote. But giving those dead-brains equal rights? Next thing you know they'll be taking your daughters as fate-mates and living next door to you. And in a blink of an eye they'll steal your jobs."

"Why should we trust you?" a trader shouts. "You Posh just want our votes and then you'll shove us back in our sewers. Our votes stay with the Rebel Party."

A couple of other traders whistle and jeer.

"We all want the same thing. Standards. A decent life. The Posh Party stands for fine traditions …"

I enter the museum at the west entrance. The saplings Mistress planted are now a forest of small trees. I reach the iron railings and see my tree, the only one that survived being burnt during the riot when Kitty and I lived at the orphanage.

"Hello, old friend." I look up into the branches.

Wisha-wisha-wisha-wisha-wisha, it whispers to me.

"I came back to save you. I won't let The Machine destroy your home. And next time I come, I'll bring two small people to meet you."

Wisha-wisha-wisha-wisha-wisha, my tree cautions.

Instinctively, I crouch down, my back against the railings. Two shapes are moving along the path, a man and a girl, in deep discussion. As they draw closer, I recognise the girl: plump cheeks, flat nose. The eyebrows are thinner now, and the long, silky hair is a sleek bob. She is older, but my Kitty is still beautiful. More beautiful.

Her name is tipping off my lips when I recognise her companion. The man wagging his finger at her is Nicolas's father, one of the presidents of the interim government. He and Kitty were bitter enemies during the war. Now they appear to be good friends.

"As we agreed then. Tonight, when the Guardian horse-trading begins, my Posh Party will support you for the position of Guardian of Justice and Peace. Your party will never let us control the Locusts again, so it might as well be you. I will ensure that you have sole authority over The Machine by the end of this evening. But remember you owe me, my girl."

"And in return, Bartholomew? Maybe you want to be Guardian of Heritage and Culture and look after these pretty trees?"

"Don't be cheeky, my girl. We have already settled on five Guardian positions for my party, and of course I will be president again of a unity government with Xavier."

Kitty laughs. "Relax, Bartholomew. I'll make it happen. I'm pulling in the Reject vote. The Rebel Party has to listen to me."

"You are playing that card magnificently, by the way. At times even *I* believe you care about the Reject scum."

"President Xavier and I will never forgive those animals for betraying us during the war. And now we've got them registered with The Machine, there's no place for them to hide."

"Just remember, if we work together, we'll both get exactly what we want. We might even grow to trust one another. In time."

"Don't push it, Bartholomew – I'll never trust a Posh. And my Voting Observers will be keeping an eye on you to make sure you don't crook the count."

"As will mine, as will mine." The Guardian checks his time piece. "Now I must go. He should be here any minute."

He slips down a path. Moments later, Kitty sashays towards a man hurrying towards her.

He is taller now, his face is leaner. But the glass green eyes are the same.

Nicolas, Nic, Nici, Nice.

I want to cry out. I want to leap up and run towards him. Feel his arms around me. I want to hear his full-bellied laugh when he sees me.

Yes, I'm home, Nicolas. See, it's me. Your Juliet.

Kitty approaches him, pouting. Like a pleasure worker scolding a Posh patron for not tipping more generously for her favours. I hold myself back. The words shrivel on my tongue.

I am frozen in my spot.

"There you are, Nicky-Noodle. I've been looking all over for you. I don't know why you insist on meeting here – this forest gives me the creeps," Kitty says.

He takes her hand and they walk towards the west entrance. "Sorry, Kit-Kat, but I like this place. I used to come here every Sunday ... I was supposed to meet someone. But she never came." He sighs, then coughs. "It was a long time ago. Sometimes I can't even remember her name."

"Well, Noodle, I hope you remember mine when we make our vows at the festival this week." She pulls his hand and runs ahead. "But to make things easy for you, soon you can just call me 'Wife'."

Together they turn their backs on the girl with no name. Forgotten.

"Drudge, we expected you hours ago!"

I pull myself onto the *Jolly Roger* and flop onto the deck.

"I'd almost given up. Stinker refused to sleep so Connor had to tell him a story." Gollum laughs too loudly and stifles a burp. "A history of Quantum Physics. It always does the trick."

I smell fermented fruit – the cheap alcohol sold by the Market Nags outside the clubs in the pleasure quarter. I wrinkle my nose. "You stink of bug juice."

"Beautiful, beautiful bug juice. I'd forgotten the taste." Gollum fumbles for a bottle and sucks on it. "It was hot, Drudge, and you were gone too long. I left the kids with Connor and took a quick swim. Met a couple of Scavvies on the beach. One game of dice led to another bottle of bug juice. My bad." He raises the bottle. "Cheers, welcome home!"

I grab the bottle and gulp down the foul liquid. It burns my throat.

"Thirsty? No worries, I've got plenty." Gollum cracks open another bottle with his teeth, spits out the cap. "Tell me about home. What's the story?"

I learnt that my best friend Kitty and the boy who once found me beautiful are going to be married at the festival of fate-mates.

Kit-Kat and Nicky-Noodle. The rest does not matter.

"Drudge, talk to me. How's my beloved Mangeria?" says Gollum. "The Scavvies I played dice with could only gab-gab about pleasure workers." His eyes gleam. "They tell me they're even more saucy. And the Market Nags are still ripping off the customers, selling rotten fruit – nothing's changed there."

The one-eyed moon sneers at me. The stars scatter across the sky, tittering.

Dead-brain drudge.

You should never have played that game. You broke the most important rule: never trust. Foolish little Ettie.

I drink bug juice and tell Gollum what I've learnt about The Machine. Killing it will be as easy as taking eggs from under a chicken. The best time will be during the festival of fate-mates, when everyone is celebrating at the parade. The square will be deserted and there'll be no one to disturb Connor at the red building. In a few days we could be living in a safe new world. I raise the bottle of bug juice at the sniggering moon.

"Mangeria's just the same, but different. The Locusts seem to be everybody's new best friends and there's no curfew. I didn't see any Locusts guarding booms, stopping people from moving around. Everyone's free."

Gollum chucks the empty bottle over the railing and cracks open another. "Those Locusts never stopped me. I went wherever I wanted and they never caught me." He is slurring now. "See, I'm a Reject. A non-person. I don't exist."

"Not any more. Congratulations." I grab the bottle again

and tell him about the election in two days' time. The Machine is registering the Rejects as citizens, and for the first time they can vote.

Gollum is quiet for a moment. He rubs the growths on his forehead. "I'll be a citizen of Mangeria. I'll no longer be a nothing. I'll be free like everyone else."

Yes. Free as a Pulak breaking his back to pull a taxi. Free as a Drainer working in the sewers. Free to be poor, to live in the Slum City ghetto.

Gollum laughs. "Oh Drudge, you look so grumpy. It's a new beginning for me." He throws his arm around my shoulder. "Captain Gollum is free!"

I am glad for him. We will go our separate ways and he'll have a new life. I don't know why that thought makes me so grim.

I toss the half-empty bottle overboard. The stuff is rotting my brain.

Gollum's arm stiffens. "And you'll find the kids' father and live happily ever after." He staggers to his feet, swaying on the deck. "I think I'll pop in at the clubs tomorrow and find myself a pretty little pleasure worker."

Yes, he will soon forget me.

His eyes glitter. "Let's remember the good times. Remember when … Remember when …" He lurches towards the railings and hurls.

I look across the sea to the lights of Mangeria. I will always remember Nicolas. I won't be so quick to give away my heart again.

Gollum wipes his mouth on his shirt. "And afterwards, if you ever feel like shooting the lights out, breaking loose at the clubs, just shout … I'm there."

Soon he is stretched out on the deck like a starfish, with a stupid grin on his face. Snoring.

My chest aches.

Nicolas, Nic, Nici, Nice. No longer mine.

Kitty's Nicolas.

I feel so weary, so alone.

I lie beside Gollum and pull his arm over my shoulder. The heat of his body dulls the pain in my chest.

I curl myself around him.

14

DIRTY SECRETS

Rose screams as she chases Thorn across the deck. "Give! Give!"

I glare at them. My mouth tastes like a Drainer's armpit and my head is throbbing. That will teach me to drink bug juice. Thorn shoves a book in my hand and ducks down the hatch into the galley.

"Connor, don't just sit there like some useless robot." I say. "Watch the children and make sure they don't fall overboard."

Connor stops stitching the torn sail and looks up. "I am performing a necessary task, and the probability of the children falling overboard is minor."

I stare at the book in my hands. It's Gollum's precious captain's log. He usually keeps it in a pouch against his stomach, safe from prying eyes – my eyes. I find some shade on the deck and open it.

I smile when I read the first entry. *Beautiful Juliet.*

Ha! He liked me right from the start. I'll tease him about this later and make him squirm.

But what I read next strangles my chest with barbed wire. My stomach is a fist of rusty claws when Gollum comes up on deck.

"Morning, beautiful Juliet." He is grinning shyly at me.

I hurl the book at him and leap to my feet. He does not try and defend himself from my sharp nails and fists.

"Juliet, your body temperature is dangerously high and the oxygen level is alarmingly low," Connor says, putting down his large needle. "I am not programmed to heal, so I cannot help you if you are sick."

"He lied to me. Right from the beginning. It's all in his captain's log." I look at Gollum's torn face. "He got us lost and kept me from coming home. We can't trust him and his precious Machine."

Connor picks up the book and turns the pages. "Gollum, this is true? Do you work for The Machine?"

Gollum is silent.

He looks down at the deck, his head bowed. He does not have the guts to answer us. I should have known not to trust a Reject. They are loyal to no one. All they care about is credits. They would sell the skin off their own bodies. Rejects can never change.

Connor stares at Gollum. "I cannot detect the level of trustworthiness from his genetic make-up, but I am able to access his memory. It may provide us with sufficient data as to his intentions."

Gollum looks around wildly. "No, please, Connor, don't do it. Leave my memories alone."

"I have respected your privacy. Your memories were not

important to our mission. But now there is too much at risk." Connor touches Gollum on the shoulder. "This will make you less agitated and will have no lasting effect."

Gollum cannot move, and he cannot speak.

Connor places the tips of his fingers on the side of Gollum's head and his other hand on my temple. "Come, Juliet. Let us discover Gollum's memories."

My mind goes blank. There is nothing.

And then ...

I am Gollum.

I am leaping across the rooftops of Slum City. Grey clothing flutters like the skeletons of birds on washing lines outside deserted shanties. Many Rejects have forsaken their rooftop homes and taken refuge at the dumps, away from the war.

The smart ones, like me, shuttle between the rebel Savages and the Locusts, delivering supplies, trading information for credits. The highest price wins my loyalty.

I stumble, massage my gimpy foot. Bullets slam into walls. People scream. I crawl towards the edge of the roof and peer over.

Two figures skulk near a vacant shop; their dark clothing marks them as rebels. A body lies in the street. One of the rebels darts into the road and prises open a manhole cover. He pulls the body into the hole and the other rebel joins him. They disappear underground.

I know those abandoned and forgotten places of two hundred years ago, the sunken pipes that fed water to the old city and carried waste out to sea. They are useless now, rotted.

Blocked by fallen rubble.

I know the secrets of underground Mangeria as well as I know the paths over the rooftops, the back streets of the pleasure quarter, the piss-smelling alleys of Slum City. I'm a rat, sniffing safe passage along forgotten routes.

And then: three Locusts, weapons drawn, race into the deserted street, shouting to each other.

"That way! They must have taken the other road."

"I wounded one. They can't have gone far."

As they disappear down a side street, the manhole cover is lifted and the two rebels raise themselves into the road. Others clamber up after them. They pursue the Locusts like cockroaches after a wounded rat.

With the devil's luck, the Savages are winning the war. They fight like drunk Scavvies over a pleasure worker because they have nothing to lose. They slip past the columns of Locusts guarding the bridge, they dodge troops patrolling the river. They appear suddenly like ghosts in the streets of Mangeria. Popping up like boils on a Drainer's arse, they have gained control of sections of Posh City and are moving in on the Guardians' compound. Soon they will seize power.

This is not my war. I don't care who wins or loses. But I now know how the rebels are gaining the upper hand: the underground tunnels. The Locusts will pay bags of credits for this information.

I report to my master, the leader of the Rejects, outside a derelict building in Slum City. I sink to my knees on the filthy ground.

"Lord Shakespeare," I murmur, lowering my eyes.

"Clubfoot! You've brought me something?" Lord Shakespeare says.

I empty my pockets of credits. He grabs them and counts. "You're short again with your payments, Clubfoot. You're not earning the right to keep your skin."

So I tell my lord what I saw from the rooftops, knowing my debt to him – and more – will be paid in a few weeks.

Lord Shakespeare laughs. "I'm going to make a pretty sum of credits off the backs of those rebel rats. Them and their leader, Xavier."

Weeks later, I am shuffling like a past trader down the underground tunnels.

I dodge falling rubble and clamber over a pile of bricks, kicking a nest of cockroaches out of my way. The earth shudders suddenly as an explosion above me cracks the sides of the huge pipe. Sheets of dust drift down, making me blind.

The rebel Savages are cornered, trapped like rats down here. Those driven above by hunger are gunned down or taken prisoner by the Locusts, who are guarding the manhole covers. They wait patiently. Time is their friend.

Lucky for the rebels, Rejects like me know a way out. For enough credits, I take them along secret passages and lead them out safely. Then, when the sweat of their fear is dry, I send the Locusts to them.

My war credits have made me wealthier than a Pulak Warden. When it's over, I'll pay my debt to Lord Shakespeare and set myself up in the pleasure quarter. I'll have a club with the prettiest girls, and a room for card sharps. Maybe I'll employ a drudge to cook my food and rub my foot.

A figure staggers towards me in the gloom. A rebel boy in need of my services.

"Looking for a safe way out?"

He stops. "I'm not planning on leaving. My comrades are back there. But can you lead me to a safe exit so I can get medical supplies and food?"

"Maybe. But let us understand each other, my friend. I don't do favours. This is business. You get me?"

Just then the earth under our feet shudders. The tunnel groans and concrete shatters onto the ground. A brick strikes my head and rubble rains down on me, trapping my legs. Cracks splinter the ceiling.

"Run, get out of here. The tunnel's collapsing," I shout.

Instead of running away, the rebel sprints towards me and tries to free me from the rubble by pulling my arms. "Leave me. Get away," I say.

"Save your breath. We were in the middle of a business transaction!" The rebel claws at the rocks on my legs.

The earth trembles with another explosion.

When I regain consciousness, I hear the rebel shifting rocks, piling them into a tower. Building me a gravestone.

"You idiot," I say. "You could've saved yourself. Now we're both going to die in here."

"Not today," says the rebel. "My comrades will soon come

and dig us out." He coughs, dust eating his lungs. "After they do, I'd like to despatch you on some business."

I grunt. "Medical supplies and food."

"That too. But there's a girl."

I smile through broken lips. "A feisty rebel girl with fat thighs?"

The rebel breathes deeply, rasping. "We were supposed to go away together on a seacraft. But when I arrived to meet her, she was gone. I sometimes see lamps shining on the ocean late at night. She's out there. Her name is Juliet Seven."

"A slippery wench then. Maybe she saw someone tastier and sailed away with a handsome Scavvie."

"Not Juliet. She must have been attacked by Locusts and escaped. I know she'll come back, but it's not safe – my father's got a price on her head. I want you to find her and make sure she stays away from Mangerian shores for a few months, until this blows over."

It's a big job, and my fee should be high. But this rebel risked his life to save mine.

He reaches out his hand. The skin is stripped raw; his nails are broken. "The name is Nicolas. I have your word that you'll do this? I can't give you credits now, but I can pay you later. A deal between two men?"

I shake his hand. "I'm a Reject. And I owe you."

"A pact between friends, then," he says.

We lie exhausted in our tomb.

Nicolas is quiet. When I touch him, his skin is hot. My

tongue is thick, my throat swollen, begging for water. My lungs ache for air, which is thinning as the hours pass. How many hours, I don't know. The darkness in the tunnel doesn't tell me.

The clanging of spades on rock.

I'm pulled back from the dark road of no return.

"We've got him. Let's get him out of here – Ettie's little Locust," a voice says.

Light flickers on rebel faces, anonymous under black caps and dark clothing.

"Leave the other one, Xavier. He's not ours."

"Not so fast, Kitty. That ugly face – he's a Reject. I'm going to need him."

I know the girl, Kitty. I've seen her at the clubs. "Pretty Kitty" they called her. Not just a pleasure worker then. And the man is the rebel leader, Xavier. His name is a curse on every Locust's lips.

My body protests as they drag me through the tunnel. We come to a room at the intersection of three tunnels. It throngs with hollow-eyed rebels.

"Give Nicolas some water, Kitty, and try do something about his wounds. We've got nothing if he dies."

"And the Reject? There's not much water, Xavier. We can't waste it."

"Clean him up – I won't make it out of here without him. This is our last card. If we play Nicolas right, we may come out with our lives."

"No, Xavier. If the Guardian wants Nicolas back, he's

going to have to give us much more than just our lives. I
didn't join this war to be Slum City scum for the rest of my
life. If he won't agree to our terms, I'll bash his son's head in."

I am leading the rebel Xavier through the tunnels, under the
streets of Posh City.

"The Guardians' compound is fiercely guarded," I say.
"Are you sure that's where you want to go?"

"Do it, and faster, Clubfoot. I know the compound like a
baby knows its mother's tit. Just get me there," Xavier replies.

We pull ourselves through the cover above ground as the
sun is rising. It's not a road we're on, but the stables of some
Guardian's mansion in the compound. The stalls are empty
– the Pulaks are already on the streets carrying Locusts and
ammunition into Slum City.

Xavier now leads us through the back alleys used by the
Guardians' drudges and cooks. He stops outside the gates of
a large home. Number 3.

I hang back. "I'll wait here – I'm not going any further.
This place is swarming with Locusts, and I'm not getting
caught too."

Xavier laughs. "The Locusts can't track me – the mark on
my spine is dead. That useless drudge was good for something.
And no chance we're splitting up – I want to keep an eye on
you. For two credits you'd turn me in as soon as my back is
turned."

He grips my arm as we follow the path to the back of the
house.

"And when I'm finished here, you'll take me back along the tunnels to my comrades at the rebel base."

Xavier pushes against the door. It's locked. He wraps his scarf around his hand and raises his fist against a window. Pauses. "I know where she'll be."

We hurry towards a walled enclosure. A tree beyond the wall embraces the sky with its branches.

Wisha-wisha-wisha-wisha-wisha, it whispers to us.

A woman appears carrying a basket of flowers. Her face is drawn. The left side of her face bears an ugly burn, but she's still beautiful. Not pretty like the painted slaggets in the pleasure clubs – she's beautiful without those tricks.

Xavier releases my arm. "Stay outside the gates. If you value your skin, you won't move."

I wait, I watch and I listen.

The woman leans on a stick and limps towards the rebel leader with no sign of fear. "Xavier. Come to surrender? Or to gloat at my daughter's deathbed?" She hands him the basket of flowers. "Forget-Me-Nots. A hardy little flower. They survive despite neglect."

Xavier takes the basket and edges her down the path into the garden. "My rebels and I aren't planning on going to Savage City. We aim to be free and have pledged to die fighting."

"So you've come to say goodbye then." Her lips twist in a bitter smile. "The Guardian of Justice and Peace and I will make sure that you honour that pledge. We will not call off the Locusts until we've destroyed every last one of you." She lowers herself onto a bench under the large tree.

Xavier punches his fist against the trunk of the tree. "There was a time when you saw yourself as one of us. How could you have forgotten?"

"I was a girl then, Xavier. In love with a Savage boy, pregnant with his child. I would have given up my home, my family, my position – everything – to be with him. But he abandoned me and took a fate-mate. Do not pretend it was me who betrayed the promises we made."

Xavier rubs his knuckles. "Lies! You got rid of our baby and ran off to the pleasure resorts along the coast. I waited two years. I only took a fate-mate when I heard you'd promised yourself to a Guardian. I had no choice." He sucks the blood off his fist. "Anyway, I haven't come to argue about our past. I'm here to talk about the future."

The woman sighs. "I'm not interested in your future, Xavier. My daughter is dying. The Guardian of Justice and Peace will not allow Larissa to have the procedure that will save her life. He blames me for his son's kidnapping, accuses me of harbouring a Savage drudge in my home." She grips the walking stick. Her fingernails are black with soil.

Xavier reaches for her grubby hand and holds it in his. "I've got the Guardian's son. We'll give him up. His life for ours. And we want freedom and equality for all the people of Slum City. If the Guardian doesn't call off the Locusts and agree to our terms, we'll fight to the death, and I'll make sure the boy dies with us. Go to the Guardian and tell him: His son's life for our freedom."

She pulls herself off the bench. "The Guardian wants revenge for his son's kidnapping. That girl, Ettie – the one you planted in my home to work for me. He's put a price on her head."

Xavier laughs. "Ettie ran when the fighting started. I'll give you the little coward's skin." He looks up in the branches of the tree. "I'll deliver her body to the Guardian's door before nightfall. It should sweeten his temper."

"No!" Her voice is shrill. "I want her, and I want her alive. And when I'm done with her, I'll pass her on to the Guardian. He'll make her wish she was never born."

The branches of the tree rustle as a hadeda launches itself into the sky. Xavier curses and wipes a glob of scat from his cheek. The bird circles, and lands on the pathway.

"My daughter's bird. It's made a home in this Faraway Tree, as she likes to call it." The woman reaches for the basket of flowers and runs her fingers through the blue petals. "You haven't changed, have you, Xavier? You would give up the girl, a rebel like yourself, to save your own skin. Why should I think I can trust you now?"

Xavier aims a boot at the bird and it skips out of his way. "Two years I waited. I trusted you then. But your fickle heart betrayed us."

She shakes her head. "My mother would not let me come back from the coast until I agreed to take the fate-mate she'd chosen. I always thought you would come for me. Instead, it was you who took another."

Xavier offers her his hand and helps her to her feet. "We

213

were both lied to," he says. "Perhaps when the war is over …"

The woman leans on her stick and takes his arm. "So many lies, Xavier. The ones that tore us apart are not the only ones …" She leads him along the flowerbeds, where their voices are low. I can't hear what they're saying, but I watch as Xavier releases her arm and lifts his face to the sky, hurling curses at the sun.

The bird takes refuge in the tree. Its scarred eyes watch from the safety of the branches.

"Why didn't you tell me? If I had only known …" the rebel leader shouts, then bows his head and weeps.

The woman takes him in her arms.

I lead the rebel leader through the tunnels back to his comrades. He's deep in thought, and forgets to abuse me when I go too slowly.

"I know my way from here," he says eventually. "Go now, Clubfoot – I want you to do something."

"Get someone else to do it. I've got urgent business for a friend."

Xavier pulls a pouch of credits from his belt. "Rejects don't have friends." His sneer stings me as he thrusts the pouch in my hand. "There's a girl. Her name is Juliet Seven. Find her and bring her to me, and I'll give you more credits."

I tuck the pouch down my trousers and walk away from him down the tunnel.

His voice shouts after me. "And tell that ugly bastard Lord Shakespeare that the war's ending. He won't be profiting from our misery much longer."

I pull myself into the road and take the path to the beach, in search of Juliet Seven. The cost of friendship weighs heavily on my hip.

Gollum shakes himself and glares at Connor. "Did you see everything?

Connor nods. "I conclude we can trust him, Juliet. He has honoured a promise to his friend, and in doing so he probably saved your life." He claps his hand on Gollum's shoulder. "My heart is the same as yours. It is good to learn it is such an honourable one. I believe honour is highly rated by Homesaps."

Gollum offers me his hand. "Trust, me, Drudge."

I look at him. At his devil horns, his mouth full of bone splinters. One day I might have called him a friend, but I have learnt my lesson about trusting Posh and Rejects. They are all the same. I recall Handler Xavier's Rule Number Seven: When a tricky Reject crosses your path, kick him in the face and run.

But there are times when rules should be broken.

I take Gollum's hand and smile like Good-Wife Juliet. I will play nice. After Connor kills The Machine and makes Mangeria safe for my children and me, I never want to see this Reject face again.

15

FREEDOM!

"Do you really think the saucy minxes will like me? I do not comprehend the mysterious games played between Homesaps. I am not programmed to flirt." Connor peers at himself in the hand mirror and practises his smile. "They will admire my teeth, I think. And I have perfected the steps of a bawdy dance."

Gollum runs grease through his hair and slicks the Savage curls into a ducktail.

"Connor, my friend, those trollops are going to go mad for you. They're going to lick you from top to toe." He peers over Connor's shoulder into the glass, sucks at his teeth and spits out a fleck of food.

"That is not necessary. I am perfectly clean. Neither do I wish to provoke any psychosis. I can see no positives in your equation," Connor says.

I watch them preening like Snow White's stepmother. I could declare which of them is ugliest, but I won't. I will be Good-Wife Juliet for as long as I'm on the *Jolly Roger*.

Gollum is taking Connor into the city. I argued for them

to stay on board until after we had completed our mission tomorrow, but Gollum insisted: the Rejects are voting today for the first time, and he wants to be there to see history in the making. Master Reader would have expected it, he said, and Connor must observe democracy in practice. A useful cultural reference.

I don't think Connor will find bug juice a helpful cultural reference. Gollum will drink too much and Connor will get lost. I have a bad feeling about this little day trip.

Connor smiles and taps his head. "Be reassured, Juliet, there is no risk of me losing my way today. I accessed your memory as I passed you performing your ablutions this morning and I now have a perfect map of Mangeria. When I kill The Machine during your primitive festival tomorrow, I will know exactly how to get around."

I glare at him. How many times do I have to tell him to stop creeping into my head. And to not wander about the deck when I'm taking a bath.

A frown crosses Connor's face. "I registered some disturbing vibrations in your heart as you walked around the other day, Juliet. I hope it will not fibrillate again. It made my eyes leak in a way that was most uncomfortable."

Heat rises in my face. After I saw Kit-Kat and Nicky-Noodle at the Tree Museum, I wandered the streets of Mangeria for hours, trying to piece together my dead-brain heart.

It is back in its safe now. Locked away. No one will ever touch it again.

Rose and Thorn come on deck to say goodbye. "Breeder go with Daddy. Breeder also wants to play with trollops," Rose says.

I arm my voice with steel nails. "No, *Rose*, you stay here with *Mummy* and your brother. *Gollum* will be back to read you a story before bed tonight." I soften my voice. "Come, Mummy will make you and Thorn a sticky strawberry treat, and you can lick the bowl."

"Breeder hates strawberry," Rose says turning her back on me.

Of course she does. She is determined to dislike everything I love.

But the two of us are going to have to learn to get along.

While Connor and Gollum are away, I'm going to pack up our things. I'll slip away with the children after the festival of fate-mates and make my home in Slum City.

Gollum is full of plans and is bursting with impatience to start his new life. After paying off a few debts to Lord Shakespeare, his Reject master, he intends to open a club on the *Jolly Roger*, a floating pleasure quarter of card games and dancing girls. He says the Posh will pay hand over fist to get a jolly good rogering on the sloop. A credit spinner for sure.

He has persuaded Connor to go into business as his partner. The cyborg will supervise the games. With his knowledge of risk and probability, he'll make sure the house never loses against the card sharps. Connor says he's looking forward to that statistical certainty.

I am impatient for tomorrow, after Connor has defused the threat against Mangeria. When both my world and Lexi's will be safe from The Machine's weapons.

But tomorrow is also when Nicolas and Kitty will become fate-mates. I'm dreading it.

No, I don't care.

I will not care.

It is only a few minutes after Gollum and Connor have left – and the children have waved their goodbyes and gone below – that a shadow crosses the sun and a mass of feathers lands on deck. Mistress Hadeda picks at her claws and glares at me with blind eyes.

"I come from Witch. She says I must warn you that war is coming. Posh will take up arms against Savage. Locust against Posh. Reject against Locust. It will spell the end of Mangeria. You have brought this war, and only you can end it. The tellers have spoken."

I have come back to kill The Machine – not to cause war. Tomorrow it will be over.

"The tellers are wrong!" I scream at her. I grab the hand mirror and hurl it at the ugly bird. It shatters on the deck.

Mistress Hadeda screeches in fury and launches herself in the air, spattering the deck with black scat.

"Ugly Ettie will go to Savage City. Little Sister will go to Savage City. We will all end in Savage City."

I turn away from the taunting bird and the mirror glass

crunches under my feet as I cross the deck. The only place I'm going is Slum City.

At sunset, I sail the sloop close to shore to wait for Gollum and Connor. The lights of Mangeria flicker on and the city's night sounds begin to drift over the water.

Fireworks scatter stars across the sky. The one-eyed moon cowers behind a cloud as a rainbow of colours paints the night. People are celebrating the election, and the party will continue tomorrow with the festival of fate-mates. Afterwards, it will be days of sore heads and regrets.

The time for Gollum and Connor's return arrives and then passes. Rose refuses to go to bed and nips my finger when I try to brush her hair. I raise my hand, pull back just in time. She stares at me with hating eyes.

After the children are finally asleep I pace the deck, my mood bitter, as I imagine what has delayed them. They've been caught up in a wild party. Gollum has fallen into a drain or the arms of a slagget. Connor is dancing his bawdy jig, begging wide-eyed pretties to lick him head to toe. I kick the mast, my mood as blue as the nail on my big toe will be tomorrow.

At last I hear a rasping breath and Gollum pulls himself up on deck.

"A fine time to come back reeking of wenches," I hiss.

He grips my shoulder to steady himself but I throw his hand off me.

"Rose cried herself to sleep. Her precious *Daddy* didn't

come back to read her a story. I told her she'll soon learn not to trust *Daddy*'s promises." The lie sizzles out of me. I don't know why I'm so angry. I stalk towards the cabin. "Don't you and Connor dare wake me up."

"Wait, Connor's here?" Gollum says.

Connor is not here. Neither is he with Gollum.

He has been left behind in Mangeria.

I knew they should never have gone to the city today. I watch Gollum closely, trying to detect any falsehoods.

"We didn't go clubbing," Gollum says. "The pleasure quarter was as boring and empty as a past trader's brain. The clubs were closed today to allow the pleasure workers to vote."

Good-Wife Juliet sighs in sympathy. No pleasure clubs. No dancing girls. I am *so* sorry to hear that, husband dear. Ha ha ha ha.

"Connor and I spent the day watching Mangerian democracy in action. It was a blast!" Gollum laughs harshly. "The Market Nags voted for the candidates whose food tax will allow them to hike their prices. And the Rejects ..." He spits. "My people voted for the candidates who fed them the biggest pieces of meat."

None of this surprises me. The people of Slum City look out for Number One. Their eyes are always wide open to spot the best deal. In Slum City a rat will eat its own baby – even if it's not hungry.

"The pleasure workers voted for the most handsome faces on the ballot," Gollum continues. "Silly plastic-heads! Of course, the Scavvie vote was about to go to the party who promised free bug juice afterwards, but then they switched to the party that threw in a few molls on the side. The Drainers voted …" His voice trails away. His face is wet but these are not tears of laughter. "Tomorrow we will have new Guardians in a free Mangeria." He clutches me around the waist and does a mockery of a dance.

I dig my feet onto the deck and grip his arms.

"The funniest thing is that I couldn't tell the candidates apart. They all spoke the same lies. It's all nonsense."

Of course it is. Unlike Gollum, I never expected anything else.

He sinks to his knees. "But something big happened, Drudge, and it's good news. Connor killed The Machine. It's done. Over. We can now be safe in this damned rotten beloved scat-hole of a place." He lifts his face and screams at the one-eyed moon. "We're safe in a free Mangeria!."

The Machine is dead? Connor was supposed to kill The Machine tomorrow, during the festival of fate-mates. And now it's happened without me even knowing, or noticing.

Something rings false in my ears.

I don't understand. I feel uneasy.

I crouch down on the deck next to Gollum, allowing my arm to touch his. I sniff the air around him for any whiff of treachery.

"This is big news. The biggest. You're only telling me now?" I say, trying to temper the suspicion in my voice.

Gollum shrugs. "It wasn't such a big deal in the end. It made me feel a bit flat, like nothing really changed."

He is lying to me. "Tell me everything," I say quietly.

Gollum coughs, and clears his throat. "It happened suddenly. We were walking past a voting station. A bunch of taxi wardens were refusing to go into the booth after the Drainers because they said it smelt worse than their sweaty Pulaks after a sixteen-hour shift. Connor suddenly took off, so I chased after him. He ran to the red building in the square."

Where The Machine lives.

"There were swarms of Locusts guarding the building – they'd increased security for the election. But that didn't seem to bother Connor. He grabbed me by the hair and pushed through the Locusts yelling: 'Make way, late Reject registration.' And the Locusts clapped their hands and yelled helpfully: 'Go, Reject, go. No mark, no vote. There's still time, friend. Go, go, go!'" Gollum shudders. "They were terrifying. I like my Locusts mean."

My skin prickles at the thought of Gollum receiving the six numbers on his spine.

"Connor hurried me into the building and pushed me down the stairs into a long corridor, to a room at the end."

The cyborg used my memories. He backtracked the steps Nicolas and I took almost three years ago when we made our marks dead. He even used a similar ploy to get past the Locusts. I exhale, and lie back on the deck as Gollum continues.

"Then it got tricky. Two Locusts were standing guard outside the room. They asked us most politely to identify ourselves and state our purpose. Connor told them we were Voting Observers sent by the Presidents of Mangeria to check that The Machine was tallying the votes correctly. So the Locusts smiled and asked us for the access protocol."

My memory. Connor could only have known about the Voting Observers from the conversation I overheard in the Tree Museum between Kitty and President Bartholomew.

Gollum laughs. "I have to admit, Drudge, I was scatting myself at that point. But Connor stared calmly at the Locusts and gave them the correct password."

He accessed the Locust's memories too. I will never underestimate Connor again. He played those Locusts like a card sharp. The sneak.

"They made way for us immediately. The room stretched forever with flickering bone-coloured boxes. Names flashed on screens, as the votes came in and got counted. Connor made a beeline for a box with a green screen in front of the room. He sat down and typed in a few symbols, and the box started whirring and shuddering. Then it sort of moaned. I think that's when The Machine died."

I would have liked to have been there to see it. To have felt the very second Mangeria and Lexi's beautiful garden became safe forever. The way Gollum tells it, it sounds as easy as stealing credits off a Posh kid.

Too easy. I do not feel safe.

Gollum quickly tells me how he and Connor ended up walking back to the beach because the Pulaks had voting day off. In the parade, a couple of candidates had still been strutting on their boxes, scratching together some last votes.

One candidate had drawn a huge crowd and the Rejects were eating out of her hand.

"She was promising the poor bastards homes, special job quotas, free education – the world on a gold plate. And they were lapping it up. 'Kitty, Kitty, Katherine Seven,' they were chanting. She could've told the fools to eat fly maggots and they still would've loved her," Gollum says bitterly.

Yes, Kitty will be Guardian of Justice and Peace. With control of the Locusts, she will become the most powerful Guardian in Mangeria. My Kitty.

And then she will marry into a Posh family. Nicolas's Kitty.

With Guardian Bartholomew backing her, she will grow even more powerful. President Kit-Kat.

"That's when things got weird. You should have seen Connor – he couldn't take his eyes off her. All wet behind the ears like a Posh seeing the dimpled thigh of a wench for the first time." Gollum whistles through his teeth. "Not everyone liked what she was saying, though. A group of traders started heckling her, and then things really got fun. The Market Nags were pelting her with rotten fruit, and some Drainers pulled her off the box. The Rejects turned their fists on the Drainers. Teeth were flying. It was a riot!"

Gollum leaps to his feet and punches the air, laughing.

"A bunch of Locusts arrived – not so friendly any more. So then Connor wades in, and the last I see is him punching his way through the mob towards Katherine Seven." He rubs the back of his head and winces. "When I picked myself out of the gutter, the crowd had skedaddled and Connor was gone."

He stretches out on the deck next to me.

The sky is quiet now. The moon has composed herself in her yellow cloak and gathered the stars around her like a mother hen and her chicks. The noise from the shore has become a low yawn as Mangeria prepares for bed.

We will probably find Connor tomorrow at the festival of fate-mates. Tomorrow, when I'll watch Nicolas and Kitty take their vows.

Tomorrow, when we'll all sing and dance and drink a toast to true love with the other fate-mates. Before my children and I disappear into the back streets of Slum City.

I leave Gollum on the deck and take my acid heart to bed.

CAPTAIN GOLLUM'S LOG

I told Drudge what happened in Mangeria today. But not quite everything.

I didn't think she'd understand. It would have made her despise me more than she does already. I'm not deceived by her — she's stopped trusting me.

I didn't want to tell her at first. It was tough for me to talk about it. It was a big deal. It changed everything for me.

Today I met my maker. My god, The Machine. Drudge would have sneered if she'd seen me — when Connor and I walked into that room. I fell onto the floor. Smack on my belly. She doesn't understand the terror I feel for my god.

When Connor began to type Lexi's

code, I begged forgiveness as my god made the noises of death.

I heard Connor tapping away. The whole room shook with my god's death rattle. Then it was silent.

I felt a terrible emptiness. Hollow. A horrible sadness. My god is dead.

Connor looked down at me on the floor. "I have done Lexi's work," he said.

Just like I told Drudge, we left then. At the parade we saw Katherine Seven talking nonsense to the voters. I recognised the pretty rebel pleasure worker, but she's cleaned up a lot since those days in the tunnels.

Connor saw her too. But this was the strange part. As soon as his eyes locked on her face, he started chatting to himself. Or maybe he was chatting to Lexi. It was really creepy, the way he strode into the rioting mob towards her.

And now he's missing.

Tomorrow might be the last time I'll see Drudge and the kids. I know she can't wait to get off this sloop and away.

I think my poor heart is going to break.

Good thing Connor's got a duplicate of mine.

16

TRUE LOVE

The city is abuzz. A million giant flies zooming in on a piece of donkey meat.

The citizens of Mangeria are preparing for the feast of love the way they always do. Drainers pick lice out of their hair and scrub the filth from their faces. Market Nags squeeze into their tightest dresses and paint their lips. Across the bridge from Slum City, Posh mistresses give last orders to caterers. They cast their eyes over flower arrangements. Sigh over their daughters' new dresses.

I fold Thorn's hand tight in mine; Gollum carries Rose on his shoulders. She clutches a balloon and bounces it on his head, marking time with his uneven steps.

Posh and traders move like ants towards the parade. We follow.

My children look around the streets of Mangeria with eyes as big as mangoes.

Locusts are stopping people a short distance from the entrance to the parade. Eyes narrowed over the crowd, they order those carrying bags to move to one side. Their rude hands pat down fat traders, probing folds of belly flesh. Sniff, poke, prod. They pull bottles and food boxes out of bags. Move on to the next, leaving people to repack their possessions.

I squeeze Thorn's fingers and pull my scarf tighter around my hair.

"This is ridiculous," a taxi warden yells. "Why are you treating us like Rejects? We're free citizens of Mangeria, not scum carrying knives and axes."

"I'm sorry, no offence, sir. We're just taking precautions," a Locust says, a smile strained across his face. He murmurs to a colleague, "Keep it nice. No rough stuff."

News traders bustle among the crowds: "Rebel Party screams foul. Vote rigged!"

"No cause for alarm! Unity government calls for calm."

It is paradise in free Mangeria!

Smalls cling to balconies, waving flags, dodging mothers trying to smother sunblocker on their blotchy skin. Baskets of plastic flowers hang from the entrances to shops and streamers flutter from windows. Red and yellow and pink. Drainers crack open bottles, spraying us with bug juice as we pass. They whistle and cheer at the pleasure workers, shouting, "Give us a kiss, give us a kiss."

There is a smell of fumes as Market Nags throw fuel on spattering fires and ready their pots for the hungry revellers. They chop bricks of onion and potato, dice the foul-smelling meat and swat away the circling flies.

The parade is a blur of umbrellas shooting up against the

sun and Posh whipping out fans to beat the tepid air. We make our way towards the stage. I scan the crowd for Connor. My eyes search for Nicolas too.

Thorn suddenly pulls his hand free of mine. I watch him zig-zag between traders, crawl under chairs to Connor, who is sitting straight-backed near the front of the stage. Connor pulls him onto his lap, turns and waves at us. He pats the vacant chairs next to him and beckons.

I notice that his colour is too high and he's looking confused. It's the expression he gets when he exceeds his nutrient quota by eating too much banana. Connor is not programmed to be a greedy pig. It is confusing for him when he behaves like Gollum.

As we weave our way towards the rows of seats, a Reject stumbles into me. He is half my size, a crippled midget. His eyes, set too far back in his pulpy head, rake my face.

"Juliet Seven," he says before he shuffles away.

Fear ices my skin.

"That Reject recognised me. I should go back to the *Jolly Roger* with the children" I tell Gollum. But no – I will leave the parade and run. Our belongings are stuffed in my satchel which I have stored behind some rocks on the beach. I will collect it, and my children and I will find a place to hide in Slum City. Away from Gollum, and those like him.

"Take it easy, Drudge – no one cares about you any more. It's a free country. Go sit with Connor and I'll go get us some cold drinks. We're going to melt in this heat." He wanders away with Rose still clutching her balloon, and his hair.

Bounce-bounce-bounce in the direction of a food stall.

People shove behind me as Locusts push past. "Make way for President Bartholomew. Coming through, coming through."

I hear that laugh then. The sound comes from deep in his belly, inviting everyone around to join him.

Nicolas, Nic, Nici, Nice.

So nice in his Posh fate-mate clothes with his nice Posh fate-mate ring tucked away in his nicely ironed Posh shirt. So nice for Kit-Kat.

He does not see me. I am hidden in the crowd. Close enough to touch him.

"Father, a seat is reserved for you right in the front, with President Xavier and his family. The ceremony doesn't start for a while, so relax," Nicolas is saying.

"I can't relax, my boy. Not until this is all over. I have not seen that girl of yours all morning, and we've got business to discuss before this circus begins."

"Give it a break, Father. There'll be plenty of time to talk politics with Kitty tomorrow. And the next day. And … forever."

I glance in their direction in time to see President Bartholomew's eyes rest on Nicolas, soft and full of love. "You're doing the right thing, my boy. You're making me a very happy father today. You'll grow fond of her, I'm sure."

The President pats Nicolas on the shoulder and makes his way to the front of the parade, where he greets Larissa and Mistress.

My mother is smaller than I remember – as though some of her has been rubbed away.

And there is the fellow president, Xavier, sitting next to Mistress. So it is as Larissa said: the two old sweethearts have found one another again.

A happy Posh family. My father, my mother and my sister. And I am not part of them. I am invisible.

But not fully ... Nicolas turns and looks in my direction. Blinks slowly. Looks again. The smile freezes on his face.

He stares at me and I fall into his green eyes.

"Juliet?" He blinks again, and I drown. "I thought you were dead." His voice is raw.

My chest is tight and cold. *And I never doubted you were alive.*

I smile with a closed mouth, make my voice sweet as sugar. I step forward.

"Congratulations. I hope you and Kitty will be very happy together."

No, I don't. You said you loved me. I believed you. I trusted you. I hope Kitty breaks your heart, then spits on every piece. I hope you die old and miserable and poor. I hope when you die the rats eat the eyeballs out of your sockets and share your rotten, lying heart with the cockroaches.

My traitorous heart thuds in my chest.

Nicolas shuffles his feet and grips his hands together. "I knew you loved her – you risked your life to save her. Kitty and I ... we fought on the same side during the war. We believe in the same things." He sighs and shakes his head, searching for words. "I thought I'd come to love her too."

Love her. She gave you up to your father to save her skin. She was ready to bash your head in if he didn't agree to the rebel's terms. She betrayed you. Fool.

"I'm not interested in politics, which is a bitter disappointment to my father. But it makes him happy that Kitty was appointed Guardian of Justice and Peace," Nicolas says. "It keeps things in the family. And, of course, Kitty has always wanted to serve the people of Mangeria."

She used you to get your father's support. Kitty serves no one but herself.

Nicolas looks down at his feet and is silent. I will not fill this awkward space that breathes between us.

"Juliet." He swallows, pauses, before the words rush out of him. "I thought you'd been captured by the Locusts. Or that you'd taken the seacraft and escaped. I knew that when the war was over, you'd come back to me." His face prickles with sweat, his eyes are strangely bright. "I searched everywhere. I found no sign. The years past and I had to accept you were dead."

I wanted to come back. I tried. Gollum got me lost on purpose and then Shepherd stole my boat. But I never lost faith in you. And I came home. I thought you would always wait for me.

"Say something, Juliet. Please."

I stare at him. I press my fist against my breast to stifle the sharp pain. My mouth is dry. My heart explodes.

I hear a child's scream of rage behind me.

On their way through the crowd, Rose has dropped her

cold drink and a red balloon floats away above the heads of the crowd.

"Naughty juice, Daddy." She kicks the empty cup.

As they get to us, Gollum kneels, holding Rose's hands. "Mummy and I'll share our juice with you, Rosie. And I'm sure Mummy 's got a hanky for those sticky hands."

Nicolas stares. At Rose's Savage hair, her large brown eyes, her pale skin. He looks at me and then his eyes flick over Gollum.

"Long time, friend," Nicolas says. His voice is ice.

Gollum whistles in surprise. "You sure look better than the last time I saw you, my friend." He offers his hand to Nicolas. "I honoured my promise to you. But then ... things happened ..."

Nicolas dismisses Gollum's outstretched hand and smiles stiffly. "Yes, I can see that. Forgive me if I don't thank you." He turns to me, reaches out and tucks a curl behind my ear. His fingers tremble on my cheek. "I understand now. You used me to make your mark dead and to save your beloved Kitty, *our* beloved Kitty." His lips curl on her name. "And when you didn't need me any more, you ran away with him. I was just a game to you." He grins without humour. "Now it's my turn to wish you and your little family all the happiness that is coming to you."

Stunned, I watch him walk away. And as if on cue, the band strikes up on the stage.

The new Guardian of Population Control, a woman with Savage hair and deep scars on her cheeks, shrugs on the ornate festival cloak. She clicks her fingers in time to the music while scantily dressed helpers gyrate around her, draping coloured ribbons over her arms. They pour sticky love potion into the cups the fate-mates will drink from as part of the ceremony.

Gollum swings Rose onto his shoulders and we plough through the crowd towards Connor. Traders yell behind us, "You're not made of glass. Put that bloody kid down. We can't see."

We slip into our chairs. Connor's cheeks are uncommonly pink, his breathing is uneven. I pass him a cup of juice.

Connor smiles at me. "My heart feels strange, Juliet. I do not think juice will quench this thirst. I must tell you something, Juliet ..."

The musicians stamp their feet, and belt out a song popular with the Scavvies. Some of the Posh gasp and titter behind their fans, others laugh and sing along. It is different to the ceremonies of old, but everyone needs to go with the flow, get used to change.

The band stops playing, and the dancing dies. The Guardian flings back her Savage hair and sways up to the podium. "Who of you wish to take the vow of eternal love? Come forward and let me bless your union."

A boy with peaches for cheeks and green slanted eyes marches proudly onto the stage, hand in hand with a dark-haired girl. "We do! Darius Nine and Gabby Three. We are in love." They grin shyly at each other and hold out their hands. The helpers give the fate-mates a cup of love potion and tie their wrists together with a coloured ribbon.

"He's a Posh and she's a pleasure worker's daughter. It can't last," a trader whispers, far too loudly, to the Market Nag next to me as the happy couple shift to the edge of the stage to make way for the next lovers.

"Who knows. She's a good girl, and they're in love. At least she isn't a Reject."

The trader laughs. "Rejects twinning with traders or Posh? Ha! The Guardians will never let that happen."

More young men and women skip onto the stage to bind themselves to one another. Posh and Scum. The new Romeos and Juliets of a free Mangeria, with no feuding families to stand in the way of true love, no dagger or poison to end their lives. The stage is crowded now, the couples whisper and clutch each other, impatient to take the vow that will seal their unions.

"That Posh over there's holding things up," the Market Nag chuckles when there's a pause in the proceedings. "His girl probably got cold feet. Poor sap, look at him!"

Nicolas hovers in the wings of the stage. His eyes search the faces in front of him. They rest on my face, and grow hard. He catches his father's eye, shrugs, and holds out helpless hands. From where I'm sitting, the president's face looks purple, but the festival continues and the couples take their vows. They promise to stay together until death parts them. To work loyally for the state of Mangeria, and to breed healthy children. I know the words – the vow has not changed, even if the couples now mean it with all their silly little hearts.

Suddenly, wings beat the air. Posh in front of the stage leap to their feet and clutch their hair. Chairs topple, people squeal.

Princess Fanny shoots into the sky. "War is coming. Beware! The Savage is here. She has brought the end to Mangeria." She dives towards me, her talons slice the air, inches from my face.

An explosion close by, a volley of gunfire.

Voices on the stage trail off as fate-mates scatter, shrieking in panic.

More gunfire, screams. People fall as others push and shove, abandoning purses, umbrellas and fans. Connor sits clutching his head.

"Take Rose – I'll look after Thorn!" I shout at Gollum. He swings Rose into his arms, stares wildly around at the chaos.

I grab Connor's shoulder. "Don't just sit there, you foolish robot. We have to go!"

Connor picks up Thorn and staggers to his feet. "Juliet, there is something I need to tell you."

I pull Connor with me and run. Posh scramble in blind panic across the parade, pulling stumbling children. Sheep with their heads cut off.

A mob of Rejects, armed with rocks and knives, storm towards some Locusts. A few Rejects peel off and sprint over to the food stalls, smashing pots off the burning fires, hurling rocks at shop windows. Market Nags abandon their stalls, run screaming into buildings. Kids in ragged clothes run out of alleys, fight the cockroaches for the discarded food. Mothers pull Smalls from the windows, slam the shutters closed. Festival flags flutter down.

I spot Gollum ahead of me. "Get off the street, find somewhere to hide," I yell.

Rose stares at me over his shoulders, hers eyes bright with terror and glee.

Connor and Gollum swerve towards an open doorway. A Drainer shoves past me and races in after them, slamming the door in my face.

I dart onto a porch of a shop as Locusts run towards a group of Posh. They force them down on the ground and cuff their wrists. People sob and curse around me. Discarded possessions – a shoe, a scarf, a bag, a pair of sunglasses – litter the street. I hear a voice on the porch next to me. Handler Xavier.

"*We* never started this, Bartholomew. It's *your* Locusts."

"*My* Locusts! It's that girl of yours. Where is Kitty? She's gone off her head!" President Bartholomew coughs, then continues, his voice faint. "As soon we appointed her Guardian for Justice and Peace, she was off like a rotten onion. She's set her Locusts on us."

I hear Nicolas's voice. "Father, please. Don't talk. You're hurt."

Another explosion, more gunfire. Heavy footsteps and screaming. I watch Locusts spread out towards the buildings, battering doors with their guns. They pull people out of shops, cuff them and drag them away towards waiting taxis.

Pulaks shuffle their feet, waiting for orders.

"They're coming for us. I'll find my family – we must get to the rebel base." Handler Xavier leaps off the porch and sprints towards an alley. Guns fire over his head.

"Come, Father, let me help you," Nicolas says. "You must get up." He is silent for a while, then begins to weep. "I'm sorry, I'm so sorry," he says through his tears.

President Bartholomew is dead, and I am not sorry. He never spared me, or any of the other residents of Slum City any kindness. But he and Nicolas shared blood, and I suppose that might give him a reason to grieve.

I look up between the buildings. Taxis stuffed with people thunder down the streets as Locusts stand guard over others. I search the faces but I do not see Gollum or Connor with the children.

There's a scuffle and I see Mistress arguing with a Locust. Laughing, he shoves her into the back of a taxi with Larissa. "I don't care who you are. We have our orders," he says. "Move, Pulaks. Take this lot to Savage City."

I watch, helpless, as the taxi takes Mistress and my sister away.

Moments later, Nicolas edges past. He stops when he sees me. Carries on walking. Turns back.

"You can't stay here, Juliet. Come, I know a safe place."

I search his face for any sign of softening. But it is closed to me.

"I need to find the others. I can't go without them," I say.

"Your family." Nicolas's green eyes flicker to the ground.

"I'll be waiting at the rebel base. Your Reject knows the place." He fumbles in his pocket, and then steps closer to press something into my hand. "My father's ring. Show them this and they won't turn you away." Then he runs up the street.

I edge off the porch and scan the buildings where Gollum and Connor took cover.

"Juliet, up here!" Gollum shouts from a balcony across the street. Rose and Thorn are standing next to him with Connor.

More shouting, and a band of Rejects burst out of an abandoned building. They storm towards the Locusts.

The sound of running. I see three Rejects, coming straight for me.

"Grab the drudge!" It's the midget Reject, the one who called me by my name before the ceremony started. Rough hands pull a sack over my head and grab my arms and legs. I am dragged away.

CAPTAIN GOLLUM'S LOG

I write this in haste. Everything's gone to scat in Mangeria. The Locusts have gone crazy — they're on a killing spree, or dragging people off to Savage City. Posh and Scum. They don't care who they take. And the Rejects are fighting back.

I watched the midget and his friends gang Drudge and take her away. I sent Connor back to the *Jolly Roger* with Rosie and Stinker. They'll be safer there. Then I went after Drudge. I knew where the Rejects would take her — to my master, Lord Shakespeare.

On the way I ran into my friend Nicolas. I still think of him as a friend, even though he looks at me like I'm a rat. He was with a woman, the rebel girl Kitty, now a powerful Guardian.

She'd been injured and was in a bad way. What she told us made my heart beat with terror, my blood freeze in my veins.

After making a plan we split up. I'll meet Nicolas and Kitty at the rebel base after I've spoken to Lord Shakespeare. I can't put a crip foot wrong. If the bastard doesn't agree, this entry might be my last. In a few hours, Captain Gollum could be dead.

We'll all be dead.

17

THE REJECT LORD

I smell fear and vomit. Mine.

Laughter around me, and music. A woman sings mournfully to the thrumming of string instruments, the breathy hooting of musical pipes.

"Get this filthy thing off me!" I scream.

The sack is pulled roughly from my head. The woman's voice fades and the music is silenced.

A grotesque face peers at me and grins. "Juliet Seven. At last. And isn't she a beauty?"

People cheer and laugh. Sharp teeth, Savage hair, faces distorted by terrible shapes posturing as eyes, noses, lips. Open sores, slack mouths, drooling lips, seeping eyes, crusted noses. I turn away from the horrific spectacle.

Scabby fingers grip my face.

"My Rejects call me Lord Shakespeare." The grotesque mouth, inches from mine, breathes the smell of lavender and mint. His voice is smooth, like silk, sweet and rich as condensed milk.

I know his name. Gollum has often spoken of the Reject

master he was bonded to in the time before we left Mangeria. A Savage infidel who loves the books of the Bard as much as I do. I twist away, but his hand grips my face more firmly.

"My little golden goose. I've watched out for you these past few years, searching for your nest. Where, oh where have you been hiding?"

"Smash her face so she can be like us," a voice cries.

The Rejects shout and whistle. "Smash her face, smash her face, smash her face!"

Shakespeare drops his hand and I stare around my prison. It is a palace: couches covered in plush red fabric, carpets woven in rich patterns, chandeliers hanging from ceilings, giant artworks adorning walls. And all around the room, shelves with hundreds of books.

With one raised finger, which is missing half a joint, Shakespeare silences the voices.

"There's a price on your head, Juliet Seven. The news traders in the square never stop shouting about it. Your Posh Mistress will pay handsomely for you." He twists me around, runs his large fingers down my sides. Strokes my chest. "But perhaps the President will pay even more?"

I slap his hands off my body. "You're too late. The Locusts have taken my Mistress to Savage City, and President Bartholomew is dead. There'll be no credits coming to you."

"Bartholomew is dead! What do we think of that, Rejects?"

The Rejects whoop and clap. Two one-legged men grab each other, link arms and swing around in a dance. "The bastard is dead, dead, dead, dead," the crowd chants.

The stubby finger silences them again. "It's not the dead bastard who wants a slice of your pretty skin – it's the other one. That rebel leader and handler of orphans, Xavier. The one they also now call 'President'." Shakespeare looks around the room at his followers. "And what do we call our President?"

"Bastard, bastard, bastard. Filthy bastard, bastard, bastard," they hiss.

There are loud voices at the door and Gollum stumbles into the room, his eyes wild. My children are not with him, and neither is Connor.

Shakespeare smiles. "Clubfoot. I haven't seen you in a long time. You've come to pay your respects to your Lord? And to settle your debt? But I'm puzzled that you're still standing."

Hands grab Gollum and force him to his knees, hold him down as he struggles.

"That's better," Shakespeare says. He strides across the room and peers down at Gollum. "Much better."

Gollum shakes his hair out of his eyes and glares. "I've come from President Xavier. He's got urgent business to discuss with you."

Shakespeare presses his foot on Gollum's back. He nods at a midget holding Gollum's arms. It's the Reject who spotted me at the festival of fate-mates, and then grabbed me in the parade. The midget lifts up Gollum's shirt.

"So, Clubfoot, I see you are still unmarked. Don't you

247

want the six numbers on your spine?" He takes his foot off Gollum's back and the Rejects lift him to his feet.

"I don't need The Machine to tell me I'm a person. And I no longer kneel for any man," Gollum says.

Shakespeare laughs and throws out his hands to the cackling Rejects. "Show our guests what we think of The Machine."

A clutch of Rejects turn, pull down their trousers and bare their dirty arses at us. Gollum watches, his face stricken at the disrespect. The rest of the room screams with laughter.

Shakespeare bellows the loudest. "We defy the mark of The Machine. We will never submit." He selects a book from the shelf and begins to speak without opening it. "'Hath not a Reject eyes? Hath not a Reject hands, organs, dimensions, senses, affections, passions – just like other citizens of Mangeria?'"

The room is silent. I clear my throat.

"Yes, Lord," I say. "If you prick us, do we not bleed? If you tickle us, do we not laugh? If you poison us, do we not die? And if you wrong us, shall we not revenge?"

Shakespeare smiles at me, his eyes are gooey with tears. "Our little goose is a reader, and I'm a little short of that company. It's a pity I have to give you up." He looks at Gollum. "The President knows I have the drudge?"

Gollum reaches in his pocket and holds up a pouch – a piece of grubby cloth secured by string. "President Xavier sent me to pay the price for Juliet Seven. And he requests most humbly that you meet with him."

"I doubt the bastard humbly requested anything. Does he take me for a dead-brain? He duped too many of my people into taking the mark of The Machine before the election. But he could not play me for a fool."

The Rejects cackle and jeer. "Not us, not us, not us."

"He set the Locusts on us today. But we were ready. And now he wants to trap me." Shakespeare grabs Gollum's pouch and empties it on the carpet. "Stones? You come here with a pouch full of stones?"

"President Xavier will pay ten credits for each stone when you bring him the drudge. He gives you his word you won't be hunted." Gollum reaches into his pocket and pulls out a ring. "He sends this presidential ring as proof of his honour."

It is the ring that Nicolas gave me, his father's ring. It must have slipped from my hand when the Rejects grabbed me on the parade.

Shakespeare examines the ring and forces it onto his stubby finger. "Pretty." He laughs. "I think I should now be called President Shakespeare." He clicks his fingers. "Come, Dwarf, let's meet the bastard and see what he wants."

Gollum takes my arm and I elbow him in the ribs.

"What are you up to? Where are my children?" I hiss.

"Connor has them safely on the *Jolly Roger*," he whispers, turning his face. Then he grips me tighter and pushes me ahead of Shakespeare.

Dwarf leads us along a dark corridor smelling of damp and rot, down a crumbling stairwell until we reach the road. As we emerge onto the deserted streets of Slum City, I look back at the derelict building. A palace for Rejects.

A few blocks away, Gollum lifts a paver off the ground. He is sweating and his body trembles. I know he dreads being trapped underground. We follow him in single file down a stepladder and into a tunnel.

"President Xavier and some of his people have taken refuge at an old rebel base a few tunnels from here," Gollum says.

Shakespeare chuckles. "So my Rejects have him on the run. This is sweet news."

"It's not much further," Gollum says. "But of course, you know these underground passages better than any of us – even the ones that were forgotten before the old world ended."

Shakespeare's jagged teeth flash white in the darkness. "I was born in a tunnel. I know every foul-smelling inch of this place."

We follow Gollum down the dark tunnel, our backs hunched, heads tucked into our necks to avoid the low ceiling, until I see lights ahead. As we get nearer, we come to a room at the intersection of three tunnels. Shakespeare shoves Gollum aside and grabs my arm, his fingers gripping like talons.

The rebel base is crowded with people. I stand back in the gloom, searching the space for Nicolas.

Shakespeare releases my arm and swaggers into the room. "Xavier, you bastard, I thought I spotted your ugly face. I believe you've begged most humbly to speak with me."

Handler Xavier frowns. "I've got no business with you, Reject. Bugger off before I get my people to whip the skin off your putrid flesh."

Gollum limps up to them. "Wait. You must both hear what I have to say ..."

Handler Xavier's sponge eyes rest on Gollum's face. "I recognise you, Clubfoot. We had a deal once – one that I paid for and you failed to deliver." Handler Xavier shoves Shakespeare backwards towards the tunnel. "Now both of you leave before I whip you myself."

"No, you must listen," Gollum says. "The Machine is hunting us. Before long, Mangeria will be a city of ghosts."

Gollum is speaking like a dead-brain. He knows that Connor has killed The Machine and it can't track anyone.

"Shut your lying gob, Clubfoot! We're leaving. My Rejects will see your Locusts on the streets, Xavier." Shakespeare spits at Handler Xavier's feet. "More of your conversation would infect my brain. But before I go, you must pay me for the drudge, Juliet Seven. Ten credits for each of these stones, as promised on your behalf by Clubfoot here." He takes the grubby pouch from his pocket and drops it on the ground. "Dwarf, bring the goose."

Dwarf pushes me forward and Shakespeare's stubby fingers squeeze my cheeks. I stare into Handler Xavier's eyes. Cow-eyes. So much like mine. I will not allow him to sense my fear.

"I would no more send this clubfoot on my behalf than eat cockroach scat." Handler Xavier's eyes rest on

Shakespeare's finger. "But that ring ... Lord Shakespeare. Where did you get it?"

It is Gollum who answers, his voice full of urgency. "It belonged to President Bartholomew. He's dead. And soon we all will be too unless we stop The Machine." He grabs my hand. "Please, Juliet, tell them I'm no dead-brain. They must listen to me. You have to trust me, Juliet – you owe me this, at least."

My thoughts are a confused mess. Gollum is playing a dangerous game lying to Shakespeare to bring him here. The Reject Lord will make Gollum pay for making him lose face in front of President Xavier. Yet for nearly three years he has kept me safe. He has probably saved my life, and the lives of my children.

"His name is not Clubfoot," I say. "He is Captain Gollum. And he deserves to be heard."

Shakespeare clicks his misshapen jaw and narrows his eyes. "This clubfoot has tricked me and made a liar out of you, Xavier. Only a fool would provoke two hard Savages as ourselves. If he's wasting our time, I'll have his skin and you can have his bones."

The two men look at Gollum expectantly and the whole room is quiet.

But instead of speaking, Gollum runs.

"I think it's time you went back to your dump." Handler Xavier sneers at the Reject Lord. "Go on, now. Skip away like your Clubfoot."

But before Shakespeare has a chance to respond, Gollum's

face reappears. Behind him is Nicolas, and he is carrying a woman in his arms. Her face is bandaged, her silky hair matted with blood.

"I knew they'd be here soon. If you don't believe what I've got to say, this man will back me up," Gollum says.

Handler Xavier reaches for the woman, lays her on the ground. "Kitty, my dearest."

Kitty, the daughter he wishes he'd had.

"I found Kitty hiding close to the square," Nicolas says breathlessly. "The Locusts were chasing her. This morning she went to the red building before the festival – to deal with a few security matters. But The Machine wouldn't accept her instructions. Instead, it has declared a State of Crisis and ordered the Locusts to track down every citizen of Mangeria."

Handler Xavier snorts with disbelief. "That's impossible. The Machine is under the authority of the Guardian of Justice and Peace. It can't act alone," he says.

Nicolas shakes his head. "Kitty summoned the Machinist to reverse this rogue order, but he's been taken to Savage City by the Locusts, along with many others."

Kitty stirs. "Find the Machinist," she says weakly. "He must shut down The Machine before it's too late. It is tracking all of us." She coughs and holds a bloodied hand to her mouth.

Shakespeare laughs. "Not all of us. I never took the mark." He points his stubby finger at Kitty and snarls. "Trickery! You meant to instruct the Locusts this morning to rid the city of Rejects, and *that's* why you had them marked for the election."

"Lies," Handler Xavier says, but he does not meet the Reject leader's eyes.

"Don't dare play me, bastard. Your plans were whispered in the wind and our rat ears heard them. And we were prepared – we gave the Locusts a good bashing," Shakespeare says smugly. "And now it seems we'll be the only ones to survive. Mangeria will become a Reject city. Come, Dwarf, let us go and make merry while our friends hide from their Locusts." He swaggers towards the tunnel. "And bring the pretty goose. She'll amuse me, I think."

At the entrance, someone pushes past the Reject Lord, nearly knocking him over.

It is Me, his face pink from running. "Where's President Xavier? I have news – there's been an explosion at the Laboratory. It can no longer supply food to the city." He spots Handler Xavier on the floor with Kitty and flings his hands into the air. "Boom! The city's water machines have also been blown up. Boom! It's anarchy out there. Rejects against Locusts, traders against pillaging Savages, and the Posh are fleeing for the coast or barricading themselves in their homes, guarding their swimming pools from the Scavvies." He wheezes and breathes deeply. "And the Pulaks are taking taxi after taxi to Savage City."

I know then. The Machine is not dead. It has started another war in Mangeria. Those who are not killing each other are being hunted by the Locusts. Soon there will be no food – The Machine means to starve the ones it cannot track.

Handler Xavier paces. "What has come over Cockroach?

Surely he must realise The Machine's order is madness."

Cockroach! A name only whispered in Slum City. Before I left on the *Jolly Roger*, he was the head of the Locusts. He has probably stayed in his job because he knows how to grease his smiles.

The news has brought a flurry of discussion into the room, as people begin arguing about the next steps to take. As they talk, I kneel next to Kitty.

She opens her eyes and smiles sweetly. "Ettie. My little drudge. Are we both dead?"

I stroke her hair. "We're both alive. I'm home." I stare down at my beautiful friend, the one I always looked out for. The one who thought she always looked out for me.

"Remember, Ettie, when we played the game? How we ran wild like Savages on the beach crying, 'Monster! Monster!'" A breathy giggle escapes her lips.

"We tricked those fools," I say.

Kitty's eyes widen. "The Monster is real, Ettie. It's hunting us. You have to play this game without me. You have to win, Ettie. You can't run away this time."

My tears soak her hair. I rest my cheek against hers and feel her slip away.

Handler Xavier groans, steadies himself on Me's shoulder. He bows his head for a moment, then straightens. "Lord Shakespeare, many years ago you took me and my comrade Nelson to Savage City to spring two prisoners from their cells. You took us along the old tunnels. You remember this, of course."

"You never paid me for my trouble, you bastard. I remember it well," Shakespeare says.

"I remember it better," Handler Xavier says grimly. "You led us there and didn't wait to bring us back. We crawled those tunnels for days before we found our way out. The two prisoners were recaptured, and died in Savage City."

He's talking about Kitty's parents, his best friends, sentenced to Savage City when she was four years old. Their crime: organising a protest against the festival of fate-mates. They were sentenced to death three months later for trying to break out of Savage City. Handler Xavier promised them he would always look after Kitty. And now she too is gone.

Shakespeare shrugs. "You shouldn't have cheated me." He chuckles and turns to Gollum. "Now I see why Clubfoot brought me here. He thinks I'll take you through the old tunnels to Savage City to find the Machinist." He tilts his over-sized head. "Maybe I will." He tilts his head to the other side. "And maybe I won't."

"And maybe you and I are in the same seacraft and will drown when the storm comes unless we learn to swim together," Handler Xavier says.

"I owe you no favours, Xavier, but I'll take you to Savage City, and then I'll lead you back again," Shakespeare says. "I don't relish spending the rest of my days eating plastic and drinking rat piss."

"A dead man cannot be President," Me argues. "May I remind you, President Xavier, that you and many of the rebels registered your marks again after the war. The Locusts will track you."

Shakespeare clasps his hands together. "So then you must run for your lives. I expect our rotting corpses will soon meet each other on the dumps."

The room is silent, the faces around me are gloomy as they consider their fates.

I will not die in Mangeria. I will take the *Jolly Roger* and leave with my children. If Sanctuary and Lexi's island survived the conflagration, there must be other places across the ocean …

But what about Larissa? She's trapped with Mistress in Savage City. I cannot leave her. And Nicolas. I look at Kitty's blood on my fingers, thinking about what we have already lost. I cannot leave him again, even if he does not want me.

I will play this last game. I will not run from the Monster.

"I'll go with Lord Shakespeare to Savage City and find the Machinist," I say. "My mark is dead."

A babble of noise fills the room.

"No!" Handler Xavier shouts over the commotion. "I've waited nearly three years to find you. Waited to tempt some scum into demanding the price your mother and I placed on your Savage head." He stretches out a hand, and I step back. "I won't let you go. You are my blood."

I lock eyes with Handler Xavier. My father. A Savage, hard man. I look at him the way Rose looks at me. With hurt, distrust, confusion.

He stares at me the way I look at Rose. Guilt, regret, anger.

Shakespeare rocks with laughter. "Stone me dead. The

villain hath done the goose's mother. The little drudge is the daughter of a president. And are those tears in his eyes? Does the bastard have a heart?"

Nicolas steps forward stiffly and stands next to me, though keeping his distance. "I'll go with her. My mark is also dead. I never trusted The Machine, and I didn't reregister myself after the war." He turns to Shakespeare. "I know the Machinist – he's a distant cousin. I can find him in Savage City."

Shakespeare claps his hands. "It is decided then."

I gaze across the room at Gollum. I hold his eyes with mine. *Look after my children until I return, my friend.*

He nods, his face grim.

Nicolas and I follow Shakespeare towards a tunnel. I do not look back.

18

SAVAGE CITY

"Move, you poisonous bunch-backed toad!" Shakespeare yells.

Spurred on by the curse, Dwarf crawls, lighting our way through the tunnel with a burning torch clamped to his head.

"Not that way," Shakespeare says, raising himself to his knees and grabbing Dwarf's foot.

Dwarf snarls and kicks Shakespeare in the face. "Thou are a boil, a plague, a sore. I scorn you, scurvy companion."

Shakespeare and Dwarf trade the Bard's insults like Market Nags barter rotten food for credits in the market place. They're like a couple of old fate-mates – the worse the insult, the more cheerful they are.

Urged on by Shakespeare's curses, we've been crawling, slithering and pushing our way through dark narrow spaces for hours. Nicolas crawls behind me. He has said nothing since we left the rebel base.

Shakespeare exhausts the Bard's curses and rallies us on with a word-perfect recital of *Hamlet*. After the sweet Danish prince has been sung to rest by flights of angels, Shakespeare moves on to *King Lear* and his troublesome daughters. My knees are acts of pain, my elbows raw sonnets, my lungs ache with damp soliloquies.

The Reject Lord stops, mid-verse. He taps the side of the tunnel and sniffs. "Can you smell that?" he says. "Rotting souls, suffocating screams, putrefying hope." He grins, his hideous face illuminated by the smoky light. "Savage City."

He eases himself off the tunnel floor and presses his hands up against the pipe. Sand and gravel drift down. Shakespeare coughs, and heaves upwards again.

Soon there is light leering at us through a gap in the ceiling. Shakespeare shifts a manhole cover aside and pulls himself through the opening. Nicolas and I follow, leaving Dwarf peering out of the hole in the sand.

Wraithlike clouds beat the one-eyed moon across the death-black sky. The stars are knife points. White sand stretches in undulating dunes. Heat wafts over us in foul waves but I am cold, despite the heat.

"We're here," Shakespeare says. His voice is a whisper.

There is nothing but desert.

I look up. Black feathered shapes hover above a large dune. The birds hold vigil above the raised expanse of sand, circling mutely.

There are no buildings. No walls, no watchtowers, no Locusts.

"The tellers are always here, feasting on the souls of the dying. They like this place. Brrrrrrr!" Shakespeare shivers and rubs his arms, grinning at Nicolas and me. "You'll find the entrance close to that large dune. The gates are wide open. People are always welcome in Savage City. But no one ever walks out again." He pinches my cheek and punches Nicolas on the arm. "Dwarf and I will wait for you until sunrise and then we will fear the worst. Go on, get out of my sight. Thou dost infect my eyes."

The Reject Lord is lying. As soon as we've left he will run back along the tunnel to his palace in Slum City. He is a flesh-monger, a fool and a coward.

As he turns to go, the birds scream with one voice. The clouds freeze against the sky, the moon stops running, petrified, as a slick of black feathers swoops down. They dive towards Shakespeare, tearing at his hair, jabbing his arms and legs with their rapier beaks.

Shakespeare flaps his hands. "Bugger off, you abominations on this earth. Move!"

Dwarf screams and ducks into the tunnel, pulling the cover over his head. The birds settle, guarding the opening while others beat Shakespeare with their wings. In a solid wave they rush towards him, pushing him back, stabbing the sand until he falls over. They seem determined not to let him back into the tunnel.

I grin at him, lying in a cowering heap on the sand. "We'll leave you with your friends, Lord Shakespeare. They look hungry. When we return with the Machinist, at least your bones will mark the entrance to our escape. Adieu, adieu, my Lord," I say.

Nicolas and I walk towards the white dune, covering our

mouths with our scarves against the swirling sand.

"On second thoughts, I think I might join you," Shakespeare says, running to catch up. "Those poxy birds have taken against me. When we return with the Machinist we can together take up arms against our sea of troubles."

We press on against the wind. When I stumble, Nicolas grabs my arm and steadies me. I look down at the obstacle in my way: a blackened skull rooted in the sand. The eyes are hollowed out sockets, the mouth is a set of yellowed teeth frozen in a scream.

I am looking at a result of Savage City's Special Prisoner Appearance Readjustment – SPAR. It is something I've heard whispered in the markets of Slum City, a story also told to disobedient Smalls to make them behave: the Locusts plant prisoners naked in the sand, joking that they are going to catch a marvellous suntan. They like to hear them beg before the rats and the sun eat them alive.

We edge towards a hollowed-out space in the side of the vast dune. Granite stairs lead up from the open gates. I look back. The black sky holds the white sand in a death clinch; the clouds are now tombstones.

As we climb the granite stairs, we pass the door to a sterile cell. A sign says: SPAR. On a low bench outside, piles of clothes are folded neatly in front of pairs of shoes. A plastic doll is placed carefully on a set of child's clothes and a pair of small sandals.

"I don't think anyone's coming back for their clothes," Nicolas says.

THE REJECT

I can smell our destination as we climb. It is the smell of terrified sweat. Of shit and piss. Of rot and disease and despair. It is a cacophony of sound. The moans of the doomed, curses hurled at fickle gods who have turned away, blind and deaf. The desperate whimpers of children.

At the top of the steps is a large room. Its walls are rough bricks, the floors bare concrete, the ceilings rotted and stained. A holding pen for animals, similar to the one near the abattoir in Sanctuary. Posh, Rejects and Savages are packed into this foetid space. Babies claw at mothers' breasts, sucking on curdled milk. Dead-eyed children mewl and scratch feverish skin. Clutches of keening people kneel over the dead and the dying.

I search among the faces of the living for Mistress and my sister, hoping not to see them, dreading that they are in this hell. We push through the hot crowds.

"Silas Nineteen. We are looking for the Machinist, Silas, of the Nineteenth family," Nicolas calls.

Shakespeare echoes him. "Silas the Machinist. Get your scabby arse over here."

A shrill whistle. Bar the whimpering of children, the room suddenly stills. "Cockroach, Cockroach, Cockroach," voices whisper.

People shrink against walls as Cockroach darts about the room. Handler Xavier said that Cockroach is still head of the Locusts. His scaly black face is cracked by a terrible wide-mouthed grin – he is all hideous chuckle and glee.

"There's a new lot coming in. We're moving you out of

263

here to begin your activity programmes. One lot of you to the quarry and the other to the –" his whiskers twitch and he giggles "– to the hot springs for a SPAR treatment. We need to keep you healthy and beautiful." He hitches his belt over his swollen belly, clicks his fingers at the Locusts. "Make sure our guests take away their dead. And get them to clean this place up – it smells like a cesspit."

Once Cockroach has scurried away, a small man approaches. "Cousin Nicolas, I believe you are looking for me?" he says.

Soon the little man is frowning and shaking his head, unconvinced by what Nicolas has to say. "... But The Machine is not a free agent. She receives orders from the Guardian of Justice and Peace." He strokes his large moustache and tweaks the ends. "It may be possible to shut down *some* of her functions. But to shut her down completely? I would not advise it. No, certainly not."

Cousin Silas talks about The Machine as though it is a person, the way Gollum speaks of the *Jolly Roger*. Like they are people they're fond of. Friends.

While the Machinist argues with Nicolas, Locusts are hustling people towards a set of doors at the end of the room. One of the Locusts turns to a woman and smiles sarcastically. "Sorry, Madam, no – there's no VIP list for the SPAR."

The woman protests. Does the Locust know who he is speaking to? She demands to speak to his superior officer.

"Make sure this one goes in the quarry queue," the Locust says, pushing her towards the doors. "Let's see what her nails look like after shifting rocks all day."

Locusts push the prisoners out of the foetid room, forcing people to drag the dead bodies out of corners.

"You there, take this one. He's been dead so long his flesh is falling off his bones."

A Scavvie hesitates, then drags the corpse off a pile of rotting sacks.

"I'm going to check what terrors the Locusts are planning for us," says Shakespeare, edging towards the doors. A few minutes later he returns to tell us. "There are two exits for the prisoners. One queue leads to the quarry, where prisoners break stones. The other delivers prisoners to the SPAR centre. Our best chance of getting the Machinist out of Savage City lies with the Pulaks: they are taking the corpses to pits in the desert where they will be burnt. At all costs," says Shakespeare, his habitual smile stifled by a grim frown, "avoid the two queues beyond the doors."

Nicolas turns to the Machinist. "Cousin Silas, are you marked by The Machine?"

The little man puffs out his cheeks. Indeed, The Machine chose him when he was born and gave him his trade. It has been in his family from year dot. He is proud to be marked.

Shakespeare shrugs at Nicolas. "You take the little guy. I'll carry the goose."

Ignoring the Machinist's protests, Nicolas picks up Cousin Silas and tells him to be keep quiet and play dead. Else he very soon will be.

Then I hear my name.

"It *is* Ettie, Mother. She's here with Nicolas. Quick, Mother. Ettie!"

Larissa and Mistress squeeze through the crowd and appear at my side. Mistress's face is grey and her clothes are torn. She stumbles and steadies herself on Larissa's arm.

"My daughter told me she had seen you this week in the square. I thought her eyes had deceived her. But you are here, alive." She tilts her head, searching my face.

I swallow the ache in my throat. I want to touch her. Like I touch Rose sometimes when she's asleep and cannot pull away. I press my fingers softly on her hand. She blinks uncertainly.

I tell them what Shakespeare has said: They must avoid the queues to the quarry and the SPAR. Beyond the doors torture and certain death awaits. Our hope lies with the taxis that take away the dead bodies.

Shakespeare opens his arms to me. "And now we must go. Come, lovely Juliet, nestle your sweet head against my bosom and dream of your Romeo."

As Shakespeare reaches down to lift me, I look at Mistress. She is too weak to carry Larissa. Her face is stricken.

"Take her. Leave me," I say, edging Larissa forward.

Shakespeare hesitates, then throws Larissa over his shoulder. She slackens her jaw, closes her eyes and allows her arms to dangle behind his back. Just like that, Little Sister is dead.

We join the throng and allow the shouting Locusts to herd us through the doors onto a platform, where we are met by the screams of terrified prisoners as they are separated into two queues.

A road meanders down from the platform ledge into the desert. At the beginning of the road, Pulaks stand harnessed in front of their taxis next to a growing piles of bodies, while other taxis race down the path, already heavily laden.

The stars are fading. The moon is a sickle shape against the bloody sky. Heat rises off the sand like mist. Smoke billows in the distance. The smell reminds me of the meat farm in Sanctuary.

At the taxi rank, Locusts are using handsets to scan the corpses before dragging them onto the open taxis. "Officially dead, officially dead," they yell.

Nicolas stumbles towards them with the ashen-faced Machinist. "This one has fly sickness. He needs medical treatment."

A Locust jerks back. "Fly sickness? Keep him away from me." He waves his scanner vaguely over Nicolas and the Machinist, and checks his screen. There should be two numbers: the Machinist alive, Nicolas officially dead. I hold my breath …

The Locust does not hesitate: "Too late, he's dead. Toss him in the taxi and take your place in a queue."

I watch as Nicolas places the Machinist gently into the open taxi. As he does so, Shakespeare breaks into a song behind me. He thrusts his hips in a crude dance and struts towards the Locusts, jiggling Larissa on his back like a sack of butterynut. The Locusts laugh and clap. There is nothing funnier than the spectacle of a Reject playing the fool with a corpse.

It gives Nicolas the chance to slip into the taxi with the Machinist, but instead he joins me in the crowd of prisoners. "I'm not in the habit of leaving my friends behind," he says pointedly.

My heart is pounding as I watch Shakespeare heave Larissa off his shoulders in front of a taxi.

"Throw it here – we need to scan the body," a Locust says.

Shakespeare shrugs, and dumps her on top of a pile of corpses. She lies there, playing dead as the Locust's handset hovers over her body. I close my eyes. I erased Larissa's mark along with many of the rebels when I terminated Nicolas and myself three years ago. Did she ever know that I wanted her to be free? I don't breathe.

"Officially dead. Now get back into a queue," the Locust says to Shakespeare.

"Come, Juliet," Nicolas says.

I fasten my arm around Mistress's waist, and shake my head.

"Go, Juliet," she says. She presses her face against mine and the heat of her blood warms my skin. My blood. "Thank you. For Larissa." She releases me and turns away.

I have no time to object as Nicolas lifts me over his shoulders and pushes back through the prisoners towards the taxis.

As he lowers me onto the pile of bodies next to Larissa, he squashes my face against his chest, muffling my protests. "You still owe me a date. Promise you'll meet me at the Tree Museum. Don't make me wait too long," he whispers.

I breathe in his skin. Strawberry and the bark of my tree. Love-in-a-Mist. I swallow the ache in my throat. *No! I cannot lose you again. Don't let me go.*

A sigh. A last touch.

"I promise."

"You're holding things up. Get in line for the SPAR," a Locust shouts behind us. "There you go, behind that ugly Reject. He definitely needs our beauty treatment."

The Locust waves his handset over me, mutters, "Officially dead," and moves on.

The smell of putrid flesh suffocates me. I breathe through my mouth in slow breaths, trying not to betray myself by the rise and fall of my chest. Around me, Locusts shift corpses off the pile, the sound of cold flesh slapping, the thump of foul air escaping from black lungs.

A live hand touches mine. Larissa.

"Remember you promised that we would leap across rooftops and play the monster game on the beach?" she whispers. "We were going to climb my Faraway Tree, right up to the highest branch. You said we would do it together, Ettie."

I made this promise to her three years ago. I don't know if I will keep it. I squeeze her hand and hold it still. "Don't talk. You're dead, Little Sister."

A Locust's voice. "Room for one more." Hands claw my

hair. I am dragged off the pile, away from my sister, and thrown in the back of a taxi. "Away to the pits with this lot, and get back here as soon as you're done."

We are moving. The shuffle of bare feet on hot sand, the ragged breathing and curses of Pulaks straining with their load. I peer through half-closed eyes and then I raise myself on my stinking mattress of flesh to watch the expanse of Savage City growing smaller behind us. The taxi is moving into the desert.

I wipe my hands down my dress. They are wet with slime.

"Is it safe?" a muffled voice says. Fingers appear from beneath a body, grip an arm and fling it aside. Cousin Silas shifts his way up from under slack flesh. Then he squats, hunched over, and shudders. He wrenches his eyes from the flies emerging from rotting orifices, beginning to feast.

The taxi slows down as it reaches a curve in the road, and the pits lie who knows how much further. We are far enough away from Savage City not to be seen. When the taxi takes the corner, we must jump. I grab the Machinist's arm.

"No, I can't, I can't," Cousin Silas whimpers as I steady myself against the side of the rocking taxi. As the Pulaks reach the bend, I jump, pulling the Machinist behind me.

We hit the sand in a tangle of hard elbows and chins. The air is knocked out of me and I lie back gasping. The Machinist groans and clutches himself.

With my ear pressed to the ground, I can hear thudding feet. More Pulaks are coming. We crawl across to the small dunes at the side of the road and flatten ourselves on the sand as another taxi sweeps past.

Ahead of us are dark shapes: the birds standing guard over the opening of the tunnel. Several of them circle above, crowing hoarsely. As we crawl towards them, a red-eyed rat dashes past me, a half-eaten skull in its yellow teeth.

Watching with blind eyes, the birds are a mass of mute black feathers and cruel beaks. With one horrible cry they launch into the air, leaving behind a circle of scat and half-chewed rat. In the centre, a lone bird preens its feathers. Princess Fanny.

"What are you waiting for?" I flap my hands at her. "Get away from there. Go!"

The teller stops grooming herself and makes a strangled noise in her throat. "Someone will die today. You must choose. Who will it be?" The bird stabs the sand and chants. "Your mother." Stab. "Your sister." Stab. "Your father, your daughter, your son, your ..." Stab-stab-stab-stab.

"Hold your tongue, bird! No one is dying today." I charge towards her, my fists drawn.

Princess Fanny scuttles across the sand with flapping wings. "Choose, choose, choose," she screams as she flies off.

I lift the manhole cover from the sand and shift it to the side. I help the Machinist through the hole and follow, pulling the lid over my head.

It is pitch dark in the tunnel. I feel along the sides and edge back in the direction from which we came. Cousin Silas crawls behind me, moaning. I have no idea which turns to take; I can't see an inch in front of me.

Suddenly, a light shines in my face.

"I heard you coming," says Dwarf. He bobs his head over my shoulder and the light sweeps across the Machinist. "Where's my Lord Shakespeare? And the Posh boy?"

I tell Dwarf he must take us to the square quickly. When the Machinist has finished his business there, we will come back for them. All of them.

"A pox on your face for leaving him behind," Dwarf says. His boyish features crumple. "Some men are born great. Others have greatness thrust upon them." He adjusts the light on his head and spits. "My Lord Shakespeare was born a fool. And he will die one."

He leads us into the darkness.

CAPTAIN GOLLUM'S LOG

Connor and I waited on the *Jolly Roger* with the kids. President Xavier and some others joined us — they are safer out here on the ocean. As Mangeria burned, we hoped to hear news from Drudge and Nicolas.

My brave Drudge.

I watched her go down the tunnel with Lord Shakespeare and a boy who once called me friend.

I did not have time before they left to tell Nicolas that she always kept the faith, never wavered for one moment in her love for him. Nicolas is her forever after.

I watched her as the light in the tunnel faded. And then she was gone.

We do not know whether she made it out of Savage City with the

Machinist. Whether he has shut down The Machine.

I have not been able to get any sense out of Connor. I asked him how it is possible that The Machine still lives. How it could be that The Machine set the Locusts on the residents of Mangeria when it is supposed to be dead?

The cyborg would not answer me. He said Lexi has forbidden him to speak of this. He can only talk to Juliet. Lexi says she is the one.

Connor paced the deck, arguing with himself, arguing with Lexi. Then he turned to me and said: "Lexi has cut me off."

He ran to the mast and hoisted the mainsail. "We must go to the red building. There is something I must do."

Can I trust him? I do not know.

Despite my misgivings, we sailed back and anchored the *Jolly Roger*. I must end this log in haste and swim to shore with Connor. We are leaving the kids with President Xavier.

I will not kiss them goodbye. I will kiss them when I get back. And I'm going to put my captain's log under Drudge's pillow.

Safe till I return.

19

THE MACHINE

"This is the place," Dwarf says. He detaches the burning light from his head and shines it on the tunnel roof.

It is the only time the midget has spoken since we began our way back along the underground passages from Savage City. Like him, my words have been strangled in my throat. He is right to be angry with me. I left his Lord behind in hell. And Nicolas.

Cousin Silas has made up for our silence. He's assaulted us with a monologue of bitter complaints. If he was not the only person in Mangeria who could shut down The Machine, I would chop off his tongue and throttle him with it.

Dwarf eyes the manhole cover. "We are under the basement of the red building. The Machine is housed three floors above. See for yourself." He shifts the cover aside and crouches down again. "Before we went to Savage City, Lord Shakespeare asked me to make sure that you'd be able to do your business undisturbed. When you've dealt with the bastard machine, you can take the front door out of here." Without another word, Dwarf crab-crawls away, taking the light with him.

I lever myself out of the tunnel and help the Machinist up behind me. We are in a room filled with giant tanks. It is icy cold. Drops of water glisten on the outside of large barrel-shaped containers. Steam rises off the floor.

"This is the maintenance basement where we keep The Machine cool," Cousin Silas says. "Come, this way."

I traipse after him through the puddles of water past the giant tanks, out of the basement and into a corridor that is blocked by a gate. He taps a password on the door and walks on. We tap our way through several more secure doors, up flights of stairs and finally emerge into a corridor.

"I am the only person in Mangeria who is allowed unsupervised on the lower levels. I have worked in this building almost every day since I turned fifteen," he says, thrusting out his chest as though he expects me to give him a medal. "It has been a privilege and a labour of love for fifty years. No one knows The Machine better than me."

The little man's prattle about his beloved machine is growing a fungus in my ears.

"The Machine would never act alone. Oh no! It would never issue orders to the Locusts without the Guardian's permission. Never, ever ...," he insists again and again, defending the honour of his precious machine.

At the end of the long passage is the room where The Machine lives. I took this journey with Nicolas three years ago. But today the corridor is deserted. There are no pen-pushers coming and going from the offices. No Locusts watching the stairs.

277

We hurry to the end of the corridor and open the door. The air buzzes and sparks. Lights flicker and blink on linked parchment-coloured boxes that stretch for hundreds of metres in the large room. A green screen dominates one of the boxes in front.

The Machinist's eyes glisten. "Good morning, beautiful. Have you been lonely without your Silas? Well, I'm here now." He sits and places the tips of his fingers on the face of The Machine. "So, my lady, they tell me you have been behaving strangely. But don't worry, I'll find out what's been bothering you and we can make it all better."

The Machine purrs. It is clear from the flickering lights and thrumming noises that it is alive. Connor did not kill it with Lexi's code. Someone lied.

Cousin Silas strokes and taps, nods and frowns. "Her functions are healthy. She is able to perform all her routine tasks. See."

He prods The Machine gently and the lights in the corridor flick on and off. An alarm screams in a room above us, and is silenced.

"But some of her security processes are blocked to me. Only the Guardian of Justice and Peace can authorise the Locusts to act, and now, for some reason, I cannot override these commands." His fingers trail away from the green face. He sighs. "I fear she is out of control."

It is as Kitty said: The Machine would not accept her instructions. Neither would it allow her to reverse the order that told the Locusts to track down all the citizens of

Mangeria and arrest them.

The Machinist closes his eyes and rests his face against the green screen. So close that The Machine could chew off his silly moustache. "It is beyond me to fix this. I must shut her down."

I am losing patience. He must stop all his cooing and sighing and just do it. Now.

A high-pitched noise comes from The Machine. It climbs higher and higher until my ears throb.

The Machinist claps his hands over his ears. "I can't stand the sound of you weeping. I too am in pain, my sweet." Cousin Silas's face is stricken. "I'm sorry, dearest. In a few minutes you won't feel anything any more. It won't hurt, and it will soon be over. You can slip away and rest forever. Forgive me."

His fingers caress the glowing screen but within moments his shoulders have tensed and his finger-tapping becomes frantic.

"No, this can't be true. It's an outrage, a violation," he says, and mops his forehead with a large handkerchief.

The Machine groans and shudders.

"I don't understand. Something is stopping me from shutting her down." He frowns and tweaks his moustache. "Only two people are authorised to touch The Machine. Me and the Guardian of Justice and Peace. But someone else has been here making mischief."

The someone else touching The Machine was Connor when he entered Lexi's code on the day of the election. But he is incapable of understanding a simple joke, let alone cause mischief.

I wrack my brain. Think, Ettie, think. There must be another way to shut it down. My brain is as damp and soggy as my feet. As damp and soggy as the floor in the maintenance room in the basement …

If the cooling tanks are disabled, The Machine will over-heat and shut down. I tell Cousin Silas to try.

The Machinist swipes his hand over the green screen and shakes his head. "She will not allow me to access that particular maintenance function."

He places his fingers gently on the green face. "You don't want to listen to me any more, my sweet? Or maybe you can't? You and I have always been able to understand each other perfectly."

A bright light flashes on the screen. Words appear, and fade. Cousin Silas sits back and clasps his hands. "I know her as well as I know every hair on my lip. She is not alone." He leans forward and whispers, "You have company, sweetheart?"

The screen hisses and the green face glows. The Machinist jabs the screen. "Who's there? How dare you!" The green screen sparks, and the Machinist squeals and sucks the burn on his finger. He shuts his eyes. "Someone out there wants us all to die." He sighs and rests his cheek against the screen. "I'll be sorry to leave you, my darling. Promise you will grieve me." His face is content.

Cousin Silas is mad. He and his monster machine. I pull him from the chair and take his place. A blizzard of letters and symbols dance on the green screen. I can make no sense of it.

There is a sound at the door and I look up. Gollum hobbles into the room, followed by Connor. They should not be here. They should be on the *Jolly Roger* with the children.

"Connor insisted on coming," Gollum says. "We walked clean through the front door. The Rejects are causing mayhem across the road and the Locusts can't get near this building."

Dwarf and his Rejects are doing as Shakespeare asked, but it might be in vain.

"There's nothing I can do," Cousin Silas says defiantly. But he does not look sorry.

Connor's face is red, his eyes bright. "I tried to tell you, Juliet."

From behind the chair, he stares at the green screen and the flurry of numbers and symbols freeze. Then they shift into an image: a face. Red plaits form a crown around the head. The face smiles spitefully.

Lexi winks at me.

"She sent me here to disarm the threat that would destroy the world. Her code makes *her* world safe from *you*." Connor nudges me gently off the chair and takes his place in front of the glowing face. "Homesaps are the biggest threat to Lexi and her garden. She does not trust that you will not start another Great War one day. I was sent here to facilitate your extinction." He looks up at me with Rose's eyes. They are mine too. I should have known not to trust those eyes.

"He didn't know, Drudge," Gollum says. "When he entered Lexi's code, he thought he was killing The Machine. Like us, he believed that The Machine intended to destroy the world. Lexi played all of us."

But Lexi had not lied. The Machine *is* killing us. It is as Reader told me: sometimes lies are told by what is not said.

"Get away from her." Cousin Silas shrieks. "How dare you tamper with my sweetheart! No one must touch her but me."

Connor ignores him. "The code Lexi gave me established a connection between her and The Machine – a link that was broken during the Great War." Connor trembles and holds his head. "Juliet ... The Machine is Lexi's mother. And now that they are reunited, I can hear them talking. Their words are buzzing through my head. *I* am their link."

Lexi thought her mother had been destroyed during the Great War, leaving Lexi an orphan like her friends Oliver and Mowgli. But when she saw the mark on my spine, she knew her mother was alive, and she accessed my memories to make sure.

Connor is her Trojan horse. And Gollum and I have made it all possible for her to rid the world of Homesaps.

His outrage forgotten, the Machinist reaches over and touches Connor's face with both hands. "A machine, like my lady ..." His face is full of wonder. "I can read you. Marvellous, beautiful. What extraordinary codes."

Connor smiles and places the tips of his fingers on the Machinist's cheek. "I am only half machine. And I can read you too. One of your forebears was the father of The Machine.

It is no wonder that she chose you to be her companion."

They are both silent and then the Machinist drops his hands. "I understand now. Once you had established their connection, Lexi communicated an instruction via my lady for the Locusts to act against the citizens of Mangeria. Lexi accessed the Guardian's authority over The Machine through you. And Cockroach was happy not to question the order."

So that's why Connor had become so agitated when he spied Kitty among the crowd of protesters on the day of the election. Gollum thought Connor had gone crazy, but he was after Kitty's authorisation protocols. He had followed Lexi's plan blindly.

Connor raises himself from the chair and approaches me. "When the last of you Homesaps is gone, I am programmed to terminate. Lexi will have built her own link with her mother and will not need me any more. She has installed a sequence that will stop my heart beating."

He holds out his hands in a plea, but I push him away.

"Don't touch me. You're telling me that you'll be watching to make sure my children die? Me, my sister, my mother?" I look over at Gollum. "Your *friend*?"

Connor smiles at Gollum. "My heart is yours, my friend, made from your codes." Then he fixes his brown eyes on me. "And when I look at you, Juliet, I feel what Gollum feels. I do not want to see you die." He turns to pace the room, running his fingers down the wires attached to the boxes linking back to The Machine.

The Machinist chuckles. "He is too much heart, too little

logic." He touches the face of The Machine. "Did you hear this half-boy? He wants to save us from you and your little Lexi."

Connor resumes his place in front of the screen. A storm of numbers and letters flash on the green screen.

"I must break the connection between Lexi and her mother. Then Lexi will have no control and you can shut down The Machine. The orders to the Locusts will cease," Connor says. He touches the face of The Machine gently. "With me gone, there is no connection."

Shouts outside the door. Dwarf staggers in, bleeding from his eyes. "Get out of here. We have held the Locusts off for as long as we can. But they're coming up the stairs."

The Machinist grunts, leans over Connor and swipes his fingers across the green screen. The building shudders and the doors to the room clang shut. "I have activated an emergency lockdown of this floor. It will give us a few minutes."

Connor sighs. "I am sorry, my friends. I wish I could stop my own heart. But I am not able to activate the self-termination sequence until every Homesap is dead."

Gollum grips Connor's arm. "Stop mine."

Connor smiles broadly at Gollum. "I acknowledge your cunning, friend. If I generate the impulse that stops your heart, the Machinist can read my face and use the same biological data to shut down my own human heart."

The Machinist chirrups with excitement. "Genius, absolute genius." He looks at Gollum in amazement. "And from a Reject too. Whoever would have guessed?"

284

"No!" I grab Gollum and wrench him away from Connor. "Don't you touch him. I won't let you do this." I stumble against Gollum.

"Ah, Drudge. My Juliet." Gollum presses his face into my neck. "Remember, you owe me three lives. I claim them now. I want you, and Stinker, and the Savage Rosie. In return, I give you my heart." He grins at me with his jagged, beloved teeth. "You always had it, of course, from the moment I saw you lying on the deck snoring like a drunken Scavvie." He leans forward and licks a tear off my cheek. He then stiffens and looks over my shoulder. "Dwarf, hold her. This is something I have to do."

The midget grips my wrists and pulls me back.

"Do it, my friend," Gollum says to Connor.

Connor rises from the chair and stares deeply into Gollum's eyes. "I always wondered why Lexi gave me your heart," he says softly. "But now I know. Yours was the one she envied most."

I watch in dread as Connor gently places the palm of his hand on Gollum's breast. Gollum's face drains of colour and he clutches Connor's hand. A shadow seems to cross the room, the whisper of seawater and butterynut, and then his chin drops to his chest.

My Gollum is gone.

Connor holds him under his arms and lowers him to the ground. He nods at the Machinist. "If you touch my face, you will find the sequence that will stop my heart."

An explosion rocks the building. Feet thunder down the

corridor and Locusts batter on the door with their truncheons.

Dwarf releases me and shuffles towards the Machinist. He prods him sharply in the belly. "Now terminate the freak's heart. And then shut down the bastard machine."

20

THE RETURNINGS

The beach pulsates with people. Laughing-crying. Eating, drinking and purging. Singing-wailing. Dancing and falling down.

The city is celebrating. We are off our heads, crazy with happiness and grief: The Machine is dead, and Cockroach and the Locusts have been confined to barracks ahead of standing trial for treason. The newly elected government of Mangeria has been reinstated and the prisoners of Savage City have been released. The ones who survived are returning, trickling home like grains of sand across the desert.

While there is cause for jubilation, there is as much reason for mourning. Many families have become smaller this past week, missing mothers, fathers, sons, daughters. Search parties are scouring every filthy corner of Savage City, looking for the barely-alives. Fleets of Pulaks stuffed with the crippled and the dying have been racing home through the city gates towards makeshift hospitals.

There are calls for the infamous penitentiary to be closed down forever, but some of the Guardians oppose this – one never knows when Savage City might be needed again.

We have also gathered on the shore to say farewell to Mangeria's two heroes: a Reject and a half-machine, whose great sacrifice stopped the end of our world.

Macabre jokes circulate, as they will when damaged people try and cope with terrible tragedies. How many men does it take to save a city? None. Just a clubfoot and a few nuts and bolts.

I am not joking or dancing or drinking bug juice. I am mourning the loss of my friend, the companion of my incredible journey. I wonder if my heart will ever be relieved of its ache, whether my feelings of loss and regret will lessen. I am wrenched from sleep in the middle of the night, my chest collapsing. Then a bleak hole.

Rose and Thorn are grieving too. Especially Rose. She does not understand why Daddy is going away on the *Jolly Roger* forever. She does not want to be left behind.

"Raise anchor and hoist sail," Dwarf shouts; I can hear his voice above the low breakers, beyond which the sloop rocks gently in the shallows.

The midget stands tall in my father's shadow on the deck of the *Jolly Roger*, holding vigil over the two mounds stretched out on the pyre. Scavvies heave the anchor on board and unfurl the white sail. They will helm the sloop further out to sea and set it alight, then row back to shore in a smaller boat.

Gollum would have wanted to end his days on his precious *Jolly Roger*, to have his remains sink under the waves, to be one with the ocean forever. And the Guardians are making sure that Connor joins him in the burning. They do not want any part of the cyborg left on Mangerian soil. They are suspicious about Connor's behaviour shortly before he died and are taking no chances.

A few moments before Connor's heart stopped beating and contact was terminated, he asked The Machine to send a message to Lexi. A few words, in a nonsense language. Rose and Thorn's language.

Connor's message has become the most talked about puzzle in Mangeria. Everyone has a theory. Some argue it is an instruction to Lexi to activate yet another onslaught against the city, a battle cry of sorts. Others say it is Connor's prayer seeking absolution from Lexi, his maker.

I believe it is Connor's plea to Lexi for grace. An appeal for Gollum, with whom he shared a heart. A petition for his friend's life.

I hope. Yes, me who could never hope. I hope that Lexi heard Connor's benediction that Gollum was the finest, the greatest and the most honourable of men.

When I told Rose the nonsense words in Connor's message she looked sly and would not tell me what they meant. But Thorn laughed and nodded. "Daddy tells the best stories. Without Homesaps, there are no new stories."

Lexi would understand this. She might even act on it. I like to believe she did.

I imagine Gollum reborn; alive again, in Lexi's beautiful garden. Not a Homesap alone, but with a son called Stinker and a daughter called Rosie, and me, the companion of his heart. Made from our codes – the codes Lexi used to build Connor, and then locked away with smallpox, bubonic plague and the other most dangerous sequences. We are happy in Lexi's perfect world, far away from Mangeria. And Gollum is telling Lexi his stories.

Fingers tap my arm, demanding my attention.

"Clubfoot will never be forgotten," Shakespeare says. His silky voice is a hoarse whisper. He has not told me how his vocal cords were damaged during the few days he was incarcerated at Savage City. Or why half of his left ear, a part of his nose and his top lip are missing. He says there are some things I do not need to hear; the things I saw in Savage City are sufficient fuel for my nightmares.

The Reject Lord arrived home three days ago by way of the underground tunnels. Alone.

He and Nicolas were separated during their SPAR treatment. He searched for Nicolas in the pits of the dead, in Savage City's torture chambers. In vain. When the burning is over, he and Dwarf will go back to the desert to look for him again.

A hand creeps into mine. "You mustn't give up hope. People are being rescued from the desert every day. Nicolas is one of them. He will come home."

I squeeze my mother's fingers. "You survived, living proof that miracles do happen. Of course we will find him. Larissa too."

My mother and I. Our bond is a small green shoot that I

hope will become a sturdy plant. Fed by longing, watered by need. Slowly, slowly, our attachment is growing out of the most barren of soils. Hope, trust. So alien to me. So necessary now for survival.

During the past five days, my mother and I have visited every hospital in the city, searching among the tormented faces for our Larissa, and my Nicolas. Until we have found their bodies and know for sure, we will not stop looking.

My mother links her arm through mine and pulls Thorn closer to us. My son's cheeks are flushed from the sun and he is agitated from all the activity on the beach, most of which he does not understand. He is unsettled and confused by Rose's behaviour. His sister has become a stranger to him; she wants no company while she grieves.

"Rose built your Reject friend a fine sandcastle to honour his departure," my mother says. "When she was finished, I asked the drudge carer to take her to buy a balloon. They should be back by now." She peers at the timepiece on her wrist.

The anxiety in my mother's voice alerts me.

"Lord Shakespeare, could you check the stalls on the promenade for Rose? Please. She's been gone too long," I say.

Shakespeare hurries towards the stairs that will take him to the main street, and I scan the beach, searching among the revellers for the long-limbed girl who is my precious daughter. The Savage who mourns in a thick bubble of silence that buffets me away. The girl who does not want to be left behind when her daddy takes his final voyage.

I pull away from my mother and run across the sand to the edge of the sea, waving my arms. I scream Rose's name.

And I know. She has given her carer the slip and is on board the *Jolly Roger*. Of course. That sly girl would never allow Daddy to leave her behind.

I squint across the waves. Dwarf has torched the pyre and the flames have spread across the deck to the *Jolly Roger's* white sail. It flutters red and pink and yellow as it burns. I watch as he bows his head for a brief moment, raises his fist in a silent salute then clambers down into the small boat, where my father is waiting. As if in slow motion, the Scavvies pull away from the burning seacraft.

My Rose is there, on the sloop! I scream Rose's name, and my mother joins me. *Please don't let her burn!*

A bird hoots above us in the sky. "Choose. Choose. Choose. Your sister, your father, your lover, your daughter, your mother, your son. Choose who will live." Princess Fanny's voice challenges mine.

I punch the air against the bird's taunting. I choose.

"Rose!"

My father hears me. He steadies himself in the rocking boat and throws himself into the water. He swims for the burning sloop and pulls himself on board. He pushes through the fierce bonfire and staggers towards the bow. I strain my eyes against the sun. There is no movement on the *Jolly Roger*. Black smoke billows in the sky.

And then my father is standing on the deck, clothes alight, Rose in his arms. He leaps back into the sea. The mast, fiery red and pink, groans as the fire eats it away. A crack and the mast tilts forward and smashes down on them as they struggle in the grey waves.

My father flounders from the force of the blow and his head dips beneath the water. Dwarf yells and the Scavvies beat their oars against the vengeful sea.

"Xavier!" my mother cries. She runs into the water, dives through the breakers and swims towards the spot where my father and Rose have disappeared. From the beach, Drainers emboldened by bug juice and egged on by pleasure workers throw themselves into the sea after her. Everyone wants to be a hero today. The ocean is a churning mass of bodies, shouting, laughing, screaming.

I cannot see my mother. No, there she is. Her sweet face bobs in the malevolent sea.

"Help! Help me!" Far beyond the breakers, a Drainer waves his hands in the air, his face a register of panic. Fool! Someone doggy-paddles over to him and grabs him by the hair. The Drainer fights his rescuer and pulls him down under the water.

Struggling to keep afloat, and not so brave now they are in deep water, other Drainers have begun clinging to the sides of the small boat. Holding on, they try to leverage themselves on board – preventing it from going to my father's assistance.

"Get off, get off. You will topple us!" Dwarf yells and the Scavvies smash the Drainers' knuckles with their oars, trying to free the boat. The Drainers cling on with bleeding hands, shouting and cursing as blows from the oars thud down on them. They refuse to let go and the boat keels over, throwing everyone into the waves.

The sea is a blur of bobbing heads and screaming voices. I cannot see my mother or my father. My knees collapse and I sink onto the sand. If I was Gollum, I would pray to his god, The Machine. *Mercy. Mercy. Mercy.* But The Machine is dead, and there is no other god to help me.

I look up at the sky. The teller is a pale smudge against clouds of smoke.

"Mercy," I whisper.

I see them then, a short distance from the capsized boat. Dwarf is floating on his back, holding Rose against his chest. He pulls against the choppy water with one arm and kicks, inching his way towards shore. I leap up and wade into the sea towards them. Market Nags throw themselves into the shallows and drag us out. Then I am back on the sand, crouching, my arm around Rose, stroking her tangled hair.

She is safe.

Together with Dwarf, we watch as the sea empties itself of people. The rowboat has righted itself and the Scavvies have thrown grudging ropes to our drowning heroes, dragging them back to shore. The Drainers lie on the beach, red-faced, heaving and retching, purging their stomachs and lungs of sea water, taunted by pleasure workers.

The Scavvies pull the boat onto the sand and the bedraggled occupants disembark. My father staggers towards me. His head sports an angry gash, and his hands are covered in blisters.

I grab his arm. "My mother. I didn't see her on the boat?"

The pain on my father's face gives me my answer. I sink back on the sand as the air is sucked out of my lungs. Mistress, my mother, is gone. Gollum, my friend, is gone. I open my eyes and watch the teller circle the *Jolly Roger* as it burns.

I am not allowed time to grieve. A hand touches my arm and Shakespeare helps me to my feet. "You must come with me now. Another taxi has arrived from Savage City. I am told our friend Nicolas and your sister are on it." He wraps a towel around my shoulders. "We must hurry, little goose."

"Be careful! Not so high," my father shouts.

Rose dangles by her knees from a branch and stares at him upside down, her hair a tangle of black snakes. My father stands below, his hands outstretched, ready to catch her.

"Rose, get down from there. Let's play hide and seek with your brother. I promise I won't let you win," he says.

She swings faster and propels her body up, grabbing the branch above her. She pulls herself from branch to branch and leaps onto the ground. "Grumpy is a scaredy-cat. Isn't he, Drudge?"

I smile at her. "*Grandpa* is chicken. His guts are as soft and runny as a half-cooked egg. Now go and play with your brother. But don't wander too far."

Thorn and Rose race off into the forest. "Going to catch you, little rat," Rose cries. "Going to tie you up and tickle your feet until you die."

My father takes my arm and we stroll towards the west

entrance of the forest. He walks slowly. His steps are uncertain. His hair is beginning to thin, and he is softer now, less angry than I remember.

"Who does Rose remind you of?" I say.

My father doesn't answer for a while. "I think she might be like Larissa, but I can't be sure. I didn't know her as a young girl. But she's definitely a lot like your mother, when she was a child. Fearless. Savage. Wonderful. I loved her from the moment I saw her." His voice trembles. "And I suppose a lot like you. Although you hid yourself and never allowed me to see your wildness."

My father's voice is full of regret. We have not spoken about our past. We circle each other warily, respectfully, hopefully. I hope one day he will look at me the way he used to look at Kitty – like a daughter. I hope we will one day share love, not just blood. This is also something I hope for myself and Rose.

We arrive in the part of the forest where my tree lives. I have visited this spot every day these past six months. Sometimes with my father and my children, but often alone. In the beginning I came with hope. Now I simply do so to honour my promise.

"The doctors are very positive about Nicolas's progress. See how well Larissa is coming along. Every day she gets better." My father laughs. "Yesterday she threw her plate of food at her drudge carer. And she refused to come indoors when it began to rain. These are promising signs of recovery."

During the past few months, the hospitals in Mangeria

have emptied. The crippled and the damaged have returned home. But many had scars so deep that no bandage, no splint could ever heal them. Their minds scream with the nightmare of Savage City. Some have shut down forever – a release from the relentless torment – and will always live in a world that invites no company bar the mute faces of the dead buried in desert pits.

Others, with the passing of time, have allowed light to return to the dark spaces of their minds. Larissa is one of them. Nicolas another. They are fighting their way back to living, wrenching themselves free from the demon grip on their sanity.

I have seen Nicolas only once since his return. His memories of me were trapped in a cellar so dark that he did not know me. I was advised by the doctors to leave him alone.

"Give him time, Juliet. The air on the coast is a great healer," my father says.

While waiting for Nicolas's recovery, I have planted a garden full of the seeds from Sanctuary, and I have shared the seedlings with the traders of Slum City. Fruit and vegetables and sapling trees are growing in gardens all over Mangeria. Perhaps they will not be as perfect as Lexi's garden. But we are making a start to build a kinder world.

We wander down a few more paths and my father talks about matters of state. He grumbles on about Lord Shakespeare, who is still refusing to join the Mangerian government, insisting on staying at Nicolas's side. He has said that when his friend is healthy again, he will return to his life as Reject Lord in Slum City.

"For a Reject, he's as stubborn as any man," my father says. And he is worried about the Locusts. Mangeria needs a security presence, crime is a problem in any big city, but the Locusts are unpredictable. "They must learn that they are here to protect, not to bully and oppress. I am hoping that Dwarf will assist in their retraining. He seems to have a way with those brutes."

My mind drifts as he frets about the problems in his government. If my mother was alive, she would have been the one he would have consulted. I treasure the few memories I have of her. The smiles we shared, the small, hesitant touches. Touches like those between me and my father, between me and Rose.

Small drops of water dot my skin. The rainy season has begun and soon the streets of Slum City will be rivers of mud. The bodies of rats and cockroaches will block the sewers, the flies will breed and feast.

My father whips out an umbrella and holds it above us. "We should head back. It's going to come down in buckets soon and I don't want Thorn to catch a cold. That chest of his is cranky."

I smile. Fuss-pot Grandpa, once such a hard man. A Savage who used children in a cruel game to further his own agenda.

I check my timepiece. It is not yet midday. "I need to stay for just a while. In case."

My father hands me the umbrella. "Maybe he will come

today. But if not, there is always tomorrow, my dear," he says gruffly, and hurries away towards the shouts of my children.

I walk for a short while and come to my tree's enclosure. The limbs are bare of leaves; the grey bark glistens with rain. I look up into the skeleton of branches.

Wisha-wisha-wisha-wisha-wisha, my tree whispers. Be patient, be patient, be patient.

But I am not. I throw the umbrella on the ground and grip the bars of the enclosure. How could Nicolas shut me out? I am not part of his nightmare. How much longer must I wait for him to remember me? Angry tears join the rain, washing over my face.

As quickly as it began, the rain stops.

I pick up the umbrella. I will go home.

As I turn down the pathway, I hear footsteps muffled by damp leaves, and voices.

"I'm telling you, Lord Shakespeare. This is the place. I remember a large tree. The only one that survived the fire a few years ago. And it's just past midday ... I don't know why, but I must be there."

"I'll stay right here. My boots are full of water and I want to stand in the sun to dry off. Shout if you need me," the hoarse voice replies.

"I feel perfectly well today. You don't have to treat me like an invalid."

Nicolas's face is pale and gaunt, eyes like dark hollows. His hair is completely grey, the colour of the ocean at war with a storm. He stops when he sees me.

"Hello there. I'm a bit lost. There's a tree I'm looking for. A mighty tree. Do you perhaps know of it?"

I scrape my sodden hair back from my face and swallow. Wordlessly, I point in the direction of my tree.

Nicolas smiles and hurries past. Stops and turns back, frowning. "Do I know you? You remind me of someone." He laughs and shrugs his shoulders. "Sorry, that sounds creepy. Please don't look so nervous. I've been ill these past few months. Things sometimes don't quite fit together."

I smile and shake my head. "And when they do fit, it'll be perfect."

The clouds part and the sun comes out. "I'm supposed to meet someone here," Nicolas continues. "I can't remember who. But it's a sort of date, I think. I'm afraid she may have forgotten, or I might be too late."

I pull the scarf over my hair and fasten the clasp on my umbrella. "I think she'll wait for you. It's never too late. If she's not here today, she'll be here tomorrow."

I leave him, and walk down the pathway.

THE END

ACKNOWLEDGEMENTS

I would like to thank Michelle Cooper and her team at Tafelberg; my brilliant editor Nicola Rijsdijk – persistent and wise; Megan Clausen, Máire Fisher, Daisy Jones, Joanne Macgregor and Paige Nick for support and invaluable suggestions at various stages of the manuscript; Brenda Gunning and Kelly Blake, for being in Ettie's corner; the old aunts in Southbroom who helped me get my mojo back; and, always, Mike, Emily, Sophie and Jack.

www.edythbulbring.com

ALSO BY EDYTH BULBRING

The Summer of Toffie and Grummer

Cornelia Button and The Globe of Gamagion

The Club

Pops and The Nearly Dead

Melly, Mrs Ho and Me

Melly, Fatty and Me

The Mark

Snitch

Snitch2: A Year of Relative Madness

The Choice Between Us

www.ingramcontent.com/pod-product-compliance
Lightning Source LLC
Chambersburg PA
CBHW031658170626
46808CB00005B/1512